Paul Micou is the
previous novels, *The Music
Programme*, *The Cover Artist*, *The
Death of David Debrizzi*, *Rotten
Times* and *The Last Word*, all of
which are published by Black Swan.
After graduating from Harvard in
1981, he lived in Paris; he has lived
in London since 1988.

David Saeme

Also by Paul Micou

THE MUSIC PROGRAMME
THE COVER ARTIST
THE DEATH OF DAVID DEBRIZZI
ROTTEN TIMES
THE LAST WORD

and published by Black Swan

Adam's Wish

Paul Micou

BLACK SWAN

ADAM'S WISH
A BLACK SWAN BOOK : 0 552 99603 3

Originally published in Great Britain by Bantam Press,
a division of Transworld Publishers Ltd

PRINTING HISTORY
Bantam Press edition published 1994
Black Swan edition published 1995

Typeset in 11/13pt Linotype Melior by
Kestrel Data, Exeter, Devon.

Black Swan Books are published by Transworld Publishers Ltd,
61–63 Uxbridge Road, London W5 5SA,
in Australia by Transworld Publishers (Australia) Pty Ltd,
15–25 Helles Avenue, Moorebank, NSW 2170,
and in New Zealand by Transworld Publishers (NZ) Ltd,
3 William Pickering Drive, Albany, Auckland.

Reproduced, printed and bound in Great Britain by
Cox & Wyman Ltd, Reading, Berks.

FOR ANNA U

PART ONE
MEETING

PART TWO
COURTSHIP

PART THREE
MARRIAGE

PART ONE

MEETING

Adam Gosse stood alone in the stern of a France-bound ferry, watching the white cliffs recede into the Channel mist.

'*Messieurs et mesdames*,' he practised, anticipating his bilingual speech at that afternoon's wedding. Adam had been responsible for introducing the betrothed couple, and on that basis had been granted the mixed honour of acting as the groom's best man. It would be his sixth such performance in three years. Adam had many male friends, and it was the marrying season of their lives.

Today's wedding was going to be different, in that it was the first one where Adam would unhesitatingly have taken the place of the groom. In the past he had attended friends' weddings in the way a cheetah haunted a gazelle's watering hole; more recently he had begun to acknowledge a disposition in favour of marriage in general, and specifically in favour of his own. This day's wedding had set him in a contemplative mood, because he could think of no other man in his circle who remained unmarried. Adam had recently begun to admit to himself that he was lonely. His fondest wish was that he might meet someone, fall in love, and marry her.

11

'I hope you will excuse my abominable French,' he said, in abominable French, addressing the cawing beak of a seagull at eye level in the mist. Hearing what difficulty he had negotiating those twisting vowels, Adam recognized with regret that his French was not so perfect as he had supposed. Adam was half Belgian. He and everyone else had expected him to speak French fluently. This would have been the case, had he not been shipped off to England at the age of two, when his father was appointed Ambassador to the Court of St James's. His English mother had rightly insisted that her own language be spoken at the dinner table whenever it was possible to do so. For no good reason, he had studied Russian at school. On rare trips to France with English friends, he had allowed them to order meals and ask directions, on the pretext that they needed to practise and he did not. Humiliatingly, an English girlfriend had translated his draft of today's wedding speech. Adam now had to consider the possibility that his French was quite poor. He had never returned to Belgium after his father's retirement; nor had his parents, for that matter. They had gone the way of all flesh, to a disappointing condominium in Antibes.

Adam never mentioned his nationality if he could help it, nor did he volunteer his occupation to strangers. People automatically took his reticence in the matter to mean that he was a solicitor. Adam found himself bristling at the suggestion, though it was correct. He counted among those who, just past the age of thirty, were still convinced that their conventional, comfortable, bourgeois lives were temporary hallucinations from which they would awaken to find themselves playboy shipping magnates, virtuoso musicians, millionaire expatriate abstract artists living in hot countries with sixth wives.

Adam was not an exception to the rule that those to

12

whom much has been given will crave still more. Only rarely did it occur to him that he and those like him might be pushing their luck – that he might rouse from his wish-filled fantasy to find himself working on a storm-tossed North Sea fishing boat at six in the morning in midwinter. Whether or not he did so consciously, Adam was a man who guarded what prestige he had, and constantly sought its enhancement.

Some of Adam's fellow passengers had joined him at the stern railing, so that he was obliged to practise his speech under his breath. Adam literally looked down his nose at a boy whose parents had dressed him as colourfully as a harlequin. The boy threw paper packets of salt and pepper at the hovering seagulls until Adam, *in loco parentis*, told him to stop. The boy was soon joined by his older sister, who looked as if she had cut her own hair without the aid of a mirror. They began to hit and scratch each other, bumping into Adam's legs without taking the slightest notice. Adam self-righteously remembered himself at their age, wearing his miniature tweed suit against the London winter, shaking hands with the Queen; sitting silently, teacup in hand, next to General de Gaulle; dancing with Princess Georgina for more than an hour without complaint. One advantage of being an only child was that Adam's parents had felt they could take him places where children of diplomats with larger families would have been out of place, not to say unwelcome. Adam had been a charming boy, grown-up without being irritating, good for a chat. He kidded himself that this was some innate, superior trait, rather than the product of irreproachable grooming on his parents' part. Whatever the reason, he had done Belgium proud.

Adam looked at his watch. He regretted that he had been unable to secure a day or two off work, which would have allowed him to visit a girlfriend in Paris before driving into the country for the wedding. As things stood, he would be lucky to have time to dry the sweat from his brow before pacing up and down with Norman, the groom, outside the château chapel.

Norman was an unexceptional man – Eton, Oxford, aimless world travel – with little to recommend him but his family's ancient title and its more recent international property débâcle. Adam understood that Norman had chosen him as best man by default; no other choice but a neutral one would have appeased Norman's brothers, stepbrothers, schoolfriends and fellow aristocrats. Adam's selection was also a gesture of Norman's immeasurable gratitude: Adam had shrewdly and selflessly seen how perfect a wife Didi (as the bride was known) would make for anyone who could prove that he deserved her. Adam had sent Didi Norman's way after only a token, four-month attempt on his own behalf. Adam's personal campaign had not been entirely fruitless – something he hoped he would be gentleman enough not to mention to Norman in the receiving line – but any possibility of continuing their liaison was soon snuffed out by Adam's patent lack of funds. Funds were what Didi liked, because funds were what Didi was used to. Didi ran with a glamorous crowd.

Of the dozens of ghastly secrets Adam would have to keep to himself during the wedding, one was that he had once proposed to Didi. Her laughter still rang in his ears. She had not appreciated, as Adam had, the gorgeous romance of proposing marriage to a woman one had known for mere weeks; nor had she found it amusing that Adam thought he measured up, financially speaking, to her requirements. The result was that she found his sincere proposal of marriage simultaneously insulting and ludicrous.

14

Adam fought his disappointment in secrecy. He told no-one – not even his mother, who would have been thrilled to hear that at least her son had made an effort. He hoped Didi had kept the episode to herself, while doubting she had. Norman was so pitilessly crude and arrogant that he was likely to make an issue of Adam's humiliation during one of the evening's toasts.

Another of Adam's secrets was that he had begun to hate the groom. So many things had gone Norman's way that the man had begun to believe they were his due. He belittled his friends to their faces and in front of their wives. He lived for social point-scoring. Two days ago, over the telephone, he had called his soon-to-be wife 'a very, *very* stupid girl,' when that was obviously not the case. He alluded openly to aspects of their courtship that Adam considered private. Adam had frequently resolved not to spend time in Norman's company, ever again, but always found himself lured back by the prospect of capturing one of Norman's cast-off girl-friends on the rebound.

Adam folded his translated speech and slid it into his inside jacket pocket. A young man and woman – dressed head-to-toe in black leather, covered in grease and sores, scraggly hair stiff with dried sweat or gel – approached and took a section of the rail next to Adam. The man flicked his hair in the wind, like an oily horse tail. The woman wiped her nose on her sleeve. Adam studied the filthy pair and listened to what passed for their conversation. They grunted and they pouted. They let cigarettes dangle from their mouths, and allowed ash to fall on their leather jackets. Their words were so indistinct it took a minute for Adam to realize they were British. He had a good ear for accents, even mumbled ones. He placed the couple as lower-middle-class Londoners who affected the increasingly popular cockney intonations and were better educated than their appearance and manner suggested. He brimmed with disdain.

Adam's accent was beautiful. His speaking voice would have been rich, precise and seductive in any language, but the accident of his upbringing, his social milieu and his education had granted him an accent that most people enviously and secretly agreed was the apotheosis of spoken English. He could have been an actor, had he the barest trace of talent. He even laughed perfectly.

He moved away from the leather couple, away from a French family taking turns photographing each other, away from three English ladies who reeked of sherry even in the strong morning breeze, away from a pair of African men who carried handbags. He spent the remainder of the journey avoiding people who offended him. It was not just Adam's natural snobbery in action here: Adam was easily depressed by his own short-comings, a feeling compounded by having to look upon the miserable failings of his fellow men. It was because Adam had a good, soft heart that other people displeased him. He was oversensitive to the human condition, especially as it reflected on the fruitless endeavours of his own mortal life. It was with some relief, therefore, that he finally returned a customs official's salute and accelerated alone into the parched French countryside.

Adam pointed his beloved car in the direction of Aubade, the village of Didi's birth. He had seen photographs of her mother's château, which was built inside the partially ruined walls of a medieval fortress. Norman, the groom, had visited his intended's family several times. He reported that their home was not the largest château one could imagine, but among the prettiest. Its colourful history of sheltering army head-quarters over four centuries of war helped to explain the château's survival and its excellent state of repair. It was known locally as Le Château du Philosophe, after a famous house guest of one of Didi's ancestors: The philosopher Huivis came to visit for a season in the eighteenth century; he had stayed on, entirely un-welcome, for the remaining fifty-eight years of his life.

The château had been built of local stone, and re-tained the attractive rust-orange colour of a discreet sunset. Its turrets were conically capped with grey slate, its gargoyles were mischievously sculpted in the image of the Pope at the time of construction, its courtyards were paved with reddish cobbles, its park boasted a small zoo. Norman said he thought he would be very happy living there, if Didi's parents ever died.

The village of Aubade, which Adam reached from the coast in under three hours, was hideous. Located on a flat stretch of land on the left bank of the slow-moving Baune, under the towering pylons of the French national grid, coated in a chalky dust particular to the area, Aubade sweltered in summer heat waves, drowned in winter cataracts, and festered in between. Its two abutting cafés offered plastic chairs and tables, awnings tinged with soot and advertisements in English for fish and chips. The village was home to a single dusty tree, an ancient oak that cooled the church square and shielded soccer-playing children from the sun. Le Château du Philosophe stood two miles or more up river, on a gentle escarpment that must have eroded considerably since the time it was considered worthy of fortification.

Adam pulled over into a dusty lay-by to change his clothes. He did not wish to risk being noticed in mufti by early arrivals. The atmosphere beside the road was one of asphalt, diesel and cow-pat. He undressed,

17

stretched in the sunshine, then put on the new morning suit he had bought specially for Norman and Didi's wedding. This was an extraordinarily well-fitting garment – thrice altered, thrice cleaned. He retrieved his top hat from its box in the boot, reconsidered, and replaced it. He tiptoed back to his seat, wishing not to arouse the sticky Aubade dust and soil his glistening leather shoes.

He pulled back out into the road and drove along in the wrong lane for a minute or more, until corrected by an oncoming articulated lorry. By the time he had swallowed his heart, the forest that surrounded the fortress wall that surrounded the park that surrounded the château had come into view. He found the entrance without difficulty, for it was marked with colourful balloons and printed signs that read 'Didi'. Two other cars, coming from the opposite direction, turned in before Adam did. Cars were parked along both sides of the gravel drive out to a considerable distance from the château, the central aspect of which could just be glimpsed through the trees and the dusty heat haze. Adam took his official wedding duties seriously, and believed in perquisites. He drove on. He passed women walking uncomfortably in short dresses and high heels, girls wearing flowers in their hair, men uniform and grim. Guests trailed on like refugees.

Adam drove slowly uphill through a wide gap in the overgrown fortress walls, after which the road levelled out and changed from gravel to cobblestone. The château was smaller than Adam had expected it to be, but more ornate. The one respect in which Huivis had not been out of his mind was his decision to stay as long as he did. Two naked youths of stone held a fish aloft between them at the centre of a modest pool. A fine spray shot from the mouth of the fish, and a faint rainbow arched above the château walls. Wide steps, visibly bowed at the centre, led to a narrow promenade in front of the château's main entrance. A gardener had done wonderful things with boxwood. Two huge intaglio fleurs-de-lis framed the front door, in recognition of the controversial Bastard King – a child of nine named Julien St Gregoire de la Boigne-en-Yres who had lived in the château and reigned over France, without knowing it, for six weeks in 1743.

A man wearing a dusty suit flagged down Adam's car and asked him where he thought he was going. Adam strained his memory recalling the French for 'best man'.

'*Je suis le garçon d'honneur,*' he said, blushing at the phrase.

The man clicked his heels and gestured for Adam to continue into a reserved parking area. Adam was greeted there by a squad of eager porters that outnumbered his light luggage. He was ushered into the château through a rear kitchen entrance, then up two spiralling flights of a back staircase to his stone and oak bedroom. Adam felt illicit, once he had been left alone with his gold-canopied bed, his panoramic tapestry, his tiny windows overlooking the park and the parade of wedding guests. It was as if he had broken away from a tour of Versailles and stepped over a velvet rope. This room could have belonged to the Bastard King himself. Its dark wood ceiling was decorated with carved suns and stars and moons. Adam liked his room so much that he hated the thought of having to leave it for the chapel.

A weary knock came on Adam's door. He answered it to find Norman standing unsteadily in the corridor, wine bottle and glass in hand. Adam supposed that Norman was as handsome as people said he was meant to be, but was it really right for him to wear three days of salt-and-pepper stubble to his first wedding? Norman looked frightened, hungover to the point of physical sickness, drained of all his normal self-confidence. He solemnly shook hands with Adam, but did not look his friend in the eye as he entered the room and sat down on the bed. It was as if he had come to Adam to be told his appeal against a murder conviction had been turned down. This struck Adam as extremely odd behaviour in a man who in a matter of minutes would be married to the splendid Didi and, by extension, to a splendid château.

'Try to smile,' Adam said. 'It's not the end of the world. And you are going to be clean-shaven if I have to do it myself.'

'I've done the stupidest thing,' said Norman, in a deep, tired voice.

'The *stupidest* thing? *The* stupidest thing?' Adam sounded jovial. 'Go on, tell me.'

Norman did not smile. 'We had a party last night.'

'I'm sorry I couldn't make it.'

'Here, in this house.'

'This is a beautiful "house", Norman.'

'Well. Everything got out of control. I think it must have been nerves, on everyone's part. I had a terrible row with Didi.'

'That's to be expected.'

'Yes, especially if you've been caught sort of kissing your fiancée's stepsister.'

'Oh, God, Norman. You *did* do the stupidest thing.'

'I'm afraid so.'

'Will the wedding go ahead?'

'Are you joking? Do you know what kind of planning goes into an event like this? How much money? We'll be married, all right.'

'Thank *God*.'

'Don't be sarcastic.'

'I'm sorry, Norman. I feel I've let you down. I should

20

have been here yesterday at the latest. I might have prevented all or some of this. It's just that I couldn't ignore some important . . .'

Adam choked on the word 'work'. 'Work' was something as foreign to Norman as space flight. He had responsibilities, and probably spent as much time as the next man doing things he would have preferred not to do, but no-one would have called his occupations 'work'.

Norman ignored Adam's apology, and looked even more tense. 'Do you know, she didn't say a word to me at the town hall? We had to register. She didn't *look* at me. We went there and returned in separate cars. The first time we'll be face to face will be down there.' Norman waved his fingers towards the chapel. 'You don't think she'll *kill* me, or anything, do you? Some French ritual I don't know about? Or not show up and leave me to pick up the bill?'

'I doubt it. Knowing her it's more likely that she'll take it in her stride. She's awfully modern.'

'I certainly hope so. It would be embarrassing to get divorced before we were married. I have no idea what will happen. You will protect me, won't you?'

'Where are your brothers, your . . . other people?' Adam asked this question cautiously; Norman had a complicated family.

'Drunk,' he said. 'That is their retaliation.'

'They all know?'

'They all know.'

'But that's ridiculous. You need your team to rally behind you. This is a crisis. Where are their loyalties?'

'With Didi's father, once they got a look at his cellar.'

Norman took a packet of cigarettes out of his jacket pocket and lit one like the condemned man he considered himself to be. He threw the spent match carelessly to the ancient parquet floor.

Looking at his friend, Adam wished he had a title. Titles were beautiful things, no matter what anyone said. Those who would belittle titles and the titled were the most envious of all. However seldom they were used in daily life, they were still there on the stationery, on the hotel register. No doubt Didi understood this.

'She's going to forgive you,' said Adam. 'I'm certain of that. She already has forgiven you. She wants this wedding to be perfect.'

'Do you really think so?'

'I'm sure I'm right.'

'About ten more minutes, and we ought to march down there.'

'Fine. But do me a favour?'

'Whatever you want.'

'Three things. Give me the ring. Don't put that cigarette out on the floor. Come over to the basin for a quick shave. You'd better brush those teeth, too.'

Minutes later, well-groomed groom and best man entered the candlelit gloom of the chapel through a low side-door near the altar. Norman and Adam took their places next to the right front pew, which was occupied by Norman lookalikes of all ages, across from Didi lookalikes of all ages. Everyone looked surprisingly jolly, considering that most of them probably knew what Adam had just learned. Adam wondered which one of the elegant young women in the front pews was the stepsister in question.

A frail-sounding organ hooted in the background, the high heels of late arrivals clicked on the stone floor, too much incense caused coughing among the elderly. There were no more than forty or fifty people assembled indoors; hundreds had massed in the main courtyard. The Norman lookalikes were noticeably puffier and pinker than their French counterparts. Most of the men

22

beamed the friendly smiles of people who had recently discovered the pleasure of drinking fine wine early in the morning.

A priest, or possibly a cardinal, entered the chapel through the same door Norman and Adam had used. He nodded to the two men, then went about his business behind them. Adam could just hear him muttering in Latin, pouring liquids, kissing objects. Out of the corner of his eye, Adam saw Norman rocking on his heels; he hoped his friend wouldn't faint.

Seconds before their wait would have become embarrassing, applause was heard outside the chapel. Everything started to move quickly. Adam patted his pocket and felt the ring there. Didi entered the chapel on her father's arm, kitted out for marriage rather than vengeance. Her father was born to his role: tall, slim, white-haired, tanned, ever-so-slightly stooped in modesty. The usual organ music piped down from the dark ceiling. Everyone stood. Adam could feel Norman relaxing at his side. Didi's smile was visible behind her veil from fifty feet away. Norman should never have doubted the social professionalism of his fiancée.

Like her father, Didi was predisposed to shine at public ceremonies. Adam had always thought that her beauty was of an unusual, hard-to-place variety, but now all was clear. Didi was made to glide down the aisle on her father's arm. She had the neck for it, the smile for it, the hair for it, the bosom for it; she had a six-year-old niece to gather her train. Nothing was going to interfere with her performance, not even whatever messiness Norman had got up to in recent hours.

Suddenly, Adam had a terrible thought. That smile on Didi's face – it didn't look murderous, but nor did it look quite sane. She had suffered an extreme blow to her pride, after all. Norman had revealed himself just one day too early as the shit everyone else already knew him to be. She would have her revenge, Adam thought (and now his limbs had begun to tingle), by turning to him, Adam, instead of Norman, to take her vows of matrimony. In a flash, it made sense. Adam could not say he was against the idea. He recalled their nights of passion with pride. He had proposed to the woman once, after all; Didi needed only to accept at the last possible moment. How romantic of her. She would make anecdotal history by marrying her groom's best man *at the altar.* Adam had a ring in his pocket, for which Norman could be reimbursed over the next few years or so. *He* would live happily here, in his wife's pretty castle, until he died.

In the event, Didi did not suddenly take Adam's hand. She married Norman, as planned, and when the ring was handed over Adam had to sit down and clutch his sweating hands together. The priest, or cardinal, drew out the ceremony by speaking at length in three languages. One of Norman's brothers, or stepbrothers, read St Paul's epistle; Didi's most famous cousin, a male actor, read a frightening poem whose central metaphor compared life in general with the specific lot of a Frenchman who was killed in battle during Napoleon's last campaign. The perfidy of Albion was played down; none of France's maddening characteristics was mentioned. Even Protestant Adam, because he had been rattled by his thunderbolt matrimonial fantasy, almost partook in the Eucharist.

Adam walked only two ranks behind the married couple as they debouched into bright, hot sunshine and the noisy cheers of their less favoured friends and relatives. A smattering of colourful locals was also on hand for this part of the festivities. Adam lost sight of the newly-weds as they were surrounded by the crowd on their way to a horse-drawn carriage. He found himself being kissed or patted on the back by friends and acquaintances, and trying to say the right thing to each of them. Adam remembered everyone's name, always. He prided himself on this politician's trick, which required sustained effort. It meant that at a drinks party, for example, he often had to interrupt a conversation to ask people to repeat their names over the background noise. If they said 'Pietro Volicare,' Adam asked them to spell it. Then he would shout at himself inside his cranium, 'Pietro Volicare, Pietro Volicare!'

'Hello, Pietro,' he said now, effortlessly recalling the name of someone he had met for ten minutes five years ago. 'Hello Sibyl, Thérèse, Alan, Judd, Catherine, Paul, Helmut, Crink, Nathan, William, Henri, Patrice . . .' This went on for some minutes, through thirty people or more, until the clacking of hooves caused everyone to rush to the battlements to watch the couple's ceremonial departure (ceremonial, because they were going to come right back). There was a night of revelry to be endured.

Bells tolled in the village down the road. The couple's carriage, drawn by a single skittish bay, driven by a liveried servant carrying whip and cigarette in the same hand, descended the gentle slope amid a clatter of camera shutters. Adam estimated that four hundred people were on hand to witness the spectacle. This number would be whittled down by a third for champagne in the park, meaning that the locals would be sent home. A choice eighty would later retire to the banquet hall inside the château, where a single famous table could accommodate them all. Adam wanted to see that table.

The crowd was corralled into the park to await the couple's return. Adam was told that the carriage would pause in the village only long enough for the

25

newly-weds to drink a glass of cider with an old woman who had saved six-year-old Didi's life when she fell into the Baune and nearly drowned. The woman was now too frail to make even so short a journey. Adam supposed some might think the bride's gesture a pretentious act of *noblesse oblige*, but he found it understated and admirable.

Adam followed the procession towards the park, walking arm in arm with Norman's elderly grandmother. He had met her on numerous occasions in the past – on school holidays, for example, which Adam sometimes spent with Norman's constantly changing family – but had never seen her wear quite so annoyed an expression. She lifted her hatchet face to the crenellations and arrow slits overhead, and seemed to hark longingly back to Agincourt. Adam supposed that Norman's grandmother resented the idea that her offspring had to sell everything she had given them in order to keep the external trappings of her estate on view to the worshipful masses. How galling to be a genuine aristocrat hard on her luck, then to see a French family's ersatz version thriving; not to mention all the bloodthirsty papist nonsense she had just sat through.

'Norman is looking well, don't you think so?' she said, in her clear voice. Her dry fingers trembled lightly on Adam's forearm. 'The pair of you, my goodness. You were so handsome no-one could take their eyes off you.'

'You're flattering me, Silly,' said Adam, wincing at Norman's grandmother's nickname; at the same time he felt a special privilege in having been told long ago to address her that way, rather than use her formal title and name.

'I suppose I should say that the bride looked simply beautiful?'

'Of course she did.'

'And this is lovely, here, this little *earthen track*,' she said, holding Adam's arm tighter as they climbed a beautifully groomed path to an enormous plateau of park – planted, as the French seemed to insist on doing, with breathtaking avenues of red rose bushes. 'There is a pavilion, at least.'

In fact, there were three huge red-and-white-striped tents. These were useful not just in case of rain, but to fend off the setting sun. The receiving line began to assemble at the skirting of the first tent, with four photographers arranged to capture every kiss and hug. Everyone was issued a glass of champagne to last the wait. Guests were overtly discouraged from splitting off to form satellite conversational groups.

Norman's grandmother seemed happy in the queue, especially as she found herself only feet from where the couple would reappear. She began to lecture a young relative of hers, a boy who seemed not to know who she was, so Adam felt it was safe to leave her alone.

'I must go,' he said, kissing her cheek. 'The responsibilities of the best man, you know. You will dance with me later, won't you, Silly?'

Adam had to take a nap. The tediousness of the wedding service had added to his usual sleep requirements. His presence at Norman's side would not be required, owing to the large number of brothers and stepbrothers vying for a position at the groom's elbow. Adam wanted to be fresh for his speech, and he missed his fabulous room. He was capable of sleeping at will for exactly twenty minutes, fully clothed. He smiled as if on a particularly pleasant errand as he weaved and waved his way through the gathering queue and marched up the front steps of the château. He found his way to the back staircase, climbed it, and locked himself in his room with a heavy iron key. He removed his coat, then lay on top of the bed with his hands folded over his chest. Thirty seconds later he was asleep. When he awoke he sat up straight-backed, like a vampire rising from his coffin. Those few minutes of sleep would serve to extend his liveliness until dawn, which was the earliest hour one could expect to escape Norman's clutches, even on his wedding night.

Adam stood up, fluffed the silky bedclothes, and went to the window. Outside, in the park, the queue had begun to wind past the newly-weds, who from Adam's perspective high in the château looked like ornaments on a wedding cake.

An orange sun hung expressionistically over the horizon. Two dozen waiters ferried silver trays of champagne to thirsty, alcoholic guests. The authentic locals trudged home to their village, clutching red plastic bags containing party favours and souvenirs. Adam thought how beautiful the scene was, how right for the celebration of an important couple's union.

Adam's envy was like a tight collar around his neck. He bit his lip and leaned against the window frame. He knew what an ignoble emotion envy was, not to say a deadly sin. He wished he could stop himself from thinking – as he had done with increasingly painful focus – that if he really belonged to the society fate had seen fit to throw him into, he might experience life as something more than an annoying series of humiliating phases.

With a sigh, Adam left the window and went to a gilded mirror to perfect his appearance. He took after his father, which most people agreed was fortunate. He had a boyish look about him, an easy smile, broad shoulders and long legs. He was used to being attractive to women, but within the past year he had been annoyed twice by casual remarks about his features. One girl had said he looked like someone who was used to wearing glasses and had recently switched to contact lenses; this

28

was not only untrue, it also caused Adam weeks of concern as he tried to figure out whether she could possibly have meant it as a compliment. Perhaps she liked men who went around looking startled. The other remark was of a more straightforward nature, having to do with Adam's strong jaw – and the likelihood of its eventual disappearance into Göring-like folds. Adam did not like being kidded about a double chin he did not yet have.

Adam scrubbed his hands in the porcelain washbasin before descending to the park. He took the long way out of the château, taking in its opulence before he became too drunk to appreciate it. When he entered the banquet room he stopped, leaned against the oak door frame, and put a palm to his chest. There stretched before him the fabled table and its eighty place-settings, each one a miniature skyline of crystal glasses. Severe underlings in starched white chef's outfits ignored Adam as they busied themselves arranging precious, artistic food. Wherever the kitchen was, it had filled the banquet hall with the perfume of exalted cuisine, a blend that would prove to be comprised of seven heartbreaking courses. Adam's palate quivered in anticipation of the red wine, which even now breathed from decanters set next to dusty bottles ranked like soldiers down two sidetables. It was all so impressive – the flowers, the silver, the table linen, the gold place-card holders, the art, the suits of armour in the corners – that Adam thought he would weep.

Instead, he helped himself to a piece of truffle the size of his thumb, then skipped out into the sunset to take his place in the receiving line.

'Hello Cynthia, David, William, Frances, Chantal, Xavier, Victor, John, Camille, Rebecca . . .'

His first glass of champagne was replenished before

he noticed it was empty. He knew he would have to steer a course between an amount to drink that would allow him to deliver his bilingual speech without shame, and an amount to drink that would allow him to survive the fit of nerves he already felt welling inside him. Adam belonged to the majority of people who were uncomfortable with public speaking. He dreaded it, and with reason. His previous efforts at weddings had never been, as alternately required: inspirational, amusing, nostalgic, spiritual, sarcastic or loving. Worse, he could hear himself descending into banality and hollow punch lines, without being able to control his delivery. This difficulty never affected him in small groups. Presentations at work rarely posed a problem. Only in front of crowds did he lose his composure, even when his speech had been thoughtfully drafted in advance. It was no comfort to know that in this respect he was simply normal.

In the receiving line, Adam was able to put his nerves to one side and revel in his status as best man. All of Norman's friends, who would have loved to give the impression that they had seen it all before, had forgotten about pretending not to be awed by the setting. They asked Adam to report on Norman's state of mind just before the ceremony. They hinted that backstage rumours of discord had reached the ears of even the lowliest guests. Adam was quick to say that this was nonsense, that all had gone as smoothly as Didi's parents' high standards required. He said that Norman could not have been more positive, while at the same time being humbled by the power of his love for Didi. He pointed out the sunlit smiles of the couple now only twenty yards away.

Adam was startled when the parents and step-parents of the bride addressed him in French. He mumbled in reply, which came out sounding enough like a proper language that he could smile and mumble some more. His hosts did not seem to notice, and they thanked him for a job well done. Next in line was Norman's father, a fat, smug, side-of-beef of a man. He looked as if he thought he had better things to do than stand around in the sun all day outside someone's gaudy pile; there were grouse to slaughter, for heaven's sake. Adam bowed to Norman's father as he shook his hand, a nervous tic he could not train out of himself. He knew better than to ask any questions or to attempt small talk, because Norman's father affected the speech of someone with a heavily bandaged head and screws through his jaw. Adam simply performed yet another involuntary bow, muttered congratulations, and moved on.

Norman's mother and stepmother stood gamely side by side, which was astonishing to anyone who had read newspaper reports of their bitter feud. Predictably, Norman's mother was an emotionally scarred woman in her early sixties, while Norman's latest stepmother (two more, now exiled, had intervened) was tall, vacant, ill at ease and thirty-five. This arrangement saddened Adam, who believed that families ought to remain together for the sake of children, grandchildren and decorum, no matter what horrors of hypocrisy and compromise had to be endured.

Adam's chest tightened as he moved to his left to kiss and congratulate Didi. It was so important to be blasé, or to appear to be blasé. He had to wait an uncomfortable minute, brushing at his lapels and gazing up at the sky, while Didi saw off the profound feelings being conveyed to her by a French guest. When at last the guest was pulled along by her companion, Adam took a step forward, pivoted on one heel, took one of Didi's hands in both of his and kissed it. Then he kissed her lightly on each cheek, administered the subtlest of squeezes to one side of her waist, said in his mellow voice how lovely she looked, then stepped away again. Adam liked to think that he, rather than the evening sun, had caused Didi to blush.

'I'm sorry you weren't here earlier,' she said, in her sweetly accented voice.

'Work,' said Adam, with a tone and emphasis and movement of the eyes intended to convey the image of life-and-death financial crises only he could manage, instead of the tiresome trip to Bath that had been the real cause of his tardiness. One of his more mercurial clients had got into trouble expanding a business based on the sale of false mobile-telephone holders; these were fitted over the real telephone next to the driver's seat in cars, convincing thieves that the owner had taken the precaution of removing his expensive equipment.

'You poor man. We had a lovely time.'

'That's what Norman said.'

Adam never ceased to marvel at the sophisticated codes of human speech.

Didi leaned closer and positioned her mouth next to the side of Adam's head that faced away from her husband. He could smell her make-up, her perfume, the flowers in her hair; it was all a bit much. Her ivory wedding dress had a cobweb look that Adam supposed meant it was antique and valuable rather than dirty and second hand.

'Norman and I have a surprise for you,' she whispered. She put the back of her hand to her lips and made her body accompany a silent giggle.

Adam wondered what this could mean. 'A good surprise, or a bad surprise?' he asked.

'Oh, a good surprise. You will see.'

'He isn't going to embarrass me, is he?'

'How could anyone embarrass you, Adam?'

'They could make me give a speech in French, for a start.'

32

'Oh, that. You will be marvellous. You will be so funny and handsome. You will say wonderful things. *Frances*,' she said, turning to the next guest in line. Adam was left with an uncomfortable pause while Norman finished exchanging japes with a Frenchman who thought he had a stylish command of colloquial English, but did not. Norman alternately nodded and shook his head, then at last patted the man on the shoulder and ushered him along. It was Adam's turn.

'Norman.' A long shake of the hand and extended eye contact symbolized the meaningfulness of this moment in their lives.

'Adam.' Norman's appearance had been transformed by shaving and matrimony. He had changed only just perceptibly since university days, when he had commanded respect out of all proportion even to his family's advanced social standing. Adam had envied him then, and he envied him now. He seemed so at home in the receiving line of his own wedding outside his in-laws' château. There was an inevitability about his situation that Adam promised himself he would think about later.

'Congratulations.'

'Thanks,' said Norman. 'Listen. I have a surprise for you.'

'Really?' Adam glanced back at Didi, who was not listening to someone who had a great deal to impart in a hurry.

'You're going to thank me for this.'

'Tell me.'

'No. It's a surprise.'

'When will I be . . . surprised? I hate surprises.'

'You won't hate this, Adam. You will be surprised in approximately two hours. During dinner, in other words.'

33

'I have no idea what this is all about. You're being cruel, now. Please prepare me.'

'I'm not going to say a thing more. Except thank you for making up for not being here when I needed you.' He turned his head away from his brand-new wife and whispered, 'Everything seems fine. Time will tell. There are other matters to attend to.'

'And other clichés.'

'Anyway, off you go.' Norman already had the next guest firmly by the hand.

Adam wandered away towards the second pavilion, where an ignored string quartet played energetically in the shade. He plucked a champagne glass from a passing tray, and found a group of acquaintances with whom he could stand and pretend to converse. Between casual, insincere remarks, he asked himself what Norman's surprise could be. Any number of possibilities sprang to mind, including two or three humiliating ones. It seemed unlikely that Norman would risk further damage by alluding publicly to Adam and Didi's doomed courtship.

'Don't you think so?' asked a tall, bald, bespectacled American whose name immediately sprang to Adam's mind.

'Absolutely, Travis,' he replied, nodding and frowning.

Adam wanted to relax and try to forget about Norman and Didi's surprise. The successful delivery of his speech was still uppermost in his mind. He hoped he would have an opportunity to study it one last time. Its text contained the word '*grenouille*', which he dreaded pronouncing. Worse than that, Adam no longer had confidence in the joke that required him to use the word '*grenouille*'; he wondered if he ought to find a Frenchman and test the joke for offensiveness.

* * *

Adam had envied Norman since the day they met. Their friendship was based on their parents' acquaintanceship when Adam's father was Ambassador. It was Adam's belief that Norman reciprocated friendship because he had never met anyone quite so intelligent as this half-Belgian contemporary. Adam was very bright; Norman's other friends, on the whole, were not. People who met Adam when he was younger thought how wonderful it would be to know as much as he did, and to be able to express one's ideas so clearly and persuasively. They chalked it up to luck, when it was the product of scholarship. Adam had misspent his youth in study.

'Norman is a lucky man,' said Travis, squinting up at the château walls.

'I hear there are problems. Money problems. In Didi's family,' said another American in Adam's group.

'This wedding won't help,' commented an Englishman.

'This is excellent champagne,' Adam remarked.

'Laudable,' said a German, holding his glass up to the setting sun.

Everyone tried hard not to break down and weep at the impressiveness of Didi's set-up, which all of them had heard about but never seen. For people who set great store by social and financial advancement, and who gave themselves happiness mainly by comparing themselves favourably with others, there was something eviscerating about momentary contact with the unattainable.

'Are your parents not here, Adam?' asked John Freeman, one of Norman's childhood friends. The question was designed to highlight Adam's parents' lack of intimacy with the groom's family, relative to that of his own.

'I'm afraid not, John. They're in Antibes.'

'Stuck with the tourists, are they? Pity.'

'No, well, they're . . .'

Adam decided rather maturely that this conversation was pointless and exhausting. Also, if he were to be perfectly honest, he did resent the fact that his parents had not been invited to the wedding when John Freeman's had. They may not have kept up with Norman's parents in recent years, or ever since Adam's father quit the diplomatic service, but the men used to dance with each other's wives, and vice versa. He wondered if his father, who was not a pleasant man, could have done something to offend Norman's parents.

Adam liked to think that his father could be summed up in a simple anecdote from his own childhood. When Adam was about six years old, his father picked him up and put him on top of a tall metal filing cabinet. 'Now jump down,' his father said, extending his big hands. 'I'll catch you.' Adam jumped, and his father let him fall to the floor, where he twisted an ankle. As he carried his son out of his office to find help, Adam's father said, 'You won't forget this, my little one. Don't *ever* trust *anyone*.' Adam's father hadn't had a terrifically good war.

'Oh, no,' someone said. 'It's a medieval jamboree.'

It was, indeed, a medieval jamboree. As the last fifty guests waited to congratulate the newly-weds, a colourful procession of rag-wearing, black-toothed, juggling, singing, fire-breathing, dancing Dark-Ages types turned the corner of the outer fortress wall and began to try to be entertaining. Children joined in, and were issued non-medieval helium-filled balloons. Minstrels wearing vertically striped tights strummed crude mandolins and sang songs about the infrequent joys of serfdom. Dramatically corseted women and girls, bonneted and barefoot, taunted Norman's inhibited guests with the bawdiness normally ascribed to people who lived in the shadow of great plagues.

The sun bled into the dark, flat horizon, as the medieval jamboree was succeeded by a village brass band wearing tattered, dusty uniforms. They formed a semicircle around the newly-weds and the dregs of the receiving line, and began a prolonged serenade. The couple forced smiles through the blare, and continued to shake hands until the last guest – an old man neither of them appeared to recognize – had been dispatched.

'So far so good,' said a woman named Marina, at Adam's side, as if it were her own wedding.

'Yes. At last, they can have a proper gulp of champagne. I think I'd need it.'

'But, you have champagne,' said Marina, who was German, and whose English was not perfect.

Adam had met Marina twice before, at Didi's London pied-à-terre, and he liked her. She organized foolish excursions in Europe for a wealthy circle of friends that included Didi. These were people who required an element of surprise to enjoy their holidays – the opposite of normal travellers. Marina supplied them with a list of clothing and props they might or might not require, bundled them on to a coach at a central London hotel, drove them to the airport and blindfolded them before check-in. Not knowing what pleasure was to follow seemed to relax them and make them happy. Marina was a stout woman, Adam's age, who was a sister and confidante to her more beautiful friend. She had a crush on Adam, which made him sad. In the iciest chamber of his heart, he disliked the idea that she thought she had the remotest chance.

'I understand *she's* here, tonight,' Marina said. 'But I haven't seen her yet. She certainly wasn't in the chapel.'

'What do you mean, Marina?' Adam liked to use

people's names in conversation, since he had gone to all the trouble of remembering them.

'I mean I heard someone say *she* would be here. You know who I mean.'

'Let's see,' said Adam. 'The President's wife?'

'You are joking.'

'Not Princess—'

'Pah.'

'Then I can't think.'

He could think. He knew who *she* was. What he hadn't known was that she would make time in her schedule to attend an out-of-the-way wedding. She was someone about whom Adam had been rude, over and over again, without ever having met her. This was possible because he could be rude and condescending at a safe remove, in the privacy of his own cranium, looking at her picture in magazines and newspapers. Everyone knew she was an old friend of Didi's but no-one mentioned it, lest they appear to be seekers of introduction. The source of Adam's rudeness was his old-fashioned belief that celebrity for celebrity's sake was superficial and uninteresting. The woman in question seemed to have risen to prominence on a puff of hot air having to do with beauty, exotic parentage, and the kind of daredevil social life some would call an art form in itself. Adam, fascinated but superior, dying to meet her but afraid to mention her name to anyone who knew her, leapt to the conclusion that she had been carried to notoriety to the tune of creaking bedsprings from London to Los Angeles and back again.

'It's *Natalie*,' said Marina.

'Natalie? Oh, *Natalie*.' Adam frowned and sipped his warm champagne.

'She's so *average*,' said poor Marina, pursing her lips as if it pained her to say so.

'In what way?'

'In all ways. Don't you think so?'

'I've never met her.'

'Well, neither have I,' said Marina, as if it were rude of Adam to have implied that she had. 'But the things you read, especially recently.'

'I suppose I haven't been paying attention.'

Adam had been paying attention. He knew quite a number of well-known individuals – in fact it tortured him somewhat that there appeared to be so much fame to go around that half his friends had tasted a soupçon here and there – but Natalie was the most talked about person within the perimeter of his social circle.

Adam got the idea that the engine of fame accelerated rapidly. How else to explain a woman of only twenty-five – whose main accomplishment seemed to have been the honing of a style of dramatic entrance to parties – fetching up as some sort of pseudo-starlet and being the most anticipated guest at the smartest wedding in all of Europe that weekend? Adam found himself becoming galled, in Didi's park. Natalie had begun to give *interviews*, in which she was asked about her wardrobe and her political outlook. Adam had decided that *not* having any proper qualifications was her strong suit, and that with fantastic instinct it was the one she had elected to play. The thing had a momentum of its own, and it made Adam sick.

Marina was a good example of the kind of person who had evidently fuelled Natalie's literally effortless rise. By calling her 'average', Marina implied that Natalie had done something, rather than stood around listening to people telling her how wonderful she was, and knowing that they carped enviously behind her back. She could not be average, because there was nothing with which she could properly be compared.

* * *

39

Natalie's parents had been the catalyst of the whole strange reaction. Her English father had done something modern with words; her French mother had done something modern with fabrics. They had exploited their self-employed status with a lifetime of Bohemian travel, a style of living that was apparently unaffected when they became rich. Natalie's father, George, was the first to be the beneficiary of a windfall. Just after the war he had written a curious little fable called *Army Ants*, twenty pages of verse that he printed himself in his garage. Because of the paper shortage he made only fifty copies. His first wife, Joanna, had illustrated the book with simple line drawings of the characters, who all looked the same because they were ants. She was proud of her husband's verse, and secretly used her own family's money to augment the print run. She took samples to bookshops to see if they thought they could sell a few copies. The shopkeepers indicated that the work would probably not appeal to children, because the writing was a meaningless stream of disjointed phrases about nothing whatsoever, but that they thought it had every chance as adult poetry. A few dozen books were accidentally sold, and George and Joanna waited for literary canonization; sadly, and despite the incomprehensibility of *Army Ants*, recognition did not follow. It was only twenty years later, when a subconsciously influenced British filmmaker appeared to have plagiarized what there was of a story in the work (submarine warfare), that George made his killing. The court settlement, which did not seriously dent the production budget of the American film, probably paid George more than all the postwar poets earned among them in their lifetimes.

George's first wife and illustrator had died of boredom not too long after helping her husband to launch *Army Ants*, so it was Françoise, Natalie's mother, who profited most from Hollywood's misdemeanour. She was the keenest of travellers, and convinced George that his rejuvenated writing career would best be lived out in a nomadic, shoulder-shrugging apathy suited to the age. They took Natalie and her two little brothers with them. Adam found it hard to imagine a world where such constant movement in treacherous foreign lands was possible, but evidently such a time had existed not too long ago. They traipsed and they wandered, they roved and they roamed. Natalie grew up self-confident, multi-lingual and tanned.

Françoise came into her own during these travels. A long-term amateur of décor – and since the birth of her children an energetic clothing designer – she naturally assimilated whatever ingredients moved her in each culture her family encountered. While her husband sat indoors wearing loose cotton clothing and not writing, Françoise embarked on an informal career that would result ten years later in seeing her initials over a boutique almost in the Faubourg St Honoré. She was aided by her gift for articulating a philosophy of children's clothing, in three languages, that was embraced by Continentals and mistrusted by Britons. This philosophy saturated her designs with meaning, and the suggestion that something like world peace depended on the success of her line. European children whose affluent parents were interested in the preservation of humanity were soon to be seen wearing batik shifts, hand-crafted leather bandoleers, tropically colourful silk headbands and almost any manner of hat.

Natalie and her brothers grew up in an atmosphere that neatly blended art and commerce; they enjoyed the prestige of the former and the prosperity of the latter. They were taught mainly at home, by both parents and servants, and substituted languages and worldliness for traditional education. They carried with them through their teens that special mystique often attached to people who must pause for a moment to recall their nationality, or must grope for common words in what should have been their native tongue. Their father, inspired by his wife's success and his indirect fame in America, began to put pen to paper instead of holding it an inch above its surface. He produced four further children's stories that were sold side by side with his wife's clothing. Unfairly, perhaps, each story was transparently about Natalie. They told of her adventures in far-off lands, of her nasty, mischievous little brothers, of her beauty and her grace. She was photographed, and became the face that fronted her mother's enterprise. She was famous before she knew whether such a condition might be desirable.

'Natalie probably won't turn up,' said Marina. 'She's too important, I suppose.'

'Maybe you're right,' Adam said, looking at his watch. 'Still, there are plenty of other important people here.'

'Of course. But not like *Natalie*.'

'No.'

The older set at Didi's wedding – with their counts, their politicians, their soldiers and their intellectuals – might not have known nor cared about Natalie; but for the younger crowd – those whose characters were not yet wholly formed – she was the pre-eminent guest. Her absence so far only confirmed her stature in their eyes: her signature was the late, breathless entrance, which offended Adam no end: late, breathless entrances were for American floozies, or dizzy Latin gold-diggers. Adam let the theory cross his mind that Natalie would fail to appear at all, snubbing both Norman and Didi in one *coup*. Adam guessed that Natalie had made the conscious decision to generate more column inches by staying at home – wherever that happened to be – than

42

by appearing alongside the relative riff-raff at Didi's family château.

This was not an attitude Adam could normally abide, but he reminded himself that Natalie was not entirely to blame. If she could parlay colourful parents, a redoubtable personality and some people's idea of great beauty into such splendid notoriety, who was Adam to complain? Still, the theoretical Natalie irked him.

'Hello Beth, Victor, Henri, Barbara, Allison, Gunther, Mark, Frédéric, Matthew, Paul.'

A crèche had been arranged in a modern addition to the château, so that parents were temporarily free to enjoy themselves. It contributed to Adam's composure that most of the young children and babies had gone away. Children were a reminder to him of how many good friends he had lost to family life in the recent past. Most of the women his age who did not yet have babies were pregnant. Adam saw how their lives had ended, but was sanguine about the idea that his own would end as soon as one of the few single women near him in Didi's park made a sufficiently convincing bid to make him her groom.

Still, this thought shocked and terrified Adam. He did not like to think that another person could hold sway over his life – a life he thought he had lived more or less to perfection, within its limitations, for thirty-one years: he worked hard, he knew many important people, he had travelled widely. Short of being an important person himself (which he considered beyond him for structural reasons), Adam had accomplished somewhat more than might have been expected of him at birth. On the other hand, he wished for love.

'Couldn't be better,' said Adam, ten or twelve times in five minutes. This was the truth. Adam believed that people were born with limited potential. The Normans and the Didis of the world were no different, but they

43

were limited in a distinct way. Norman, for example, had very few choices in life. Now that he was the uncle of his older brother's healthy boy, nothing short of a series of tragic accidents would permit him to become as important a figure as his father, no matter what he did or how hard he tried; and by marrying Norman, Didi had made one of the few decisions of significance in her life. Adam could see her remaining years playing themselves out as if they had already happened: two children in two years; a dirty divorce from Norman (who would probably be in gaol); remarriage to someone older; interminable widowhood; death in the château, surrounded by family she no longer recognized.

For the sake of appearances, Adam tried to appear light-hearted. He stood with one hand in his pocket, the other holding his champagne glass loosely at his side. He adopted a rapt expression when women spoke, and a look of comradely goodwill for the men. Not all of this behaviour was unconscious. To act naturally was not a form of social conduct available to him. This did not mean he was stiff or uncomfortable in company – merely cautious and dishonest, like everyone else.

The brass band went away. Norman and Didi were photographed, along with their complicated families, under klieg lights on the main staircase of the château. Waiters and waitresses weaved through the park, serving exquisite morsels of seafood, and sausages to placate the English. The summer evening had provided a perfect temperature for standing outside in formal clothes. The guests' conversation grew in volume. Those who knew that their presence was not desired at the dinner table drank and ate as much as they could before discreetly returning to their cars. The eighty favoured ones gradually coalesced into a dense group close to the banquet hall doors, while the hundred who would make do with outdoor tables searched the empty sky for rain. Norman and Didi returned from being photographed, and a small cheer went up in their corner of the park.

Norman looked ill again. He smoked openly, which Adam found unbecoming in a groom. Adam wondered if he ought to go over to him and whisper in his ear that his teeth were purple, and that he wasn't supposed to be drinking red wine just yet. Adam told himself to relax, and to stop treating this occasion as if it were his own wedding. So what if Norman and Didi got off to a rocky start? What did that have to do with Adam? He would probably see them once every year for five years, once every two years for six more years, then never again. Their relationship would be entirely pro forma from now on. Best man indeed, thought Adam.

'Hello, best man,' said Jan Deely, one of the groom's friends. 'What do you think of Norman's conquest, then?' She gestured not at the bride, but at the bride's ancestral home. Jan was a tiny woman with prominent teeth. She wore bright green-rimmed glasses that made her look like a baby alligator. She was known for her sarcasm and bitterness. Adam guessed she was lonely.

'She looks lovely,' said Adam, ignoring Jan's true meaning. 'I'd say she was born to appear at her own wedding. How are you, Jan?' He wanted to tell her that he liked her dress, which was brown, but suspected Jan, of all people, would turn her brutal wit on any sign of false flattery.

'I'm just aflutter with happiness and sentimentality,' she said. Jan's career in journalism had evidently not disqualified her from Norman's circle. 'Did you hear that *she's* supposed to be here? I am breathless with anticipation.'

'I suppose you mean Natalie,' said Adam, covering a small yawn. 'Someone mentioned that, I think.'

'The world is upside down, when people like *her* become prominent.'

'As opposed to people like them?' said Adam, nodding his head one centimetre in the newly-weds' direction.

'Well, still. I think it's disgraceful. Who *is* she? What has she *done* to deserve so much attention?'

Adam risked betraying his attention to Natalie's rise by pointing out to Jan that she herself had recently written a bubbly profile of Natalie.

Jan frowned. 'That was supposed to be a piece about exactly what I've just said. It was edited down to a puff. You don't know how these things work, Adam.' She adjusted her green-rimmed glasses on her nose.

'I suppose not.'

There was a pause, and no immediate conversational escape route opened to either of them.

'How smart you look,' said Jan, looking up at Adam. 'Quite the gentleman.'

'Thank you,' he said, having long-since decided that flattery was best taken at face value.

Jan looked at her watch. 'I have to go.'

'Oh? Well, I'll see you inside . . . after . . .'

'No, I *have* to go. I am not one of the elect. I have overstayed my welcome as it is.'

Adam flinched with social self-consciousness.

'Well, then. Back in London?'

'Of *course*,' said Jan, reaching into her brown plastic handbag for her car keys. 'I'll just pay a few last respects, say a few goodbyes.' She walked away.

Adam was essentially a good man – he knew he was. He avoided confrontation, he practised a professional honesty that would probably be the undoing of his legal career, he made every effort not to offend people or hurt their feelings, and he considered himself a loyal friend. He therefore asked himself why it was that he had just been made to feel that he had broken Jan Deely's heart. It wasn't his fault that she had fallen at the last social hurdle before the big banquet-hall table; that a place could not even be found for her outside; that she was only a journalist; that she looked like a baby alligator.

'Hello, best man,' came another voice. A conversation followed that was remarkably similar to the previous one.

When it was over, Adam made an excuse to those near by, and retreated once more to his bedroom to study the text of his bilingual speech. Already the folded pages shook in his hand. He wondered if he should have drunk more champagne, or less. His speech now sounded sycophantic and weak. It sounded like a courtier's last attempt at favour. He had to take the formal-sounding French on faith.

He opened a window for fresh air. When he leaned out of the window, he could see most of the crowd in the park near the banquet hall. Beyond the park and the ruined fortress walls, the flat, dark countryside stretched into the violet distance. Two ranks of towering pylons marched against the horizon. Adam's head contained few thoughts as he gazed down at the grey-and-floral crowd. This was not his mind's normal state, but a defence mechanism triggered by nerves. He had lost confidence in his speech.

There was little or no train of thought to be interrupted, therefore, when a white taxi appeared on the straight, linden-tree-lined drive. Adam saw two-dozen heads turn in the crowd. He saw the bride stand up on tiptoe, and put a hand to her hair. The taxi swept up to the main staircase, and Adam could see the driver's face craning out of the window to take in the splendour of the Château du Philosophe. The rear door opened, and out came first the legs, then the garment bag, then the rest of Natalie. She turned and handed the taxi driver a note, and waved away change. The driver seemed reluctant to leave, but did so. Natalie turned again, dropped her bag to the ground, put one hand to her white, large-brimmed hat, and raised the other hand to wave at the crowd, every member of which had now stopped talking to watch her arrival. Didi cried out girlishly and began to run across the park to the drive, as if until now she had thought Natalie had been killed in a plane crash years ago. She must have been wearing flat shoes, because she glided smoothly along with one hand protecting her coiffure and the other holding up a bouquet of ivory wedding dress. Natalie reciprocated by jogging up the steps to the landing of the park, where the women collided in embrace. The other guests looked as if they wanted to break into applause. Natalie's bag was swiftly ported away by one of Didi's liveried flunkies.

Arm in arm, Natalie and Didi returned to their audience and were swallowed up. Adam was glad to be sequestered in his beautiful room, thus avoiding inevitable questions about one's social proximity to the starlet. There would be Marina-like remarks about Natalie's choice of dress, which was light blue and probably too short for one's liking at so formal an occasion. Questions would be raised about her hat, and what could be seen of her hair. It would be admitted that she looked good, but mainly that she photographed well. Some would wonder where her boyfriend was, currently rumoured to be a young American actor with European art-film pretensions. Adam risked falling out of the window to see Natalie kiss the groom. Afterwards she gave him a little slap on the cheek, which was probably meant to signify that his hell-raising days were at an end, that it was time to trim his flaps for the short cruise towards oblivion. The party seemed to turn around her. She stood between bride and groom, as if forming a second, more important receiving line.

Adam would be damned if he would enter into this charade. He closed the window and returned to his speech, which now sounded like a plea for clemency from a charwoman caught stealing her mistress's earrings. He wished he could rely on an innate ability to extemporize. How difficult could it be to bestow his blessings and his best wishes for a bright and prosperous et cetera? *Mes chers amis . . .*

What he needed was a central joke or pun – what expert after-dinner speakers probably called *extended metaphor*. He tried to imagine seventy-nine heads thrown back in unbuttoned laughter, waiters pausing in doorways, fearful of interrupting the finest banquet-hall speech since Huivis himself had held forth in his prime. He tried to think of an original metaphor for Norman and Didi's union, and had to stop thinking when all that came to mind were corporate mergers, Middle-Eastern dowry-deals, and genetics experiments.

Adam decided he had to return to the wedding before he was missed. By now people would have got their perverse anti-Natalie conversations off their chests, and could return to talking impotently about world events. He walked downstairs the way he had done some hours before, to take in the banquet hall. This time he had the courage actually to explore the long room, which was empty of people: the geniuses had finished their work. The chandeliers were alight. Adam ventured further, tracing his hand along the edge of the table and inspecting the place cards. It was in this way that he discovered the surprise Norman and Didi had mentioned in the receiving line. He found his name, framed in gold, between those of Norman's grandmother and Natalie.

Adam sniffed. A waiter appeared in one of the two

doorways that led to the kitchens. They smiled at each other, and Adam made a gesture of approval with one arm. The waiter bowed and retreated. Adam turned and exited the hall, taking the long way out to the main entrance of the château. In the grand entrance hall stood a marble statue of Huivis, a fat book in the crook of his arm, a hand to his chin, deep in original thought. Adam looked up at the great philosopher, and envied him. He brushed his lapels with opposite hands, then strode through the wide-open doors into the night. He turned left, following the light orange château wall to the park. The party had relaxed. The conversation was noisy, oiled by drink. The waiters and waitresses collected more glasses than they delivered, indicating that dinner was minutes away.

'Hello Catherine, Nancy, Inger, Sam, Peter, Philip, Arthur, Susan, Suzanne, George.'

With the utterance of most of these names, Adam felt a new blister of envy forming on his thin skin. His contemporaries were just old enough to have primed their lives with success, just young enough not yet to have ruined everything with excess, accident or pigheadedness. There was an apparent effortlessness to their conventionality that made conventional Adam feel like a deranged outlaw merely because he was single. Adam wished he would meet a woman who might vindicate him, and made the others take notice. He wondered what they said about him behind his back, knowing that it was statistically unlikely to be kind; presumably they enjoyed reminding each other that Adam was Belgian.

Take Simon, here, now shaking Adam's hand and probing for his last name. Simon looked less English than Adam did, but was a certified Knightsbridgian. He was bald. He sported a tidy blond goatee. He wore delicate round spectacles. His soft body hung sack-like in a dusty morning suit. He looked like the coach of a Dutch chess team. On the other hand, Simon had enjoyed infuriating success in what should have been ordinary business, and he radiated the pleasure he took in his growing family and other possessions.

Or take Fabrizio, here, shaking Adam's hand and not remembering his name at all. If Adam met one more suave Italian princekin wearing cufflinks of . . .

'Hello, best man,' came another voice. 'May I have a word?'

Norman had left Didi's side. He looked awful. He took Adam by the elbow and escorted him away from his group, out of earshot.

'I have the worst problem,' said Norman, smoke jetting from his nostrils.

'Oh really? A couple of hours ago you told me you had done the stupidest thing. Do you now really have the *worst* problem?'

'You tell me,' said Norman, turning his back to the château. 'I've come down with something of a disease. A genital thingy.'

'Oh.'

'I just can't imagine where I picked it up. It's ghastly. I mean, it's *visible*.'

'Let me guess,' said Adam, with distaste. 'You have managed until now to keep this condition secret from your now wife.'

'It only . . . erupted a couple of weeks ago, and she hasn't really been . . . you know the stress of weddings, Adam, it hasn't been an issue.'

'But now?' Adam enjoyed postponing the moment when he asked Norman just what he thought his best man could do about such a fiasco.

'Well, now, just about fifteen minutes ago, the girl told me how much she is going to enjoy conceiving on

51

her wedding night. She says it is a family tradition, and men aren't considered, you know, virile, unless they come up with the goods.'

'Dare you risk it?'

'Well of *course* not, you bloody—'

'You mustn't raise your voice,' said Adam. For the benefit of any guests who might be looking on suspiciously, he tossed back his head and pretended to laugh appreciatively at Norman's sentimental thanks for his services as best man. 'And there are lip-readers everywhere in France.'

'Look, I've come to you to see what you think of a little plan I've hatched to cope with this situation.'

'I see. I am the venereal-disease-on-the-wedding-night expert, am I? I advise the groom on his bedroom deceptions, do I?'

'Please, there isn't time for you to be angry. I have thought the plan through, and I like it. I have decided—' Norman looked over his shoulder and lowered his voice. 'I have decided to have you spill brandy in my lap after dinner, then I will simply drop my cigarette lighter into the stuff, we'll douse the flames with wine and rush me to hospital. I will take the doctors into my confidence. You will translate.'

'I must say, Norman. You are packing several years' worth of unpardonable behaviour into the first hours of your marriage.'

'Can't you see that it is a perfect plan?' Norman insisted, insanely.

'Better than the knock-on-the-head, feigning-amnesia, disappearing-for-a-few-months technique? Better than shooting yourself?'

'I can see that you're angry.'

'You are a fool, Norman, a degenerate, an unforgivable—'

'Yes, yes, but will you *help* me?'

52

'—cad. Absolutely not. And where did you pick up this . . . these symptoms, anyway?'

Norman scratched his chin. 'I was hoping you could help me narrow it down. Have you been going out on the town much with me, during the past month?'

'I have an idea, Norman. Why don't you just make a list of your sins, a complete list, and submit it to her tonight along with a brief glimpse of your grisly privates. You are Catholic now, aren't you? Just confess and get it over with.'

'No-one is going to *help* me,' Norman said, looking down at his dusty shoes.

'And no-one said marriage was going to be easy.'

There were facilities available in the château for those who desired to change their clothes for dinner. The smartest women, including Natalie, took advantage of this service. Two waiters wearing starched white jackets with gold-braid epaulettes stood at attention on each side of the dining hall entrance, signalling an end to the outdoor reception. All of the undesirables had cleared off.

Adam held back and chatted with a pedantic, elderly German whose main topic of conversation centred on a slackening he had perceived in the morals of young people. Adam nodded regretfully and admitted to similar reservations about his contemporaries, unwilling to waste his breath mentioning what most people would have called an utter collapse of morals in the older man's day. The German's pale, darkly freckled pate was visible between strands of silver-blond hair. He spoke conspiratorially, as if Adam were a fellow member of a secret society. Adam had observed that he often had this effect on men and women his parents' age or older; he thought it might have something to do with his conservative style of dress or his neatly cut and parted hair. He did not know if it was a good or a bad thing that he quickly gained the confidence and approval of authority figures. Certainly, it could be useful when charming the anxiety out of girlfriends' guardians.

In the same way that Adam always endeavoured to remember people's names, he tried to concentrate and remember the things they said. This was one of his hobbies. He wanted to understand and store their remarks, no matter how routine or superficial, and to understand what might lie behind them. He wanted to be sympathetic to human nature as reflected in people's verbal tics and subtleties. When the German man explained his presence by saying that he was an old friend of Didi's mother and was the father of one of Didi's many international beaux, Adam took this to mean that he resented Didi's having married an English second son instead of his own perfectly suitable boy. When the German said what a wonderful fellow Didi's father was despite being merely a wildly successful businessman, Adam detected the hint that Didi's old man was rich enough to have restored his wife's château and kept her family's semblance of nobility on the rails. When the German let it slip that the choice of wines had been his own, it did not take a man of Adam's social acuity to infer that he considered his palate superior to the best to be found in the mouths of Frenchmen.

'The young today they do not understand the refined pleasures,' said the German, returning to his only theme. 'They want to believe the marketing man, the advertising man. They have no independence of conviction,' he said, in his precisely enunciated, not always correct English. 'And why is that?'

Adam knew this was not a question he was expected to answer. He was supposed to sigh mournfully and let the German continue.

'This is because the young people today are neglected by their mothers.' Adam looked up from the grass, where he had been pointing his head with unfocused eyes, and looked at the German's mottled face. 'They receive insufficient attention from their women-folk, both the men and the children, and they are navigating. They are *wandering*. Why is this that they get insufficient attention from their womenfolk? Because the women are working now, in this busy world.'

Adam and the German shuffled along in the informal queue that had formed at the entrance to the dining hall. Adam calculated that he would have to suffer roughly three more lessons in *non sequitur* before they reached their destination and parted to take their seats.

'The culture of the nation is instilled by the mother into the children. My mother sat patiently with me when I learned to play the violin, when I learned to draw, as I composed my poetry.' Adam had learned earlier that the German had used his many gifts and social connections to attain the position of Executive Vice-President in charge of sales for Denmark and the Netherlands of an American conglomerate (speciality fine laundry detergent). 'Ach, Schubert,' he said, looking up at the sky, revelling in his own cultural refinement. 'The children do not go to the concerts. I can see that you are different, though.'

'That may be,' Adam replied, feeling himself being adopted. He had only been to a single concert of any description in fifteen years, and he hadn't enjoyed that one.

'These people with their fuzzy heads and their filthy overclothes—'

'Ah, here we are,' said Adam, disguising his relief. 'I hope you enjoy your dinner. It looks superb.'

'I selected the wines myself, you know,' the German

repeated, as they shook hands. They separated, and walked in opposite directions along the vast, breath-taking table.

Adam stood behind his high-backed oak chair, waiting for the last of the ladies to return from changing into different versions of what they had been wearing minutes previously. He studied the tapestry covering the entire wall opposite, which was known as the *Layenfette*. It depicted the usual hunting, crusading, banqueting and solar-eclipsing one was used to, with the famous addition of a none-too-subtle panel reflecting the unconventional, possibly bestial appetites of one of Didi's earliest ancestors.

The long room was suitably dark, and a layer of candle smoke had already established itself between the carbon-coated rafters high overhead. Adam tried to relax, and greeted each newcomer to his end of the table with a smile and a nod of his head. He did not dread Natalie's arrival, for he had already rehearsed in his mind what he hoped would be a nonchalance verging on rudeness. One could not let fly-by-night good-time girls get the better of one. He would wait a suitable length of time, which he would spend talking to Norman's grandmother about the decline of standards back in England, then he would wheel on Natalie and ask her who she was. He would do this so convincingly that Natalie would be forced to conclude that here, at last, was someone so busy and self-contained that he did not have the faintest idea how lucky he was to have been seated next to her. It would be amazing how many friends they had in common. Then he would turn away and not speak to her again, ever, for the rest of eternity. He would have struck one tiny blow for the part of civilization that did not, as the German man had rightly pointed out during his one lucid moment, fall for the marketing man and the advertising man. If Natalie was a product, Adam wasn't buying.

For the hundredth time, Adam patted his jacket pocket to feel for his folded speech. Silently, without opening his mouth, he exercised his throat in preparation for the dozens of guttural noises he would have to make. He would speak third, after the father of the bride and the father of the groom. He had already sized them up as no competition. Didi's father would be formal and cold, ticking off points as a matter of etiquette before saying how pleased he was and sitting down. Norman's father would attempt to entertain the guests, which in his entire life he had only tried to do by telling the story about the time he was in France during the war and had decided to liberate some of his comrades from captivity in a farmhouse, only to discover that he had picked the wrong place, blasted the doors off an innocent barn, and let three Allied cows out into the wild. There was perhaps no story ever told that was less funny than Norman's father's story, unless it was the same story told by Norman's father in the evening, when he was certain to be drunk and disorientated. It was not possible that the French contingent would laugh, and the English guests would choke on their *coeur de palmier* in embarrassment. Norman's father's face would bloat and redden in amusement at his own failed heroism. He would sit down after a cursory toast to the newly-weds in which he would studiously forget or at least mispronounce the bride's name. This was the sort of act Adam thought he could safely follow.

Adam found himself salivating at the sight of what food had already been placed on the table. There was so much red wine breathing in the hall that he could smell its sumptuous bouquet as if a sommelier had raised a spoonful to his nose. He eyed his assortment of crystal goblets with satisfaction. He was just about to say to himself how typical it was that Natalie was among the last to return from preening herself, when she entered the room arm in arm with Norman's grandmother. Natalie had decided to wear something decidedly odd – a tight gold-piped black jacket of distinctly Spanish cast over a brilliantly white ruffled blouse and a billowing ankle-length black skirt. She had not dressed like any of the other women, but nor would she have blended with the crowd had she done so: her smile brightened the gloomy old hall. Adam was touched by her evident patience with the slowness of Norman's grandmother's gait. He noticed the whiteness of the tips of her long fingers, offset against the brown hand she rested on Norman's grandmother's forearm.

'Hello again, Silly,' Adam said, installing Norman's grandmother next to him, smiling at Natalie as if she were the lady's minder.

He pulled out Natalie's chair. She waited until the bride and groom arrived and were seated, then smoothed her skirt and sat down. Because her attention was on the newly-weds, she did not acknowledge Adam as he guided her chair beneath her.

With everyone seated, waiters and waitresses began to work their magic. Guests did not have the sensation of being catered to, so numerous were the servers: forty, to be exact, each responsible for whisking away two silver plate covers. People were busied immediately with food and wine, with which the newly-weds casually toasted the assembly to put them at their drinking ease. Before the first perfectly timed gambit of charm could escape his lips in Norman's grandmother's direction, Adam found himself confronted with a china plate not too preciously adorned with crescents of goose-liver pâté, thin squares of blond toast and a fistful of truffles broadcast at random.

'Eau,' said Norman's grandmother. 'I don't suppose there are brains in here, quite yet.'

'No, Silly,' said Adam, saved at the critical moment from being compelled by an invisible force to turn towards Natalie, who had been engaged in conversation by the groom's older brother.

'You won't tell anyone, will you?' said Norman's grandmother.

'Of course not,' said Adam. 'Tell anyone what?'

'Well *you* know, and all, dear boy, what has happened, about the, will you?'

'Of course not. About the what?'

'My aching back,' said Norman's grandmother.

'I know what you mean,' Adam replied, taking her remark as metaphor.

'Of course I never had an aching back, it was simply the frogs.'

'I beg your pardon?' Adam said, softly but forcefully, in an effort to remind her that she was surrounded.

'Well, you know, or the *brains*. You're quite sure?'

Adam was helped along this line of conversation when Norman's grandmother pointed at her truffles with a fork and made the face of someone witnessing cannibalism for the first time.

'Oh, Silly, that's like a mushroom. Fungus. It grows in the roots of trees, like a . . . like a potato or asparagus. You'll love it. Costs more than its weight in gold.'

'Keep your voice down,' she said, hearing Adam's last remark. '*That* won't do.'

During this surreal exchange, Adam had felt Natalie radiating at his side. He suspected that the corners of most eyes were upon him. After all, on her other side sat Norman's elder brother, who had not only married and multiplied, but had made it known to intimates that enough was enough, he was homosexual. People wanted to see what Adam would do.

59

Even Adam knew that someone as well known as Natalie wore a visible halo, these days. He could see through the back of his head, as he nursed Norman's grandmother through her appetizer, that Natalie glowed. She possessed a modern grace. She was known, for absolutely no reason her friends could divine, to hundreds of thousands – or more likely, when Adam thought about this for a moment, to millions.

'They are animals, don't you think so?' said Norman's grandmother, referring not to something on her plate but to the participants of one of the nasty wars currently flaring up in her newspaper at home.

Adam had known Norman's grandmother since he was eight years old, and she had never changed. Adam suspected that her erratic conversational style had been developed specifically to confuse and annoy her husband, who was easily her intellectual inferior. Norman's great-grandfather's short illness had seen Norman's grandfather into the House of Lords at the age of thirty-three, when he had been obsessed with the treatment meted out by humans to a particularly lovely tree. Thirty-five years in the upper chamber had not seen him speak on another subject. Each passing session found him calling for ever more ruthless treatment of those who would harm or impede the growth of his precious tree. Adam had seen Norman's grandmother shouting at the radio on the one occasion when her husband's thoughts had been broadcast to the nation. She came from a family of doers.

'Who is that thing on your right?' Norman's grandmother asked in a whisper.

'Silly, please, she'll hear you,' he replied, his head lowered, his napkin to his mouth. 'She is an old friend of Didi's. I think they met in North Africa when they were girls. She's awfully famous, at the moment.'

'Didi is?'

'No, the other one. The one practically touching my elbow. Please, keep quiet.' Adam knew that Silly was capable of tapping Natalie on the shoulder and asking her where she bought her ghastly clothes.

'Anyway, she's perfectly beautiful,' she said, to Adam's surprise.

'Do you really think so? You aren't staring, are you?'

'What if I were? She is marvellous. Oh, my. You don't often see *posture* like that, any longer.' She had leaned well forward now, to inspect Natalie with the brazenness of the elderly and socially secure. 'She must be a film star.'

'She isn't, actually,' Adam whispered, unable any longer to eat. He put his napkin to the corner of his mouth and spoke with his lower lip touching Silly's ear lobe. 'She is the daughter of a rather famous British writer and his even more famous French designer wife. You are right in the sense that roles have been offered to her, but she is more what you might call a socialite, for the time being. She is covered in the newspapers and magazines as if she were a duchess. There must have been girls like her in your day.'

Norman's grandmother snorted and reached for her glass. 'You're lookin' at one,' she said, in an American accent.

Norman's grandmother had drunk a great deal, and it suited her. Adam was able to peel sixty years from her features and see a beautiful girl who had made a desperate mistake by marrying Norman's grandfather. He could also see that she was offended at having been seated farther away from her grandson than Natalie; that she couldn't care less about the success of her grandson's marriage to someone she considered a beautiful but frivolous tart; and that she didn't care for French peasant food no matter how aesthetically presented.

'Aren't you going to talk to her?' she said. 'Don't waste

your time on me, Adam. Where is the man in you? My God.'

Adam's face twitched as he tried to think of a chivalrous reply. 'Don't be silly, Silly,' he said.

'I wouldn't at all mind seeing you married. Talk to her, for heaven's sake. This is how things work.' Her parchment skin was stretched over sharp cheekbones. Her upper dental plate rattled as she ate. 'Have I been clear on the matter that you were not the worst influence in Norman's life?'

'You have now.'

'It's true, you know. I am making an attempt to be clear with people, and I want to be clear on the matter of the way in which you have not been the worst influence in Norman's life. Far from it. Ah, more wine. No, that would be his father.' Norman's grandmother sucked in her cheeks and raised her glass sloppily in the direction of her son. 'I am dead inside,' she concluded, not for the first time in Adam's experience. He knew he was now expected to turn and introduce himself to Natalie, on his right side.

He turned, and Natalie did likewise, as if their movements had been choreographed.

'Isn't this divine?' she said, smiling in a way that was so familiar from the photographs he had seen that Adam had to remind himself that they had not been properly introduced. 'I'm Natalie.'

'Adam.' He wiped his fingers with his napkin and shook her slender brown hand.

'I know about you. You're Mister Gosse, the best man.'

'The *garçon d'honneur*, that's me.'

'I'm so terribly sorry to have missed the ceremony. It's just typical of my luck, I'm afraid. I should have left more time.' She leaned closer to Adam. 'Please, *please* don't breathe a word of this to Didi, but it's all my fault

62

for staying up so late last night. I had such a terrible hangover I couldn't dial the telephone to get a cab. I missed my flight by hours. Aren't I awful?'

'Yes, a disgrace. Where did you come from?'

Natalie had to think for a moment. 'Barcelona. I wasn't planning on using it, but there's a cute little airport in Artennes, just half an hour from here. I was the only passenger, out of Le Bourget, can you imagine? I thought of Lindbergh. I'm very lucky to be here at all. I hate myself. I still have a pounding headache and I'm stiff from dancing.'

Adam did not believe Natalie's story. He thought she had probably been in Paris for days, planning her late entrance and her glamorous excuse. 'You did very well to get here when you did.'

'Adam, listen,' she said, placing her fingers on the back of his hand. 'Do me a huge favour?' Her voice was low and beautiful.

'Anything.'

'Be my date tonight? I can't stand it if I have to dance with everyone. You can protect me from the mob. I don't like old men.'

'It will be my pleasure.'

Adam's previous girlfriend of any significant standing had been an outsider from his group, a hard-working business student named Paula but known as Cinch. She made up for being too tall by having beautiful manners and a tolerably interesting family. Adam often forgot how young she was, and as a result he sometimes behaved callously. Adam and Cinch had never come close to reaching the point of sharing living quarters: Adam believed that modern cohabitation usually had more to do with practical and financial considerations than love, and he thought the practice deeply unwise. He believed in marriage, not in playing house.

Adam's affection for Cinch had been deep, though not particularly intense, and in the year since he last saw her he had often asked himself why on earth they had parted. He could not have given Scotland Yard a satisfactory explanation, except that he knew it was his own doing. There had been a moment in a restaurant that, because Adam was the sort of person to let this sort of thing bother him, bothered him. She had asked a typically direct question about their involvement with each other; he had replied honestly that he was a strong man, he was a man who carried a stern and pessimistic philosophy around with him like a sack of human bones, and in the end he could take or leave just about anything. When Cinch burst into tears Adam had to hurry paying the bill before anyone saw them. He took her home and did not ring her for three weeks, knowing all the while, when he had time to think about it, that she would be suffering. His logic was that by being brutal he could make Cinch hate him, thus softening the blow of his withdrawal. It was an adolescent type of behaviour he had detected and despised in others, but was evidently incapable of recognizing or curtailing in himself.

Poor Cinch. She wrote to Adam, telling him she loved him and was so unhappy that her studies had suffered and she had lost her appetite. Adam did not reply. She wrote again, ignoring the telephone in a way Adam no longer found quaint, but neurotic. She told him that he might not realize it, but he was letting his life slip away in cowardice, stubbornness and short-sightedness. She hinted that her own life was not worth living without him, that she worried about her consumption of sleeping pills and vodka, and that it would take a man of inhuman selfishness not to feel responsible for her safety.

Now Adam knew he had made the right decision, if

'decision' was the word for a dumb, animal act of self-preservation. He wrote back to Cinch at last, feeling foolish with the telephone next to him, stating in categorical terms that they were no longer an item, and adding what he supposed was a white lie: he was extremely worried about his own mental health, and he did not want to burden her with his problems; he mentioned a brain scan, and left it at that.

It quite offended him when he never heard from Cinch again. Could this mean she did not love him enough to nurse him through his difficulties, drive him to hospital, bring him tea in bed? Adam's mind simmered in its own vanity and regret.

'I have to give a speech,' Adam said to Natalie. The first course had come to an end. The vigilant waiters and waitresses had allowed no-one entirely to empty a glass.

'What, tonight? How terrifying.'

'Thanks for reminding me.'

'Just tell me if there are places you want laughter. That might help. I'll prompt the hall, if you see what I mean.'

'No, no. Heavens no. It's just a little bilingual testament to two very special people.'

'You're speaking in French, as well? I can't believe it. How is it that you speak French?'

'Just one of those things,' said Adam, as if fluency in a foreign language could be accidental.

'Oh, that's right,' said Natalie. 'You're *Belgian*, isn't that so?'

'Yes,' Adam replied firmly, having learned to avoid 'Technically half, but . . .', or 'So it says in my passport . . .', or, increasingly, 'No, where did you hear *that*?'

'How wonderful,' said Natalie, whose beauty was now a fact in Adam's previously sceptical mind.

Adam wished he could add that he had missed by a

hair's breadth being a count: someone named Georges Gosse, three hundred and thirty years ago, had done something stupid to rob Adam of his rightful title, something to do with killing an aristocrat's son in a duel rather than marrying the aristocrat's daughter. Adam loathed this particular ancestor.

'I haven't lived in Belgium since I was a baby,' Adam added, not too hastily. 'Just London, Oxford, London.' He hated saying this, but it was like an involuntary reflex after so many years.

'I see. Well, I'm glad I have such a worldly date tonight. We'll have so much fun. I do think this is about the most mismatched couple in the history of matrimony, but we'll make the best of a bad thing.'

Adam wondered if he had heard her correctly. 'I'm sorry? The most what?'

'Oh, maybe I shouldn't have said so. Is it bad luck? Should I touch wood? There, that wasn't so hard, there's wood everywhere. Are you superstitious? Please tell me you aren't.'

'I'm not superstitious. It's just that I thought, as Didi's mate, as it were, you would be behind her on this . . .' Adam had to laugh. 'This catastrophic error of judgement.'

Natalie raised one of her glasses to Adam and drained it. 'Thank you,' she said.

Adam had been watching the way Natalie drank wine, keeping in mind her relative youth, the amount of travelling she had done today, the hangover she had to cure and the momentousness of the occasion. She still drank too fast. None of this was betrayed in her speech or in a face so beautiful that Adam had to stop himself from mentioning it every time he opened his mouth.

'You really are beautiful,' he said anyway, having drunk quite a great deal himself. 'I thought it might just be the photographs.'

Natalie sighed as her glass was automatically refilled. 'Yes, well.'

Adam had hoped that he could be charming in the conventional way, asking questions, feigning interest. He had lost that opportunity now. He actually was interested, and he knew the answers to most of the routine questions he might have asked. He no longer wished to pretend he knew nothing about Natalie, which would be tantamount to admitting he did not read newspapers.

'Odd we haven't met before,' he said.

'That's my fault. I've hit a patch where I just seem to be moving, moving. I'm almost never in London, any longer.'

'Do you have a flat there?'

'I stay with my littlest brother, Eddie. He's a student, and is never home. He wants to be a writer, like our papa, so he stays out late, drinking in the street.'

'Are you going back to London tomorrow?'

'No. Are you?'

'I don't know. I suppose I . . .'

'Say, did you bring a car?'

'As a matter of fact, I did.'

'Do you feel like chauffeuring me to Paris? I have some things to take care of. You can come to a rather interesting lunch, if we manage to wake up in time.'

'I can get us there in two hours, on a Sunday morning.'

'How exciting. We'll have an adventure, Adam.'

'Cheers.'

'You are doing frightfully well,' said Norman's grandmother, when it was time to switch conversational partners again.

'I'm glad you think so.'

'I am quite proud of my hearing.'

'It is most impressive.'

'Do you know the man on my left?' she asked, loudly enough that if he shared her acute aural faculties he would overhear her.

'I believe that is Didi's uncle on her father's side,' Adam whispered.

'An *evil* man,' Silly spat. 'Let me just tell you a few things he said to me.'

Adam listened to a chilling synopsis of her ten-minute conversation, while at the same time looking up and down the table at his fellow guests in the Château du Philosophe. In their dark uniformity and glittering gowns, they could have come from almost any era in memory. There were luminaries on hand, to be sure, but the world was a gigantic place; many of them must have been uncertain of their remaining status. The English guests were for the most part aristocrats. Some severe, friendship-threatening triage had been performed to reduce their number to forty. They looked hale enough to Adam, but they could no longer be said to be important figures outside the country villages that bordered their estates. Even there, one suspected, they were figures of fun – or entertainment, when their lives went terribly wrong. The French, from what Adam had gleaned about them from other guests, seemed more substantial and accomplished. They did not necessarily have legitimate titles to fall back upon, only ancient names preceded by prepositions and a shared memory of gory persecution. They looked like the sort of people who would own valuable private libraries, and who would have the prettiest daughters in the world. Unlike the English, they would rarely misbehave; when they did so, out-of-focus photographs of their departures from court would rarely be used to sell newspapers. It occurred to Adam, Eurocentrically, that the main difference between the French and English guests surrounding him was that the French were not buffoons.

Adam liked to think of himself as belonging with these people. He played by their rules, he shared their education and their values, and for many years he had possessed what amounted to an honorary title as an Ambassador's Son. What he lacked now was any stake of his own to add to the social pot. A great deal of money would have helped, but he had neglected to organize that aspect of his life. This line of thinking brought to mind work, which in turn reminded him that thanks to his instant friendship with Natalie he had already missed tomorrow evening's ferry back to England.

Adam rehearsed in his mind, with some relish, the excuses he would send his superior's way. In reminding himself of his boss, whose name was Dick McDavis, Adam had to choke down his gorge. Dick McDavis and his wife ran a firm of solicitors that had recently begun to pattern itself on American law firms – ambulance chasing, one-time clients, libel, any form of personal compensation and, these days, small business bankruptcy. 'Listen, Dick,' Adam would say, explaining why he would not be at work on Monday morning. 'About today. I'm stuck behind six miles of French lorries. They've poured pig's blood on the bonnet of my car. They've tied live calves to the train tracks . . . You haven't? Buy a newspaper, Dick, it's Armageddon over here. *Bloody* French. See you soonest.' Adam had a dislike for Dick McDavis that on certain mornings could feel like a poison working its way through his system. Dick was the only person he had fantasized about murdering.

Adam had joined what he knew was a respectable firm – Stephenson, McDavis and McDavis. It was respectable because of Mr Stephenson, a man for whom Adam had felt immediate filial attraction. For two years, Adam worked under Mr Stephenson's wing, profited from his wisdom, assumed a golden future was there for the earning. Then came the Thursday morning when Adam entered the office suite to find Dick McDavis sitting at Mr Stephenson's desk, his wife standing at his elbow, the news of Mr Stephenson's stroke delivered between greedy lips. Mr Stephenson still lived, though he would forever be incapable of work. The firm was left in the hands of McDavis and McDavis.

Adam had once believed in Dick's charisma, so nicely counterbalanced by Mr Stephenson's genteel charm. On his own, McDavis was a monster. He liked to say that profits were not everything, they were the *only* thing. He rewarded hard work with more hard work. He relished his reputation for smarm. In Adam's view, Dick and his wife had taken advantage of Mr Stephenson's soft heart; they had cornered the older man into making them full partners.

Stephenson, McDavis and McDavis was Adam's one and only job, ever in his life. It had taken only two years following Stephenson's illness for him to see how out of place he was there, and how he had probably seen to it that he would never work for a respectable firm as long as his curriculum vitae contained the McDavis name. This would not have been a problem if those only-thing profits had actually rained down upon the McDavis head. In fact, business was hard to come by. The firm seemed to attract, when it attracted at all, doomed entrepreneurs who went under before they had paid their legal bills.

Dick McDavis and his wife had recently become enamoured of entertainment, and fancied themselves film and television producers. This gave Adam plenty of latitude for sarcasm in and out of the office, and for *schadenfreude* in the privacy of his own thoughts. Still, it was not much comfort that he seemed to have unconsciously carved out a niche for himself as an expert in the field of contract breaking. Adam missed Mr Stephenson every day.

'Eau, steak,' said Norman's grandmother, when the Château briand arrived.

'Yum,' said Natalie.

The banquet hall was full of noise and smoke. Several of the French guests — and Norman — had smoked cigarettes between courses. Adam glanced over his shoulder to see a full, pitted moon through one of the room's tall, oak-mullioned windows. He took a deep breath and a sip of water before tasting the new red wine, which the German had said possessed the characteristics of 'huge, milky breasts.' Adam smacked his lips.

'Did you get them a present?' asked Natalie, having finished with Norman's older brother.

'I did. I've never been very good at that, not very original.'

'I'll tell if you will. What did you buy them?'

'A champagne bucket.'

'Oh,' said Natalie, who had probably seen the innumerable, heavily decorated antique silver champagne buckets being carried to and fro before dinner.

'What did you give them?'

'I had my mother make them a blanket.'

'A blanket?'

'Yes. Isn't that all right? It's just a bloody angora blanket. Don't you approve?'

'No, no, that's fine, marvellous.'

'I cannot believe your attitude,' said Natalie. It was as if they were having their first row as newly-weds. She pushed away her plate of untouched beef. 'My mother's blankets are really very chic, you know. A handmade blanket, with her own fingers, her own time? This is a very expensive gift they are getting.'

Adam wondered why he was always wishing people would keep their voices down.

'I'm sure it is, of course. I didn't say anything. I think a blanket is the perfect gift, very touching, very intimate.'

'A "*blanket*" – I love the way you say the word. As if I'd picked it up in the stable outside.'

'I didn't mean that at all.' Adam suspected that Natalie was drunk.

'And I'm not drunk,' she said. 'Don't look at me that way.' She turned back to Norman's brother, who had been staring into space, leaving Adam with a view of the nape of her neck.

'What a shame,' said Norman's grandmother. 'And you seemed to be doing *so* well.'

Didi's father stood to deliver his toast, just as the plates from the main course were being silently whisked away. Glass in hand, he performed exactly as Adam had predicted. He named and thanked the main contributors to the event, bowed romantically to his wife (a gesture that reeked of infidelity), said something gallant about Norman's grandmother that came across as condescending, and asked the group to drink to the health and fruitfulness of the newly-weds.

Adam's throat tightened. The meal, and his turbulent relationship with Natalie, had taken his mind off his speech. He wished half of it had not been translated into French: even Didi's father had spoken mostly in English. Now that he had fallen out with Natalie, she could presumably be expected to scowl at his side, arms crossed impatiently, trading looks of derision with his audience.

Norman's father stood up. His segue was instantaneous. He required only the word 'France', where he stood at the moment, swaying noticeably, to see him

72

swiftly into his musty tale of wartime days. At least the occasion's *entente cordiale* would not be wrecked by his story, even if anyone could follow it through the gobbles and aspirations of his growling, crepitant voice.

'Dachshund sausage meat,' he seemed to say. 'Pleated skirts on angels.'

Adam fingered the speech in his jacket pocket. He had decided that the easiest and safest course of action was to abandon all hope and stay in his seat. No-one would know except the principals, and Natalie. He could easily live with the embarrassment of being thought a coward.

'Cantaloupe fever, haw haw,' said Norman's father. He had grown fatter since the last time Adam had seen him, when he had been trapped by the fireside and forced to listen, totally uncomprehending, to the peer's views on the pressing international issues of the day: 'Sugar bum beforehand, haw.'

The French guests smoked. The English guests wore fixed winces.

Adam had been privy to Norman's father's strong views on 'Europe', a topic he never raised in the House of Lords but was perfectly willing to expectorate all over during chauffeured car journeys, astride one of his horses, or over strong drink after dinner. When Adam could understand him, the man seemed to equate 'Europe' with cholera, white slavery and insidious, subversive philosophies of every stripe. 'Few let umbilical next partum kiss valour!' he might conclude, smashing his glass in the fire. Adam hoped he would not expectorate on the subject again tonight, though he seemed to be spitting plenty as it was. There was an architect of 'Europe' in the room, a bespectacled, dyed-haired Frenchman of ancient political standing. He could be counted on to rise to his feet in defence of his edifice, should Norman's father stray into European

73

metaphor based on his liberation of the Allied cows.

The wedding itself was all too symbolic a merger, without someone departing from his prepared text to make an issue of it. Adam's own speech, as far as he could remember in his panic, contained no allusions to the European Community. As a technical Belgian, his views carried some weight. As the son of a distinguished diplomat, he might conceivably make a quote of the week in a Sunday paper if he stretched any analogies too far.

'Gnome. Deary,' concluded Norman's father tearfully, raising his glass to the couple. 'Chess.'

It was Adam's turn. He sat, stony faced, studying the *Layenfette* tapestry. Conversation grew out of the silence that had followed Norman's father's toast. Adam listened to the rumble's crescendo, and thought he had escaped. People patted their mouths with their napkins in anticipation of whatever flaming creation Didi's chefs had dared to attempt for dessert. Adam deliberately did not look in Norman's direction. The room pulsated amusingly before Adam's eyes: he had evidently been matching Natalie swig for delicious swig. He wondered if he ought to turn to her and attempt a reconciliation. He could not remember what their disagreement had been about, which reminded him of spats with lovers of considerably longer standing. He exhaled deeply through his nostrils in relief at being home free.

Ting ting ting, chimed a fork-on-glass near by. The tintinnabulation, it immediately turned out, was Natalie's. She raised her free hand to hush the crowd, and at the same time leaned close to Adam and smiled. 'You did say you had a speech, didn't you? I can't *wait*.'

Adam supposed that if he were to shear off most of Natalie's fetchingly disorganized brown hair with his steak knife, he would be famous. He and his dinner companion seemed to have travelled the entire length of a destructive marriage together, in a span of minutes: meeting, mutual attraction, courtship; bitterness, argument, deviousness, treachery.

'Come on, *garçon d'honneur*,' Natalie said, tauntingly. 'This one's for Belgium.'

The room was silent now, except for the rays of the moon crashing against the silver. With the deliberation of a blind man, Adam leaned forwards, pushed back his heavy chair, and stood up. From that altitude, he could see every bloated, wine-raddled face in the hall. Waiters and waitresses retreated through swinging doors, not to return until the end of his performance. Adam managed to smile sardonically as he pulled his folded bilingual speech from his pocket, which drew his first expectant laugh.

You are perhaps expecting smut? Adam asked his audience, using only his eyes. Ten to fifteen minutes of innuendo about the life of my good friend before he was captivated and captured by the glorious Didi, never to stray again I'm sure?

Adam hoped that was not what they were expecting. He no longer had any memory of what his speech contained, but he knew it was not in the least suggestive, not at all what tradition called for in the jester's turn that is the best man's speech. He looked down at Natalie, on his right, and was stopped in the makings of a withering look by her absolutely honest smile of encouragement. She clasped her hands to her breast. She shook back the hair he had not cut off with his steak knife. She genuinely wanted him to do well.

Moved and terrified, Adam raised his head to address the hall.

Adam thought he couldn't speak French because neither of his parents had living relatives in Belgium. They had rarely travelled there, and then only to attend functions. He thought he couldn't speak French because he went to school in England, where his first foreign language was Anglo-Saxon, his second Russian. He had taken Russian because a boy he feared and detested took French, and there were rumours that girls were shipped in from a local school to share the one Russian teacher.

Adam explained this, in clear English, in Didi's château. He got a laugh. '*Alors*,' he continued, in a Continental if not Parisian accent, full of charm, '*J'espère que vous m'excuseriez mon français abominable*.' The French pawed the air with their napkins, as if to say 'Nonsense.' The English marvelled that someone they had taken for one of their own could actually stand up and communicate winningly with the hated French.

'All of us,' he continued, in a language he had thought he didn't speak, 'understand what an important union we have witnessed today.' He listed the ways in which this was so. He discarded his prepared speech, and found his metaphor: his metaphor was Europe.

Holding Norman's father's gaze, he said in English that he hoped this marriage was proof that sometimes the twain could meet. Turning then to the architect of Europe, he said in French that any marriage was likely to be fraught with tension, as would be the relationship between the countries of the new European partnership. Here he went into some detail, fleshing out his metaphor with unconscious deftness. Norman: humorous, stoical, modest. Didi: aesthetic, relaxed, refined. Making certain to speak only of marriage in general, not just Norman and Didi's, he pointed to the traditional difficulties faced by a married couple, and applied them to Europe: finances, fidelity, mutual understanding, consensus in times of crisis.

As a Belgian, he said, he expected to be laying down

the rules in Norman and Didi's life from now on. 'Haw haw,' growled Norman's father. '*Mais non!*' cried the architect of Europe.

'*Mais si*,' said Adam, sarcastically. His French and English had blended into a kind of contrapuntal fugue. Oh yes, he would tell the couple when to have children, where to educate them, which language ought to be their native tongue. He would tell them where to live, what to eat, what to drink. He would tax them here, he would tax them there, he would tax them everywhere. He would force them to take in immigrants as lodgers. Belgians, he said, would rule the world at last. Catering to the exclusive tastes of Europe's representatives, Brussels would sprout into the most glittering capital in the world.

He raised his glass. He reined in his metaphor and descended from the general to the specific. With tactful solemnity, he admitted that if there were nothing so complex as the relationship between powerful nations, there was nothing so pure as love. 'My friends,' he said: '*L'amour!*'

'*L'amour!*' replied his audience, English and French alike.

Adam sat down, blushing sweetly at hearty applause that quickly dissolved into reassuring conversation. The swinging doors burst open and a squad of waiters and waitresses paraded in with platters held high. The smell of coffee filled the hall.

'You've done that before,' said Natalie. 'Bravo.'

'Thank you. I was very nervous. How was my French?'

'Your French was fine, very amusing.'

'It wasn't meant to be amusing.'

'Don't worry, Adam.'

'I hope I didn't sound drunk.'

'Not in the least. Not even insincere. *L'amour*, indeed.'

'You're shameless,' said Adam. 'Do you really think they are as cold as you say?'

'There have been eighteenth-century planned royal marriages based on more than this little operation. You're supposed to be Norman's best friend. You know how he is.'

'And you're supposed to be Didi's best friend. How is she?'

'Best friends or not, I hardly know Didi at all. We could not possibly be more different. I met her in Morocco when we were five years old. My parents and my brothers and I were living in a caravan – well, a glorified bus. Didi and her parents were staying in Marrakech, at probably the best hotel in the world, when the father was setting up some sort of business. It took weeks, and Didi was all alone. Didi's mother let us play together every day, because she thought our Bohemian set-up was *charmant*. Also, we took Didi off her hands. I have no idea what *Maman* did all day long, but we had Didi to ourselves. We did what kids do, and for years afterwards we kept in touch. My mother had a big success in children's fashion, so we spent some time in Paris, which is when I got to know Didi again. I like to think she was the one who changed.'

It struck Adam that he was unused to hearing women tell stories. At dinner parties he could hear himself doing what he detested in other men, which was to interrupt women at the earliest opportunity. There were women his own age who had probably spent a full year of their lives listening patiently to inebriated men who had strong opinions on subjects they knew nothing about.

Natalie sat up unnecessarily straight in her chair as she spoke, as if nursing a back injury. The most exposed tips of her dark hair had been singed golden by the sun. Her skin was quite dark, owing perhaps more to her mother's genes than to sunbathing. To someone as conscious as Adam was of accents, her voice had the most soothing effect: it was a perfectly English voice, as Adam's was, without any of the hackle-raising whinnies and whines that a member of her circle might have cultivated in London.

'Didi told me about the two of you,' said Natalie, with alarming directness.

'*Did* she,' said Adam, exploring his dessert with a feather of a silver spoon. He pretended to acknowledge someone at the far end of the hall.

'Or were you hoping the subject might be avoided tonight?'

'I cannot imagine what you mean, Natalie.'

'You know how *girls* are, Adam. I see Didi seldom enough as it is not to squeeze her like a sponge when I do.'

Some of the things that might have been squeezed out of Didi flashed in Adam's memory.

Natalie pursed her lips and looked up at the high ceiling. 'That was months and months ago, of course. Well before Norman. She would never be so candid today, not as a married woman.'

'It wouldn't be anything . . . *personal* she had to tell you?' Adam decided that of the three desserts he had sampled, the peach flambé was the most delicious. A traditional multi-tiered wedding cake had been wheeled in – not the patisserie replica of the Château du Philosophe Adam might have feared.

'You know how *girls* are,' Natalie said again, this time threateningly.

Adam managed to keep his composure. 'I hope she told you everything,' he said. 'I need the publicity.'

'Not according to Didi. She gave me a list of names.'

'Recommendations?'

'Some would say so.'

Throughout this dangerous exchange, Adam and Natalie had periodically tossed their heads and bared their teeth in mock amusement for the benefit of prying onlookers. Fortified by the reception of his speech, Adam thought he could see through whatever humiliation Natalie thought she had in store.

'The *Farouche*,' said Natalie, naming a London restaurant. 'Not eight months ago. You told Didi a story that lasted half an hour. A story about your parents in Antibes. How you were expected to be a good boy and play backgammon with them, but made an excuse. You fled into the streets and found a girl at a tourist nightclub. You brought her back to your parents' place and they found the two of you there, in the morning. Didi said she thought it was amazing that you would tell a story like that, and expect her to like it.'

'She liked it.'

'You bet she did. You both drank too much at the *Farouche*, and you told her half a dozen other stories, all about successful seduction. Didi thought you made them up.'

'*Did* she?'

'I guess it's safe to say that your stories had the desired effect.'

Adam wanted to object in the strongest way. 'I want to object in the strongest way,' he said. 'Of course I cannot confirm, deny or refute what you are saying. I may have told those stories. These stories may be true. In any case, I did not tell them for effect. I don't remember telling them, to tell you the truth. And even if I did, I did not expect someone I don't know to repeat them to me in this way.' Adam drew an index finger between his collar and his neck. 'I really don't remember.' Adam paused in his defence, and saw that

Natalie was smiling. 'Oh, please,' he said. 'Don't toy with me at a time like this. Do you know how stressful this evening has been?'

'*Stressful*,' Natalie mimicked. 'How awful for you.'

Digestifs were served indoors and out, wherever guests felt most comfortable. Natalie insisted on taking Adam's arm and going outside, where torches illuminated the scene. A band stand had been set up in the ballroom two doors down from the banquet hall. The ballroom gave on to the park, where a small, square dance floor had been installed on the grass. Amplifiers and speakers would deliver outdoors whatever music did not arrive there of its own accord. A rumour had already circulated that after midnight there would be fireworks at the end of the main *allée*, a sight Natalie had already suggested would best be viewed from high inside the château.

There were bars wherever one looked. At one of these, Natalie stopped to ask the nice man for two glasses and a whole, squat bottle of cognac. 'This will be just for us,' she said. 'It will save on all the *va et vient*.'

'Right you are.'

'I know practically no-one here,' she complained, filling two glasses held between the fingers of one hand. 'Please don't introduce me.' She handed Adam a glass, and they drank.

'They all know you, though. Your arrival was preceded by the most malicious gossip,' Adam said, as if he were above that sort of thing.

'What did they say? *What did they say?*'

'They predicted that you would arrive late.'

'And I did.'

'And you did. They also said you would be in the company of an American – Bruce, Bully, Bunny – I

81

don't remember. An actor boyfriend from the newspapers.'

'Bruno,' said Natalie. 'We'll be seeing him tomorrow, at lunch in Paris.'

'Ah.'

'He's not my boyfriend,' she said, lightly punching Adam's sleeve with the fist that clutched the bottle of brandy. 'I don't go for pretty boys.'

'No old men, no pretty boys . . .'

The band, which consisted only of microchips operated by a Frenchman who threatened also to sing, began to make noise. Although ignorant of music, Adam remarked to himself that even the best weddings always got it wrong, especially in France.

Didi and her father now took to the centre of the ballroom, most of which Adam and Natalie could see from their position in the shadows outside. They danced gracefully for only seconds before Norman broke in to dance with his bride.

'I don't know which one I feel sorriest for,' said Natalie. 'It's just possible she can tame Norman, or turn him into a dribbling recluse, so she can go around being a *Lady* without having to lay eyes on the reason why.' Her speech was absolutely clear. Adam could not remember seeing a woman drink more. 'Oh, lord, look at the way he dances. Mortifying.'

Norman danced like someone trying to learn how to walk after a crippling automobile accident. Didi, who looked as elegant and unruffled as always, did her best to lead; Norman, who looked as if he had just awakened on a pavement in the Strand, stepped randomly here and there, forwards, to one side, senselessly and without rhythm. He was used to dancing drunk in London nightclubs, where he could do precisely what he was doing now, without the encumbrance of someone trying to hold on to him.

Adam was eager to dance with Natalie while he was still able to stand. He was a good dancer, and with any luck he would catch the French musician's synthesizers in a fox-trot or waltzing mood. At the moment they played a modern French ballad about a man's scorn for his promiscuous girlfriend.

'Have you noticed how people keep their distance from us?' Adam remarked. 'If you were anyone else, they would be swarming around like—'

'Now what *exactly* do you mean by that?'

'No, please, don't get me wrong. It's simply that there are quite a number of . . . I don't know, *lofty* people here, and they wouldn't want to appear to be star-gazing, if that's the expression. Of course they're dying to meet you, they're keeping an eye on you, but it wouldn't do to come over looking for an introduction.'

Natalie frowned. Her large blue eyes shone in the torchlight. She looked honestly bemused by what Adam had said. 'If that's the case,' she said, 'then I wonder about people. Who do they think I am?'

'That's a good question. I was going to ask who you are.'

'Well, *finally*,' she said, brightening. 'I've been *bursting* to tell you but I'm so frightfully shy.'

'Of course you are.'

'I, as of last Wednesday night, am a signed starlet of the silver screen.'

'*No.*'

'*Yes.* Come off it, Adam, you've read the papers. I've made a career out of choosing my ever-so-critical début role.'

Adam had read the papers. Natalie could be found in them, turning down roles that might or might not have been offered to her. She had skipped a professional career and begun at the point where washed-up actresses attempted comebacks by complaining publicly that they simply hadn't found the right script; that there were no parts for women these days; that one's favourite director had died; that one was not affordable outside Hollywood, where there weren't any longer any good parts for women . . .

Adam wanted to say that it seemed unfair to real actresses that Natalie should be courted in this way by the masters of the world's favourite entertainment form.

'Congratulations,' he said instead, raising his glass. 'You must be over the moon.'

'Terrified, more like. It's a big enough part, and even though he said I won't have to, Serge is going to make me take *all* my clothes off.'

'Serge, I take it, is the director?'

'Yes. A sweetheart.'

'And will you be able to do it, take all your clothes off?'

'I can do *anything*.'

'Let's try an experiment,' said Adam, fifteen minute later. They were still alone together. Natalie had been quizzing Adam on the nastiest nugget of gossip concerning each person who stepped out of the bright ballroom into the torch-lit park. 'You take both our glasses and the bottle back to the bar to exchange them for something else. Chat to the bartender about something for a minute, then come back. I'll bet you a hundred francs there will be a crowd waiting for you when you return.'

'Deal,' said Natalie, taking his glass and skipping away across the lawn towards the nearest bar.

'Hello Arthur, Patrick, James. Hello again, Cynthia, Frances, Xavier . . .'

Comments were made on the splendour of Didi's

wedding, interspersed with allusions to grander weddings one had attended in recent years. The long period of time Adam had spent alone with Natalie, which was uppermost in everyone's mind, was not mentioned. She might not have existed, as the little crowd surrounding Adam spoke excitedly of other things.

When Natalie returned, this time with a smoking bottle of champagne and new glasses, Adam's crowd pointedly ignored her, shuffled its feet, suggested that it might have that dance after all.

'This is Natalie,' Adam said, proprietorially.

'How do you do . . .' 'A pleasure . . .' 'Hello there . . .'

Natalie giggled and poured the champagne. No member of the group dared ask her a direct question. Adam put himself in their shoes and saw himself behaving much the same way. He could see the single men struggling to think of something to say, and the married men struggling to look unimpressed for the benefit of their wives.

'I owe Adam one hundred francs,' said Natalie. 'We had a bet, just now. He said that if I left for—'

'Natalie.'

'No, I think it's terribly interesting. Adam said that if I—'

'*Please.*'

'Oh, well. Whatever you say. Anyway, Adam here is *very* shrewd.'

'Let's dance,' Adam said.

'You're the boss.'

Natalie took the champagne bottle with her, and placed it and both their glasses in one corner of the temporary dance floor. The musician had mercifully stopped singing and let his computers do the work. They played a plastic big-band tune. The trumpets sounded like electronic cryptograms from deep space.

The cymbals hissed like snakes. The noise was to swing what typing was to calligraphy.

They were not alone on the dance floor in the park. The older set, who knew how to dance, moved happily about and laughed at their own abandon. Adam took Natalie gently in his arms and guided her to the centre of the floor.

Now that he had touched her, all remaining barriers of prejudice had fallen down. He had already discovered that Natalie possessed a disarming quality rare in the young, a sense of humour about her station and purpose in life. If others thought her baseless fame unfair, insulting, a sign of a degraded age, Natalie found it merely hilarious. If people wanted to invite her to smart parties, if newspapers wanted to speculate about her private life in print, and if fellow guests for some reason were tongue-tied in her presence, why shouldn't she simply play along and enjoy the charade? She had stated, almost shyly by her standards, her hope that she might turn out to be good at something, but in the meantime she would take her thrills where she could find them.

'A good *dancer*,' she said, as they cut a circle from the middle of the floor, pressuring slower couples to the sidelines. 'Sometimes I can't believe my luck.'

She wasn't the only one. It had of course occurred to Adam that Natalie actually *was* an actress, that Norman and Didi had hired her services for the night. They had both mentioned a 'surprise', after all, which suggested forethought where Adam and Natalie were concerned. It did seem uncharacteristic of a notorious social butterfly to latch on to the one man seated arbitrarily next to her, especially when that one man was socially outgunned on every front.

Adam could feel how slender Natalie's waist was, and how straight her back. Her skirt twirled with each turn,

86

as her Spanish jacket opened to flash the bright white of her blouse. Her clothes might have been out of place at a wedding, but they were made for dancing. He looked at her face, which was somehow baffling in its attractiveness. What separated the beautiful from the beautiful and interesting, Adam hadn't a clue; what he knew was that Natalie's face troubled him and made him sad as well as amorous. Drunk as Adam was, he was able to concentrate on only one sensation at a time, so for several pleasurable circuits of the dance floor he focused on the smooth grip of her fingers on his hand. He was beyond caring if Natalie's attention was a put-up job or not; he was enjoying himself.

After two tolerable numbers, the music changed to something that had the effect of clearing both dance floors: it sounded like a fibrillating heart accompanied by the siren of an approaching ambulance. Adam and Natalie snatched up their bottle and glasses and fled, with many others behind them, indoors.

Didi and Natalie performed one of their noisy reunions in the ballroom, like sister survivors of a shipwreck meeting on their deserted island after years thinking the other had perished with everyone else aboard. Norman shook Adam's hand. He looked worse, if that was possible. He had been sweating on the dance floor, and most of his messy hair was stuck to his forehead and neck. Adam handed him a handkerchief.

'I'm getting my second wind,' Norman said, which might have meant that he had dipped into the aristocratic substances he had promised friends, judges and parents that he was well rid of.

'Good for you. It's exhausting, I'm sure, getting married.' They were out of the girls' earshot. Adam lowered his voice to say, 'Have you decided to do the right thing and confess? It could be very serious, you know.'

'Never you mind. You ridiculed my plan, but there are more where that came from. I'm going to have to go to Argentina for a few weeks, it turns out, to inspect some of Father's property. I've confided in him, you see. He understands completely. He rather approves. He won't say so, but I'll bet you he brought back more from France than a reputation for liberating barnyard animals.'

'Could be. There was a lot of it about.'

'Anyway this is the sort of secret where I really have to point out that you will be killed if anyone finds out.'

'You know I'm good with secrets,' Adam said reassuringly, noting to himself that Norman's wife seemed eager to spread any intimate gossip she possibly could. He wondered if Norman knew.

'I must say things seem to be going well with you and the lovely miss. Christ, look at her.'

'She does have impact,' said Adam.

'Jesus,' said Norman, in all seriousness, 'do you think I should have married Natalie instead?'

It was a quarter past midnight. Adam felt awfully warm inside. He and Natalie had explored the château together, collecting impressions of the life Didi and Norman might someday have together if her parents did the noble thing and retired to Monaco for the rest of their lives. They had run out of champagne at one point, and returned to the party for another bottle without mingling with the other guests. Adam had showed Natalie his bedroom, of which he was as proud as he would have been had he owned the château. They had held hands as they scooted along the corridors like burglars, heads below window level, whispering noisily to each other to be quiet. They had found a back spiral staircase, and climbed it to a modern stone terrace built amid the ramparts and suitable for sunbathing out of the servants' sight. From there they would have a view of the fireworks.

Some of the things they had seen in the living quarters of the château had made Adam queasy with materialistic greed. He wanted a room like Didi's father's office, with its broad fireplace, tantalizing antique portrait Adam felt sure concealed a wall safe, tall bookcases, playing-field desk, grandfather clock, discreet hi-fi system, Persian carpet, globe, ancestral portraits, ink blotter, deep leather reading chair, chest of booze and view. He wanted a bedroom like the one he had been assigned. He wanted a clay tennis court like the one he had seen from the office window. He wanted a velvet rope to pull when he was thirsty. He *wanted*.

Natalie had visited the château before on numerous occasions, which was not to say she was inured to its splendours. She dared to open wardrobes in Didi's mother's dressing room and finger fine garments. She said that if there had been any jewellery in plain view she might very well have pinched a handful. She said Didi's father was the chairman of an automobile company and even apart from that was a truly, truly wealthy man. He had a mistress in Paris and a mistress in Nice and a mistress in Rome. He had founded a military museum, and stuffed it with his own collection of swords, crossbows, armour, flags and guns. If Didi's father had anything to do with the fireworks, they would be something to behold. He was patriotic and right-wing to the point of psychosis. Fixated on immigration, he was the sort of racialist who was proud to own up to his prejudices. He had firm ideas about the reasons God had created Woman, and he lived according to his beliefs. Like many Frenchmen, he was devoutly Catholic while not for a moment thinking the Vatican had any right to tell him how to behave. Natalie confessed that although on paper he was as unpleasant a man as she had ever met or heard of, he had a wicked charm and seigneurial manner that was almost impossible not to find seductive. Adam cringed.

The fireworks announced themselves with a single thundering report at exactly half past twelve. With their elbows perched on a crenelle, Adam and Natalie took in the predominately red, white and blue rocket-blossoms over the outer fortress wall. The Gothic steeple of Aubade's church stood out on the pale horizon like a missing tooth. Far below the parapets, people had come outside into the park to watch. The château felt dark and ship-like under Adam's feet. He looked at Natalie and they shook their heads at the hugeness of Didi's wedding. They grew bored with the fireworks, and they kissed. They looked up after a few minutes to register the grand finale, a skyful of roses.

'What a day,' said Adam. 'I can't believe you were in Spain only this morning.'

'Let's have a last little toast,' Natalie said, 'then let's see your beautiful bedroom again.'

Adam agreed to the toast. He was now grateful for having drunk so much over so long a period of time. He was about to attempt something he had been rehearsing in his mind for years, in the expectation that he might someday feel the way he felt right now. He touched glasses with Natalie. They drank. He kissed her profoundly. He told her he had not expected to have such a wonderful time. He said that he would never forget this day as long as he lived, thanks to her. He helped her down two levels of the tight stone staircase, and turned down the corridor not towards his own bedroom, but Natalie's.

This was the painful part, the part he had been rehearsing for years. At Natalie's bedroom door he held her by the waist and kissed her again. He repeated what he had said on the roof, using different words. He put a hand round the back of her neck and kissed her yet again. With that, and to Natalie's evident disbelief, Adam bade her good night.

PART TWO

COURTSHIP

Adam and Natalie trundled along a tree-lined road with the top down on Adam's treasured car. Natalie sat low in her seat with one arm draped along the door frame. She wore dark glasses and a folded scarf tied as a bandanna around her aching head. It was half past nine in the morning and the long, straight road was clear in both directions. On the floor between Natalie's feet were two bottles of red wine she had borrowed from the château kitchen, after waking Adam and begging him to get her on the road before she changed her mind and went back to bed. She had not forgotten to bring a corkscrew. One of the bottles was open and not entirely full.

Adam had said little to Natalie during the half hour they had been driving towards Paris, except to grunt every so often that they were pointed in the right direction. It was already hot, and Adam too wore dark glasses. He also wore a white cotton driving cap, which Natalie had hurt herself laughing at when he first put it on. He reclined in his seat and allowed his head to loll back as far as was consistent with keeping his squinting eyes on at least part of the road. He steered with one hand limply on the bottom of the wheel, leaving the other to droop uselessly near the gear lever. If the car had been stationary, both he and Natalie might have been thought to be asleep. Had there been any French drivers unused to right-hand drive following behind, they would have been alarmed to observe a vehicle operated by a woman slumped against the door, raising her head every ten minutes to take a swig of wine from a bottle.

Adam wasn't at all sure that vintage red wine was an appropriate cure for his hangover, and it didn't yet appear to be reviving Natalie. He drove as quickly as he could without terrifying himself, which was about thirty-five miles per hour. The tops of the trees that swished metronomically overhead appeared to be light purple, when Adam knew they could not be. It was as if he had filled his body to the eyeballs with red wine, and saw the world through a film of 1963 Château Valençin. The low sun blinded him in his rear-view mirror, so that he had to turn it to one side. He thought he could hear the engine of his precious car chastising him for his over-indulgence.

They stopped at a roadside café and ordered coffee. They sat beneath a tattered, oil-stained umbrella at a white plastic table. The empty road stretched miles in each direction. The charred trees overhanging the café spoke of heavy traffic. The sun ascended, diminished in size and changed colour at a noticeable rate.

Adam was the first to see the tanker truck on the horizon. Without speaking, he raised a heavy arm and pointed out the truck to Natalie. She frowned, and lifted her bowl of coffee to her mouth using both hands.

'What are we going to do?' asked Adam, in a low whisper. The loudest noise to be heard was that of a cat rubbing itself against the cement wall of a garage fifty yards away.

'About the truck?' whispered Natalie.

'Yes, the truck.'

Natalie shrugged, and finished her coffee. Adam finished his coffee too, and then they both sat like wax dummies at their table, hands in their laps, heads bowed. The truck, still a mile away, was now audible.

'It's going to be going ever so slightly downhill,' said Adam, under his breath.

'Yes,' said Natalie. 'And there is gravel.'

Their feet almost touched the dirty, pitted white line at the side of the road.

'Here it comes.'

'It's coming now.'

A view from across the road would have shown two slumped figures at an apparently peaceful spot suddenly obscured in a flash by a hurtling tanker truck, pelted by gravel, the umbrella over their table tipping in the backwash, their empty coffee bowls rattling on the table. That view would also have proved the rule that gigantic trucks tend to travel in convoy, so that for the next few seconds the couple was deafened by noise, sprayed with gravel and exhaust.

Neither spoke for a minute or two. Adam reached out lamely to brush a speck of dust off the nearest shoulder of Natalie's light-blue T-shirt.

'*S'il vous plaît, madame*,' he said to the open door of the café. '*L'addition*?'

Adam and Natalie decided that their characters had been strengthened by the experience at the roadside café. Revived somewhat by coffee, Adam was able to sit up straight and drive at a reasonable speed. They would not be late for lunch in Paris.

'If there were a lake,' said Natalie, 'I would dive into it.'

There were no lakes to be seen, as they drove through perhaps the bleakest corner of France. Natalie insisted on back roads, which gave them an opportunity to see battered houses too close to the main drag, unlivable modern developments where quaint villages had stood before the wars, thirsty crops desiccated in the sun. It reminded Adam of a trip he had taken with his parents after his father had retired, when they had decided they deserved a grand house or château in the French countryside not too far from Paris. After visiting half a dozen humbled buildings, most of them for some reason overhung or even encircled by high-tension power lines, Adam's frustrated parents had begun to parody the patter of estate agents by saying, as they left each potential home, 'It is extremely *expensive*, and it is also extremely *ugly*.'

Adam and Natalie finished the first bottle of wine and opened the second as they breached the Périphérique and nosed into central Paris. They were starting to feel good. The weather was calm and bright, and the few Parisians who were not on holiday had stayed indoors. Adam stopped for petrol, then drove to the address of Natalie's film director.

Serge lived in the penthouse of a modern apartment building located, coincidentally, in the Rue Huivis, a tributary of the Avenue Montaigne. Hard as he tried, Adam could not remember a film Serge had directed, but Natalie insisted he was a revered master. He was not, she stressed, to be thought of only as the director of *Malaise*, which was banned in Britain as pornographic but studied like a sacred text at French universities.

Adam asked if he ought to make himself scarce during Natalie's lunch with Serge, because he didn't wish to intrude. Natalie thought this over longer than Adam would have wished, because in fact he was aching to have lunch in a penthouse with a famous French film director.

'No,' she said at last. 'You can be my lawyer.'

'Don't you have an agent, or . . . you know, *people* of any kind?'

'I have an agent,' said Natalie. 'Her name is Jane Wheeler. She's a dear, but Serge frightens her.'

'I see.'

'She won't even talk to him on the telephone.'

'I take it Jane Wheeler doesn't approve of your having accepted this particular role?'

'Oh, no, she quite approves, I think. I believe her attitude is the same as mine – that this is just a lark, and I'm better off doing the Continental art routine than actually attempting to act. We don't know if I can, you see.'

'Do you mind if I ask how or why Serge landed on you for the part? If he's such an old pro, it seems to me . . . well, who am I to say? I don't want to offend you.'

'Listen, don't worry. I know how strange and unfair it seems, but you have to remember how these film maestros work. It's happened before. Serge is the kind of fellow who is supposed to have vision. He makes films the French way, like painting. So if he has a particularly strong vision, and the money is in the right place at the right time, he tends to feel inspired. He acts impulsively. He could decide that for artistic reasons his film has to be set in eighteenth-century Hong Kong, or filmed in sepia, or silent. He is an *auteur*. He is allowed to make these decisions and stick to them and throw tantrums if he feels thwarted. In my case, it was something he has done before: he saw my picture in a magazine, and said, "*Voilà!* There is my Mireille!", or whatever her name will turn out to be.'

'Why were you in the magazine to begin with?'

'A journalist friend did a story on a trip I took to the Seychelles. There were many photographs. The text mentioned who my mother is, so Serge would have known I speak French. This isn't unusual, Adam. Serge simply got an *idée fixe*, and I'm it.'

'I hope he isn't the casting-couch type.'

'My God, is he *ever*. He's fifty-eight years old, and lecherous. But the treatment is all very smooth, supposedly romantic. There are dinners, flowers, a lot of talk about how his life will never be the same after meeting me. He's vile, of course, but I'll bet there have been dozens before me who have fallen for it.'

'Not you?'

'Not yet,' said Natalie, sitting up straight in her seat for the first time all day. 'Oh, look how nice Paris looks.'

'What do you mean, "Not yet"?'

'Well, you can't really rule out anything. Maybe I'll be transported by his genius. It would take something along those lines, I assure you. Also, he tends to live with his female leads for a couple of years after the film is in the can, and I don't think I have time for that just now. Can you believe this, Adam? I'm going to be an *actress*.'

'I believe it,' said Adam, who hoped Natalie's flippancy was a pose. He felt a sudden, unfounded righteousness about the exploitation of women in all walks of life. It worried him that Natalie was not more categorical in her dismissal of the promiscuous director. He had already formed a picture in his mind of a tall, slender, wavy-haired multimillionaire brimming with artistic passion, who put out a brown, sensuous hand to say, 'I am *Serge*.'

They had forty-five minutes to kill before Natalie's lunch which they spent staring at expensive material goods through the barred windows of closed shops.

'Have you got a lot of money, Adam?' Natalie asked, just as Adam had pointed out a men's watch that cost three-quarters of his annual salary.

'I sometimes ask myself that question,' he replied, looking at his reflection in the bullet-proof window. 'What I mean is that I know exactly how much money I have, but I have to ask myself if it is a lot, or potentially a lot.'

'I suppose that answers my question,' said Natalie. 'If you know exactly how much you've got, you haven't got a lot.'

'Exactly how much money do you have?' Adam asked her.

'I have no idea,' she said.

'It's Natalie,' Natalie said in French, into an intercom in the lobby of Serge's building. 'I'm with a friend, I hope that's all right. He's my lawyer.'

There was a growl at the other end, and a light went on over the lift. The lift arrived seconds later, and Adam bowed to let Natalie precede him. They stood side by side with their backs to the lift door, looking at themselves in a mirror.

'Uh-oh,' said Natalie. 'We look drunk.'

'I have a comb,' said Adam, but it was too late. The lift stopped, and the doors opened straight into Serge's penthouse.

They were greeted by a middle-aged Asian maid whose coiffure Adam immediately noticed for its sophistication and polish. Natalie and Adam bowed awkwardly to her, and they were shown in.

'Monsieur Serge will be a moment,' said the maid, in squeaky French. 'He says to tell you he is shaving, and that you must have champagne and strawberries and listen to the stereo.'

The room in which they stood, waiting for their champagne and strawberries to be brought to them, was the size of a village bowling green and almost as sparsely decorated. Presumably Serge shared with some other artistic geniuses a horror of clutter or germs. Either that, or he had now run out of money and was stuck with the expensive lack of décor he had once considered meaningful. The gigantic wall-to-wall carpet was gun-metal grey. The black grand piano was so far away it looked miniature. The walls were just slightly bluer than the carpet, as was the upholstery on the sofas and armchairs. The low ceiling, like that in a multi-storey car park, made Adam wonder if the piano actually was a miniature, and if Serge would come skipping out to reveal himself as a dwarf. Only one painting hung in the room, a rather good modern portrait of a woman Adam guessed was Serge's mother.

'Serge's wife,' said Natalie, in a normal voice. She lowered it to a whisper to say, 'He didn't get his money from *Malaise*, I can tell you. Name is Caroline. Serge's second cousin. Previously married to shipping fortune. Still lives, though insane. Serge romantically devoted to her. All his films about her, all end with woman looking out to sea from wheelchair with one hand clutching at blanket over knees. I suppose I'll have to do that scene.'

Music began to seep from the walls, as the maid entered bearing a wooden tray. She put the tray down and gestured for Serge's guests to be seated. She filled their glasses, and went away. Adam could not have placed the sounds coming out of the walls and ceiling. He knew little about serious music, but would have guessed that this was not mainstream. A woman was singing as softly as it was possible to do in German, as a pianist seemed to play haltingly through a score he had never seen before. It was just the two of them, the lady singer and the pianist, creeping along through something that was surely designed to be evocative of loss. The woman's voice swooped and swerved like a seagull, crashing every so often into the surf of German consonants. Adam would have bet this music was as modern as could be, probably written by one of Serge's composer friends and recorded yesterday.

'Schubert,' said Natalie. 'If I know anything about Serge, this will be the soundtrack of the new film.'

'Does the new film have a title?'

'A working title. Serge doesn't name the film until it is finished. Sometimes it takes him a year. The working title is *Tedium*.'

'That ought to pack 'em in,' said Adam, who had been picking through the strawberries instead of listening carefully.

'Sorry, you misunderstood. *Te Deum*.'

'Oh, that. It's been done, I'm sure. Whatever it is. A Catholic thing?'

'I said it's only a working title. And of course it's a Catholic thing. Serge's life, I've just tried to tell you, is a matter of wrestling with understandable adultery. He is romantically faithful to his wife almost beyond the call of duty, except that—'

'Except that he institutionalized her, took all of her money, and sleeps and lives with young actresses all the year round.'

'You don't see the beauty in that?' said Natalie. Adam was thankful when she smiled.

A buzzer sounded, and the maid emerged from the kitchen to listen to the credentials of those responsible. She pressed a button and waited by the lift. Seconds later, the lift disgorged half a dozen people who were engaged in noisy argument. Without looking at her, they heaped hats and handbags and unnecessary umbrellas on the maid. She waddled away, haystack-like, as Adam and Natalie stood up to greet the new arrivals.

Adam recognized Bruno straightaway. He was called Bruno L in the papers, and no-one seemed to know his actual surname. Adam's recollection was that Bruno L's career was in the toilet, metaphorically speaking. Bruno L had done something wrong in America, something sordid, that had caused all offers to dry up; this, just when Bruno L had thought it possible that he might soon break into adult roles. On someone's advice, he had decided to start again in Europe, to gain artistic credibility with guaranteed limited exposure, and to practise whatever sordidness had got him into trouble in a country where he need not fear the law.

Bruno had brought two girls along, who were obviously just as peripheral as Adam. They had lips, and everything else, and they seemed at home in Serge's wasteland of a penthouse. They shook hands with Adam like tourists passing an unknown painting in the Louvre, leaving him to be greeted by Bruno like a favourite uncle. Adam heard himself say 'Yes, of course,' as Natalie told him Bruno's name. Bruno was, as Natalie had allowed, a pretty boy; so much so that as Adam shook his hand he almost leaned forward to kiss him on both cheeks. His face was youthfully crinkled in just the right places; his teeth, when bared in a smile, were two rows of winsome personality; his hair looked as if Bruno had driven a motorcycle along a California beach at dawn. Bruno wore a version of clothing Adam had long envied and wondered about: a kind of crushed-linen suit, baggy over an open-necked white shirt; blue shoes. Adam carefully observed Bruno's greeting with Natalie, which he noted was not only chaste but alienated. When Natalie said that Adam was her lawyer, Bruno actually returned to shake his hand again and smile like a case of diamonds.

The other three people were Serge's older brother, a disillusioned sculptor; a French politician named Legan, whom Adam vaguely recognized; and a French woman who made Adam think he knew exactly what casting directors looked like.

It was new in Adam's experience for a host to keep invited guests waiting. To have instructed his maid to tell the guests that their host was 'shaving' seemed like going out of the way to set the stage for a grand entrance in one's own home. When he did at last appear, Serge wrung his hands and looked up at the low ceiling by way of apology. He had *not* shaved. He looked older than fifty-eight, and though short was not a dwarf. He was in every physical way what Adam had not expected. His very brown bald head was ringed with white hair one millimetre long. He had a long nose and big lips and double creases in arcs around his mouth. His wattles were as tan as his head. A loose silver chain and tiny cross hung from his neck. He wore what looked to Adam like a tropical prisoner's uniform: matching navy-blue short-sleeved cotton shirt and unbelted trousers, white espadrilles. His body was rounder than it was tall, but it looked like a comfortable one.

Various levels of intimacy were exhibited as Serge greeted a semicircle of guests: a long, significant hug with hand behind neck for older brother; a firm, comradely handshake and a topical observation for the politician; cousinly kiss for the probable casting director; perfunctory cheek-kisses for Bruno's girls; a hearty laugh and a brief pat on the cheek for Bruno; then a gaping, grovelling kiss, hug and near genuflection for Natalie, his vision. When greeting Adam he took his hand, cocked his head, and remained in this pose while Natalie issued a succinct biography as well as a recounting of their meeting at Didi's wedding. This took so long that Adam expected the muscles in his face to freeze in the idiotic smile he had adopted for what he had thought would be a routine hello. He hated it when people wouldn't let go of his hand.

Serge announced that he forbade the discussion of business on a Sunday, and that his guests were merely to have a wonderful time and get to know each other. Adam thought Serge looked like the kind of fellow who would have a fit of the vapours and retreat to his bedroom if he did not feel intellectually or sensually stimulated for more than four or five minutes. This was unlikely with the charismatic French politician in the room, from whom Serge almost certainly wanted money. Serge immediately took the politician's arm, slid open the glass doors leading to the terrace, and guided him outside. The others followed along at a distance.

The Japanese rock garden on the roof was less impressive than the swimming pool. The floor of the pool had been painted like the Sistine Chapel in reverse, depicting, according to Natalie, behind-the-scenes giants from the early days of Hollywood: moguls, directors, cinematographers and animators were painted realistically in black and white, along with some of the paraphernalia of their art. There was, too, a film screen framed in the short wall of the deep end, and a steel armchair anchored to the bottom of the pool in front of it. A scuba tank and regulator were strapped to the chair, along with waterproof headphones. It was at the bottom of this pool that Serge did the bulk of his summertime viewing, and where he watched his own films to look in isolation for ways to make them more perfectly match his vision.

Serge showed the politician his pool. Natalie spoke kindly to Bruno's girls. Serge's brother had gone back inside with the presumed casting director, as if they were allergic to sunlight. This left Adam and Bruno to gravitate towards one another and begin a conversation.

'So,' said Adam, lawyer to the stars.

Bruno smiled. There were traces of African blood in him, Adam decided.

'How is your French?' Adam asked.

'Good enough for the film,' Bruno replied, perhaps taking Adam's innocent question for an attack on his professional capabilities. 'I play an American who can't speak French.'

'Is it a big role?'

'I wouldn't say so, but you never know until Serge stops editing. Let's face it, it could *only* be me. I think I'm supposed to be part of a dream sequence, but it's kind of hard to tell from a treatment – which we weren't actually allowed to read, anyway.'

Adam looked at Bruno's watch, which was identical to the one he had gawped at in the window downstairs.

'Have you been in one of Serge's films before?'

Bruno looked insulted, as if anyone who had paid the slightest attention to modern culture would have known the answer to that question.

'I'm going to be the first American he has ever used. Anyway, he shot his last film when I was sixteen years old.'

'Which one was that?'

'I've seen it, but I don't really want to pronounce the name. It's a period thing, costumes and dirt. Same idea, though. Pure love in the background of a man's big amount of orgy.'

Adam liked Bruno, on the deliberate assumption that his remarks and quirky syntax were meant to be humorous. Bruno looked like someone who didn't mind being gormless, who would flow along with whatever came his way without stalling himself with diverting introspection. Today, it was a party on Serge's roof; tomorrow, it would be something else. Adam guessed that Bruno had been the recipient of pay packets that would boggle the mind of any labouring adult, and that the actor merely blinked as they were handed over by whatever unscrupulous leech represented him. Bruno's girls were of the sort Adam had seen on occasion in

European resort nightclubs, dancing with despicable men. They were slender, doll-like and unlikeable. They looked uncomfortable in daylight – mean, driven and selfish. They smoked and tossed their hair and tried to appear bored. Very unpleasant, Adam decided to himself, and utterly irresistible.

'They're your friends, are they?' Adam asked, hearing with some alarm that his accent and intonation had taken a turn for the worse.

'Shoot,' said Bruno. 'I guess so.'

There it was again, thought Adam. Bruno could return to his hotel after lunch and go to bed with the girls, or with one of them, or with neither, and it wouldn't make any difference to him. Not that he was so stupid that he could not enjoy basic sensual pleasures, but Bruno appeared really to be about as equivocal as could be about everything that surrounded him. For the moment he was talking to someone he thought was an entertainment lawyer. In a few minutes, who knew?

Adam's curse was that he had the ability to be objective about himself. He was aware in the forefront of his thoughts that it was a singular event for him to be standing in a Japanese rock garden outside the Paris penthouse of a famous French film director, chatting with an American film star who had done something so perverse that news of the débâcle had reached Adam even in the safety of his London flat. Adam was incapable of letting himself lose self-consciousness and wander through this or any other experience. He had to keep saying to himself that it was peculiar to find himself where he was, and getting more peculiar all the time. This trait of objectivity had dogged Adam since the day he was old enough to compare himself with others, the first instance being with other children. It lent an attractive humility to his character. He was equally objective about others, and much of what he saw at least depressed, or more often infuriated him.

While there wasn't much objectively wrong with Serge's roof garden, there was much to be worried about where Adam's reasons for being there were concerned. He had begun to wonder, in the sane way he had, if Natalie were the kind of person to use the bait of a lunch invitation simply to get a free ride to Paris. Would she ignore him, now that she had safely met her appointment in Paris, or did she need to be driven farther? He looked at her over Bruno's shoulder, chatting to Bruno's girls in the sunshine, her dark glasses resting on top of her head with their stems stuck through her red bandanna. Someone who lived as fast as she did probably kissed lots of men under showers of fireworks on the roofs of French châteaux.

Adam decided to leave the telephone call to McDavis until the last possible moment – which, for the sake of verisimilitude, was half an hour from now. That left half an hour to think how to ask a famous French film director he had only just met if he could use his telephone to make a long-distance call. Perhaps he would ask the maid.

'So, are you Nat's agent, or what?' asked Bruno.

Adam wondered if he were supposed to start calling her Nat, if the pretty-boy did. 'No, not at all. She has an agent in London. I am her lawyer, and a friend. I drove her here.' Adam wished he could add that for about forty-five minutes the previous night, and for a second here or there during their mutual hangover, he had been in love with her.

'My older brother's a lawyer,' said Bruno, employing what Adam now considered to be a natural conversational gift. 'He works back East in Bethesda, Maryland? It's a small practice but he says he likes it that way. He's married, and everything.'

'Oh,' said Adam. He wondered if he ought to tell Bruno a story about his own family. 'Is his name "L", too?' he said instead, not liking the tone of his voice. 'L for Lawyer?'

'Naw,' said Bruno, crinkling his face and delivering teeth. 'That's funny.'

Bruno had a tiny diamond earring in the rigid folds of the upper part of his ear, which Adam hadn't noticed until just now. 'Where are you staying, Bruno?'

'I'm at the Fantasmagorie, at the moment,' Bruno said, or perhaps it was a similar name he had difficulty pronouncing in French. 'A lot of people stay there.' By 'people', Adam supposed Bruno meant members of Bruno's new international aristocracy. 'What about you?'

'We're not sure,' Adam replied, pointedly using the plural pronoun. 'I suppose it's awfully hard to book at short notice, this time of year?'

Bruno looked at Adam uncomprehendingly.

Adam had almost decided to do the decent thing and leave by the servants' lift when Natalie excused herself from Bruno's girls and skipped happily to his side.

'Come look at the view,' she said, taking Adam's right arm with both hands and leaning her head on his shoulder. Adam decided he really had to make that telephone call. 'Save me, save me,' she whispered.

'Likewise, likewise,' said Adam, as they reached the north railing of Serge's roof. 'Actually, I shouldn't say that. I like Bruno. He's kind of a sweet guy.'

Natalie groaned. 'People always say that when they meet famous people,' she said, scoldingly. 'Have you ever noticed? They'll say, "I was at a party and just happened to run into Princess So-and-so, and do you know what? She's a really – no a really, *honestly* lovely human being. Just as friendly and as natural as can be."

You never hear someone say they bumped into Such-and-such, who turned out to be a shit, because that implies they did not become instantly intimate.'

'You're right, I have noticed that,' said Adam. 'Bruno's a pain in the arse.'

'That's the spirit,' said Natalie. 'Now. Let's get our bearings.'

That wasn't hard to do, in Paris. They were near the centre of the city's axis, including the modern developments to east and west. Rooftops were always good to look down upon, and in this case there was a great deal of wealthy people's drying bed-linen to study. Adam was able to look down into the gardens of houses he had walked by countless times, wondering what lay behind the razor wire.

'Do you think that's the President?' he asked. A man in a dark suit strolled all alone in the garden of the Elysée Palace.

'Definitely,' said Natalie.

'Should we call what's-his-name over here to take a look at his boss?'

'Definitely not.'

Adam turned and looked Natalie in the eye. 'Are you used to this?' he asked. 'I just want to know if you are feeling as out of place as I am.'

Natalie looked as if she didn't understand his question. 'I don't think it's possible to be "out of place",' she replied, as if Adam were conducting an examination in logical positivism. 'I mean, we're where we are.'

'Silly me,' said Adam.

'Oh, while I have the chance,' said Natalie. 'I had a quick word with Serge when we came out here, and he wants to know if we are happy staying at the Somerset, tonight. It's right there, see? That's the swimming pool on the roof. He wants to make sure everything is smooth, because if all goes well shooting begins next week. Is that all right with you?'

Adam had rarely been asked a question containing so many subtexts to which he wanted to answer in the affirmative.

'That would be just fine,' he said. 'Sure, tell him yes.'

'There's not much to be accomplished here, really. Serge is serious about no business this afternoon. I think he just likes to visualize his people, make sure they're in the country. The big guns will be here for dinner, and we'll be free.'

'Big guns?'

'The two other producers, probably the star, if he feels like it.'

'Serge is a producer, too?'

'Well, through his wife, I suppose. The money has to come from somewhere.'

'It's awfully good of him to put us up. Is it as good an hotel as it looks from here?'

Natalie winced, as if a particle of Parisian dust had flown into one of her eyes.

'Are you all right?' Adam asked. He touched her forearm.

'Yes, I'm fine.' Her eyes widened, and she looked at Adam as if trying to recognize his features as she came out of a coma.

'Are you sure? Do you want a glass of water?' Adam felt real concern. For all he knew he had caught Natalie at the end of a three-week or even three-year binge. He wasn't feeling terrific himself, after less than twenty-four hours in her company.

'No, God. More champagne. I need courage, Adam. I'm going to be an *actress.*'

'Are you very worried about that? You said I was your lawyer, you know. I could have you out of this in a minute.'

112

'I want you to be my lawyer,' said Natalie, leaning against Adam's chest.

'I can be. I will be. I am.'

'I should show you the contract. Jane's seen it, and her own lawyers. It isn't anything special. I have agreed to do whatever Serge says for the next two months or so, then some promotion for a year after that, depending.'

Natalie still seemed to be swooning. She felt small in Adam's arms. Her hair was soft.

'I ought to know terms of payment, that sort of thing, if I'm to be of any use.'

Natalie sighed, and told him how much she was to be paid, based on what. Adam coughed. 'Are you absolutely sure?'

'Well of course. It's all written down, all signed. Jane's no fool.'

'Apparently not.' The sum Natalie had mentioned made Adam's eyes water. By coincidence, her basic payment was exactly the sum Adam had visualized himself earning when he was in his fifty-fifth year and thinking of bold early retirement. He managed to refrain from saying that if he were a film producer he would find inexperienced actresses like Natalie and make them *pay* to take a small role.

'Now you have me worried,' said Natalie. 'Maybe you should take a look at everything. No, wait – I don't know if I can afford you.'

'You can afford me,' Adam said.

Natalie balanced her glass on the wrought-iron railing, and raised both of her arms over her head to stretch and yawn. Adam glanced at the other guests to make sure they hadn't seen her appearing bored, then he looked back at Natalie. He had known her such a short time that she looked unfamiliar in every new pose. Now she looked taller than he remembered. She was slim and young and just like at least two girls Adam could vividly remember staring at for lengthy periods on Continental beaches. She snapped out of her yawn and looked refreshed.

'What are you staring at?' she said.

Adam looked away with more bashfulness than he was used to exhibiting, and retrieved her glass from its precarious position on the railing. 'Here,' he said. 'I didn't want you to spill it on the President.'

Lunch was served at exactly two-thirty. Two more guests had arrived – one actress, and one person whose identity and gender Adam never learned. The actress pretended to be shy, and left after not eating her cantaloupe. The other person seemed to be Serge's sculptor brother's friend.

Adam sat between Natalie and one of Bruno's girls. Bruno's girl detested Adam because he had made the mistake of saying he was a lawyer. Her name was Geneviève, and she had no use for lawyers. Lawyers were filth. Lawyers cut out the hearts of creative people and ate them sautéed like calf's liver. Lawyers, as a whole, were a cancer on the body of humanity. Geneviève herself was an artist. What use could she possibly have for lawyers? She hated them. She hated the food, too. Serge's penthouse was ridiculous, she said, and the old man ought to know when his creative juices had dried up. She didn't like anyone in the room except for her *copine* and Bruno, the politician was a fascist, and she liked Adam least. She told Adam to his face that she found him gauche, when Adam knew perfectly well that he had never been gauche in his life. He waited a suitable interval, then whispered to her in his newly discovered French that she was a miserable whore. His cheeks reddened as he watched his remark sink in. He had never, in his life, said anything so rude.

'I'm *so* sorry,' he said straightaway. 'That wasn't at all what I meant. I was trying to be sarcastic, and it came out completely wrong. Please forgive me.'

The girl didn't seem to understand why an apology was necessary. She said she liked him more now that he had shown some feelings. So few people these days had true feelings, she said.

One of the reasons he had lost his temper so quickly was that he had not yet made his telephone call to Dick McDavis. For his excuse to be believable, he would by now be locking his doors and rolling up his windows against irate French farmers wielding dead chickens and pig organs. He managed to find an opportunity to tell Natalie of his dilemma; her reaction was to wave at Serge, interrupting him in mid-gesticulation with the politician, and to say, 'Adam needs the telephone.' Without losing the thread of his argument, Serge summoned his maid with a silver bell and told her what was required. The maid went into the living room and returned with a cordless telephone, into which Adam was evidently to lie in front of everyone at the table.

Adam did not know Dick McDavis's home telephone number by heart, but he always carried his trusty, ultra-slim address book in his inside jacket pocket. He consulted this, and memorized the number. He slipped the book back into his pocket, and cleared his throat. No-one was paying any attention to him except the girl he had called a miserable whore. He still could not believe he had called her that, and decided he had only done so because he had never used foul language in French before and those two words were the only ones to bob to the surface in time to be uttered with conviction. He hoped he wouldn't call Dick McDavis a miserable whore, in case he ever decided to go back to work.

In fact, if anyone in Adam's world was a miserable

whore, it was Dick McDavis. He was physically imposing – six and a half feet and eighteen stone, but one would not have said he was overweight – and he used his size to intimidate anyone who came close enough for the treatment. He was a natural bully, but this characteristic was accompanied, as it so rarely is, by a facile intellect. McDavis was a cunning rogue. He was a braggart, and the heaviest drinker Adam had ever met. Adam had seen Dick McDavis drink three large whiskies and two bottles of wine at a business lunch, only to belch delicately into his napkin and race off to a competitive hour-and-a-half of squash.

McDavis's rich, powerful voice had lost most of its cultivated Scottish accent, and taken on the more proletarian-English tones suitable to his new ambition to be a film producer. His style of business had less to do with the courting and representation of clients than with what he would have called 'gobbling 'em up and spitting 'em out.' He made Adam's every working day a trial, calling him weak and cowardly and a spineless toff.

Dick's partner, Judy, was less like his wife than his sister. Despite being married to McDavis, she was not to be pitied. Though so tiny that one could not meet her and her husband together without wondering right away how she had not been killed in bed with him, she matched her husband's toughness and foul mouth, and drank fully half as much as he did. The couple lived for Stephenson, McDavis and McDavis, working perhaps twice the hours Adam and the others did. No client was deemed too shoddy or corrupt for their attentions. They thrived on their reputation for cynical abuse of the system. They made it obvious to everyone that they kept Adam on board only to put a necessary gloss between them and their few upmarket clients. It was wretched laziness that had kept Adam there, and the guilty hope that the McDavis approach – even in Mr Stephenson's absence – was the one that had the best chance of bringing him an undeserved windfall.

Adam dialled the telephone in his lap. No-one was paying the slightest attention to him, not even Geneviève. McDavis answered on the first ring. He and Judy had no children, and Sunday afternoons usually found them hard at work together in the office at home, taking care of the paperwork they were too busy yelling on the telephone to get to during the week.

'Dick, it's Adam Gosse.' Even after six years, he thought he had to identify himself by his full name. 'Sorry to bother you at home.'

'What the bloody hell is it? You're not resigning, are you, you little—'

'Dick, listen. I don't have much change and I'm in a French phone box.' Adam hoped the gentle murmur of civilized conversation and the tinkling of wine glasses sounded enough like a roadside phone box. He also hoped his fellow guests hadn't heard his first lie. He raised his voice to say, 'Didn't I tell you I was going to a wedding in France?'

'Yes, you bloody well did. You wanted to scarper two days early, you—'

'Listen, Dick.' Adam lowered his voice again, and turned away at a right angle to the table. 'All hell has broken loose here – French farmers on the rampage, I'm afraid. You know how they can be. Traffic is backed up miles and there is no chance I will make my ferry. I've got to turn around and go back to find a place to stay. I'll probably be all the way to Paris before I find one. I'll be in touch tomorrow to tell you where I am and when I'm coming home. It will be difficult at this time of year to get a reservation on a ferry, but I'll—'

'Come *back*,' said McDavis. 'Lazy sod. Leave your

sodding car in France and fly back tonight. There's that wet what's-his-name coming in tomorrow who only deals with you.'

'Mainwright?'

'That's the fellow.'

Poor Justin Mainwright had wandered into Stephenson, McDavis and McDavis one day, and was so shy it took him half an hour to reveal that he wished to be represented in a touchy private matter that he was too embarrassed to entrust to his regular firm of solicitors. He warned everyone that they would laugh at him when he told them his problem, and this proved correct. It was just impossible not to laugh as shy Justin Mainwright began to tell the tale of his multiple arrests. He even laughed himself. His life had become farce, he said, adjusting his spectacles on his freckled nose, and he thanked God every day that he was an obscure person with no-one from whom to hide his shame except a wife and one grown-up son and a few colleagues at work. His myriad offences fell under the category of vice, and each individual infraction was so mild and victimless that poor Justin Mainwright ought to have been left alone; it was the sheer volume of his misdemeanours, and his inability to get away with them even when the police tried deliberately to look the other way, that had resulted in prosecution. Mainwright liked the McDavis muscle, but insisted on dealing only with Adam. He had quite a sum of money in the bank for one so obscure, and McDavis was eager to get him off these ignoble charges and move on to the meat of his affairs. McDavis was not above blackmail.

'Someone else will have to deal with him, I'm afraid,' said Adam, conscious that by speaking for so long on the telephone he was exhibiting the worst manners he could recall in his entire life. 'Look, I'm running out of change.' He took a spoon and tapped it on the receiver, which did cause some of his fellow diners to stop talking and look at him. 'Must go. Best to Judy.'

'Look, you bloody—' said McDavis, as Adam turned off the telephone.

'I'm *so* sorry,' he said to the group, most of whom looked to have gained a new measure of respect for the high-powered attorney in their midst. 'He gets up and jogs on the beach at dawn, in Malibu, with his phone strapped to his shorts. You know the type.'

They certainly did. Geneviève wanted to know if she would have heard of the person.

'Of that I'm certain,' said Adam, 'but I'm not at liberty to say just now. Client privilege and all that. This is the *most* delicious wine, sir.'

Serge wanted to be called Serge. Bruno wanted Adam's card. 'Please,' said Adam. 'No business on a Sunday. Right, Serge?'

After lunch, Adam and Natalie drove around the corner to the Somerset Hotel, and were taken to their suite. Natalie had said there were some people she needed to say hello to at cocktail time, just across the river, but that they had time for a shower and a bottle of champagne before they left. Natalie disappeared into the shower room and went about her ablutions with what Adam presumed was the efficient expertise of someone who spent most nights in hotels. He reclined on the bed and slept for exactly twenty minutes, opening his eyes to the sound of Natalie drying her hair. He opened the bottle of champagne that had been waiting for them, poured her a glass, then showered himself. Under a powerful jet of hot water he collected himself and tried to force twenty-four hours of poisons through his pores. His guess was that Natalie had not yet finished pouring drink into him, and he worried about his constitution. He wondered if Norman had successfully called off the

119

honeymoon and fled to Argentina as planned; or if, as was much more likely, he had broken down, confessed, and thrown himself on his new wife's mercy.

When he emerged from the shower wearing a hotel bathrobe, he kissed Natalie as if she were a wife of many years. She had dressed youthfully, and not to Adam's taste, in a white T-shirt, black leather jacket and blue jeans. He was afraid he would look like her father in his old jacket and khaki trousers. He said as much, and she reminded him that he was her lawyer. Adam buffed his shoes with a hotel brush, and they were off.

They strolled like Parisian lovers, crossed the river at sunset, and entered a rather seedy café called the Cinq à Sept. Adam recognized their gang by the leather jackets and ponytails of the men and the pulchritude of the women. Their three tables were littered with bottles and glasses and coffee cups. A central ashtray had been filled to overflowing. After introductions had been made, and Adam and Natalie were seated side by side in the middle of the group, it did not take long for Adam to identify the ring leader: He was Claude, a burly Frenchman trying to look thirty and failing by at least twenty years. His ragged blond ponytail drew long strands from the front of his head, where he was not entirely bald, back across the parts where he was. He had the complexion of a scrubby desert, and the swollen hands of a methadone addict. Adam disliked him so much, so instantly, that he was reminded of Dick McDavis.

It was the first time Adam had properly heard Natalie speak French, because at their previous gatherings she had always spoken to someone on her other side. Now he listened as she told the gang about the wedding, about their morning drive, about the tanker trucks, about Serge's penthouse. She spoke as vivaciously as she did in English, if anything using more specific nouns. She portrayed Adam not just as her lawyer but, unequivocally, as her lover. Adam sat up straight in his wicker chair.

If he had not known that they were in some way involved in culture, Adam would have taken these people for gangsters and their molls. Claude dominated the conversation in his grumbling, faux-Marseilles accent. He had been in Germany and Italy during the past few weeks, raising staggering amounts of money to fuel his latest project. Claude needed to talk to Natalie about the chances of her appearing at a film festival in six months' time. She agreed in principle, after receiving a nod from her only partly comprehending lawyer. He would need her on hand for a full week, and suitable arrangements would be made for her exposure to the media. Serge had granted permission. Someone else would think of a publicity stunt, but Claude advised waiting until the filming of *Te Deum*, so that they might have an idea what kind of persona Natalie ought to deploy. It was a favour, Claude admitted, listing the ways he would benefit from her appearance, but they would both gain in the end and he would not forget.

Adam knew that he might very well be sitting at a table of luminaries. They were appropriately dressed down, but from their conversation Adam could tell they were accustomed to constant international movement and the wielding of power. They represented only the little toe of the colossus across the Atlantic, but still they were coining it in the most important business in the world. Adam marvelled. These were people who lived for their work, which was something Adam could never do. Their friends, their meals, their holidays, their relaxed drinks on sunny terraces – everything they did created momentum. They brought their offices with them wherever they went, and could not separate their lovers or their dreams from their practical application

121

of will. A measure of their success was that Adam surmised all of this from ten minutes of tangential banter.

Natalie began to gossip. She told the story of a mutual friend, an Englishman named Anthony Reed, who had gone to America to become an actor. Everyone was eager to hear what had become of Anthony, because he was a pompous idiot and they all wanted him to fail. Straight out of drama school, Anthony Reed had landed a plum role in a British three-part television series, cast as a pompous idiot. It was Natalie's duty to report that Anthony had scored again. Even as she spoke, Anthony was filming in Manhattan, delving deep into his psyche to portray a pompous idiot in a film whose marketing budget was so enormous they would all see his interpretation no matter how hard they tried to avoid it. Anthony was probably going to be a big star for about five years, Natalie concluded. The others groaned. Adam asked if Anthony Reed needed a lawyer.

The idea of entertainment law had begun to appeal to Adam, if it meant travelling around European capitals drinking other people's champagne and staying in other people's houses and hotel suites. If he could get a good night's sleep every now and then, everything would be perfect.

One of Claude's sidekicks told a story he had been holding in reserve, presumably for Natalie's benefit: he had been filming some of the war in Yugoslavia, and in an attempt to reconstruct the death of a journalist friend of his, the actor playing the dead friend had been killed under almost identical circumstances. This was one of the most amazing and tragic stories Adam had ever heard, yet it was delivered as if Claude's sidekick lost actors to real warfare all the time. He said he planned to go back with a double for some final scenes he needed to shoot, but his actor-friend's death had printed fine.

Adam wanted to know how he got into Yugoslavia, where he stayed, what he ate, how he made decisions about where it was safe to go, what the dead body had looked like. These questions were not raised, because everyone seemed to take it for granted that travel and lodging took care of themselves, whether one was in Cannes or in Sarajevo. Instead, there were questions about post-production, a planned memorial fund for both the journalist and the actor, and who was best suited to do the first dead man's voice-over from Beyond. Adam had to admit that it sounded like a film he wanted to see.

Because he had no idea what would happen next in his life, Adam found himself living in the present, the way some primitive people and most farmers were said to do. He could only react, and play along. This relaxed him. He was tempted to take up smoking. He was fairly certain he would spend the night with Natalie at the Somerset suite, but things could change. He might find himself in someone's houseboat on the Seine, looking at erotic out-takes from films in progress, but it was not worth speculating. He was trying to learn how to enjoy himself.

The main thing was that Natalie now casually held Adam's hand on top of the café table. This made him self-confident enough to contribute to the conversation, in what he thought of as increasingly fluent French. He told the group about Dick McDavis, omitting the fact that McDavis was his employer, stressing the man's doomed obsession with the Holy Grail of film production. The others liked the story, because they liked any story about people who didn't stand a chance.

Adam wondered what his parents would say when he told them he had changed careers, or thought he had. They were under the impression that Adam was a buttoned-up solicitor of the old school, commuting to work on the London Underground with newspaper and umbrella under his arm, conferring with soft-spoken clients over tea in leather armchairs. They knew nothing of Dick and Judy McDavis, of small-time, fast-buck clients, of Adam's utter failure to get ahead the way he had planned. He had only told them about Mr Stephenson, omitting any mention of the man's illness. They had never visited his flat, which was anything but grand. He had sacrificed size for central location, so that against all his own advice he had taken on a Sword-of-Damocles mortgage. His parents concluded from his address that their son was getting on nicely in the wide world, and they were as proud as distant, re-pressed parents could be expected to let on. His mother assumed that her son had furnished his flat with the spare furniture she had given him when she moved to Antibes; she was wrong, because Adam had sold everything of value to buy part of his cherished car, and given away the rest.

Adam and his parents kept each other at arm's length. No real enmity existed between them that Adam was conscious of, but it was a fact that they were not friends. Part of the deliberate remove Adam kept from his parents was attributable to his London childhood, when he had been made to feel that the slightest social gaffe or expression of individuality might spell the doom of his father's career. Adam had toed the line like a good boy, and by the time of his father's retirement this standard of conduct had become habit.

Of the many piercingly ingrained parental memories Adam carried around, there was one he could not allow to cross his mind without having to clench his eyes until he saw stars. This concerned a family holiday in Nassau, when Adam, aged fifteen, had bravely struck up a friendship with a girl whose parents ran a neighbouring hotel. After two days of adorably conventional court-ship, Adam had asked the girl, who was sixteen, if she thought it would be appropriate for them to go to bed together. She thought so. Logistics were ironed out. A rendezvous was planned. Preliminary physical contact was explored. Two days later, just hours before Adam was to meet the girl in her cabana down the beach, Adam decided that he had been brought up to be forthright in such matters – to get his father's advice, blessing or admonishment, as the circumstances might merit.

He went to his father in the hotel restaurant. The Ambassador enjoyed dining alone, and encouraged his wife to find other things to do. Adam sat down, cleared his throat, and explained the situation in straight-forward language. Adam's father had met the girl and her parents. He had now been presented with the facts. Adam waited, rather smugly, for benediction. What he got instead was a seat on the next flight to London, where he was met at the airport by a chauffeur he had never met before. He was not let out of the house for four days. He spent that time thinking about the girl, about his father and about suicide. By the time his parents returned he was too angry to speak to them, and certainly too embarrassed to try to contact the girl, ever again.

If it distressed Adam to be able to see himself with cool disinterest, it was worse to see his parents that way. In Adam's view, his parents defined the word bour-geois. Their empty retirement offended and depressed him. The idea that they might live the way they now did for twenty more years was intolerable to con-template. His father's failure to have made any real money out of a sparkling diplomatic career was shame-ful. Their flat in Antibes overlooked a coach station. His mother was a source of shame and guilt. He knew, for example, that his mother had lost what looks she had even before he was born. She wore a permanent frown, and when she tried to smile she looked to be on the verge of tears. She was overweight in a way that no style of dress could conceal. She had never done anything well. It was a wonder that Adam's father had attained such an exalted posting with a dowdy wife at his side. Adam had learned through body language, long silences and sudden departures from the dinner table that she had spent many years after Adam's birth trying to conceive other children. It was fortunate for her that Adam had been such a perfect son.

'Adam's father was the Belgian ambassador to Britain,' Natalie told her friends. 'Can you imagine? And during historic times.' This remark was almost certainly a joke. 'Go ahead and tell them,' said Natalie, in English, as if she had heard his life story before. 'It's awfully interesting.'

'I suppose it was an unusual upbringing,' said Adam, also in English. The men around him still looked like hoodlums. The women reached for cigarettes. 'My father married late, you see, which is why I was only two years old when his big appointment came along. He had been ambassador to Canada and Mexico, very briefly, before that. He was well connected, of course, but if I had a photograph of him you would see why he was irresistible. He just looked like an ambassador, that's all. So my early memories are of the Belgian flag stuck on the fender of the official car. For years I thought it was the French flag. There is quite a retinue involved in this sort of thing, you understand, so I grew up believing my parents were very rich. Everyone else was. I once danced with Princess Georgina for about an hour and a half, when I was six years old. My mother wasn't good at being a hostess. She didn't enjoy it, and she did not look the part. She wanted other children, but there must have been problems.' Adam heard himself jabbering on about personal matters, as if he were introducing himself to a new psychotherapist. 'I could have used a brother or sister,' he confessed, 'to compare notes. I grew up as an English boy, and I never left because my parents believed in the continuity of education.' It was as Adam said the proud, beautiful English words 'continuity of education' that he realized Natalie was the only one at the table who could understand a word he was saying. 'They don't understand me, do they,' he said to her, still looking Claude straight in his sleepy eyes.

'No,' said Natalie. 'Isn't this fun?'

Adam switched to French and told Claude how peculiar he thought it was that they would allow him to speak at length in English, when they could not follow what he was saying.

'I hoped you wouldn't notice,' said Claude, reaching for his portable telephone. 'Anyway I like the sounds you make. Let's have another drink.'

It was almost dark. Tourists gathered on the street corner, wondering where to go. Adam badly needed a second wind. He wanted Natalie alone. It was as if they had skipped the traditional routines of courtship, and settled into chaste devotion. He found it odd that Natalie had not mentioned the previous night's premeditated act of chivalry. How often in her life could a man have declined her invitation? He wanted to take her out for a light meal before returning to their suite at the Somerset – which was, Adam now had time to reflect, the most opulent hotel room he had ever occupied.

'I say, Claude,' he said, because Claude had finished his telephone call, and because Adam felt a sudden need for an anthropology lesson. 'How did you get into this business, anyway?'

Claude replied at such length that Adam and Natalie consumed another bottle of wine before he had finished. The story Claude had to tell was one of disaffected youth in a ghastly Parisian ghetto-suburb; a stint in the army, even more disaffected, and now violent; living on the streets of Cologne, because of a girl (here Adam interpolated heroin addiction); a fling with fashion photography; another girl; a first break in his early thirties when a friend's friend made him an offer; relentless hustling during his early forties, culminating in a big success masterminding a music festival. Now Claude was a film producer.

Adam thought again of Dick McDavis. The urge to *be* a film producer was understandable to him; the desire to go through the motions necessary to reach the goal seemed barbaric. It was unimaginable that Dick and his wife would succeed; the chasm between their boastfulness and their real prospects was pitiful. Adam knew that vestiges of old-fashioned snobbery had a great deal to do with the way he felt about the Claudes and Dicks of the world – striving was déclassé, actors and actresses were prostitutes between jobs, impresarios were loathsome cretins – but snobbery was scant defence against envy.

Adam looked at Claude, and envied him. He saw a man to whom nothing had been given, who through some force of personality or unremitting application of will had transformed himself into someone who lived like a prince and worked at the epicentre of modern culture. That Claude was physically repellent only added to the heroism of his feat; that he was ignorant, crass, ill-dressed and monoglot made his achievements seem almost magical.

Adam looked at Natalie, and worried. He thought it might be his duty, even at such an early stage, to protect her from exploitation. Whatever the fast life promised, it rarely ended well. There was certainly something beautiful about her, a kind of innocent gracefulness, but it seemed to Adam that she risked too much for too little potential reward. Adam felt old and wise. He also wished, for the sake of seducing Natalie away from her cheap world, that his London flat weren't quite so small.

Claude announced that he had to meet someone for dinner – implying that his companion sprang from the very ether of celebrity – so the party broke up. Adam put his arm around Natalie's shoulders and used her as a human crutch as they weaved through crowds of disoriented, slow-moving tourists. His second wind had materialized, only to find him drunk in a way he could not recall having been before. He admitted to Natalie that he would feel better if he ate a gigantic meal. She propped him against a tree and used a public telephone to call ahead to the hotel. They would eat in their room. They arrived at the Somerset half an hour later, where two ill-kempt men standing on the pavement photographed them as they entered. Adam ignored them, as if this happened all the time, and he also ignored the people in the lobby who wondered who he was.

Their suite in the Somerset was built on three levels. The living and dining area, more spacious than Adam's entire flat in London, was decorated like a London men's club. The artwork on the walls pertained to war and fishing and topiary. A staircase as broad as the room led to tall oak-framed doors, beyond which was a further sitting room furnished with a heavy desk and two leather-clad reading chairs. A further set of stairs and oak doors led to the bedroom, which contained a four-poster bed that pulsated with historic romance. This was where Adam had napped earlier, without really taking in the grandeur of his surroundings.

129

Whatever indentation he had made in the bedclothes had vanished.

Their meal awaited them. Two waiters supervised their seating, the lighting of the candles and the pouring of the wine, then left them alone. Natalie had exchanged her unattractive leather jacket for a cotton one much more in keeping with the season and the setting. They toasted each other with a perfectly delicious little nothing of a white wine, and began to eat.

'I have to admit I'm not used to this,' Adam said, making a small circle in the air with his snail winkler. 'Jolly nice of Serge, I must say.'

'He usually thinks of everything. Imagine living this way all your life. I always assumed I would end up married to some poverty-stricken madman.'

'I wouldn't say "end up", Natalie. You're very young.'

'Anything I'll do, I'll do young.'

Adam could not reply to this, she had said it with such finality. Also, he had been thinking the same thing about her. Adam had come to believe that it was possible to use laws of averages to predict the destiny of nearly everyone. Exceptions were so rare that he could say he had never met one. He did not feel like an exception himself, and he assumed he would look back on this day as if he had dreamed it in Didi's château bedroom.

Natalie ate with deliberate concentration. Adam felt almost voyeuristic as he watched her put down her knife and fork, dab at her lips with her napkin, replace the napkin in her lap, draw her hair over her right ear, pick up her knife and fork, address her veal. Her arms were thin to the point of frailty. Her face lost all expression. All of this made Adam warm to her. He felt privileged to see the gentle, eager girl behind the reputation for world-conquering brashness. He was also touched and flattered that she wished to include him on part of her adventure. He had been mentally preparing himself for the moment when she would thank him for the lift into the city, and ask him when he was due back in London.

'I hope you're not due anywhere soon,' she said. 'I'd love it if you could keep me company for a while.'

'Oh? Well, certainly, you know, it's not as if I *have* to be anywhere. Of course, whatever you think is right.'

'Do you want to visit your parents? You said they lived in Antibes.'

'It hadn't occurred to me.'

'We could leave first thing in the morning. Do you think a brandy would be out of the question? The waiters will be back soon.'

The waiters did come back. They did allow Natalie to order Armagnac. Natalie turned on the television, and she and Adam sat ten feet apart in armchairs, like grandparents. Adam had begun to realize that his strongest physical urge was to sleep. Natalie still looked chipper. She laughed at a singer who could not conceivably be taken seriously, even by his compatriots. She looked at her tiny gold watch every so often, which was not to Adam's liking. She had taken him past his level of endurance, and if she had any other entertainment in mind outside the confines of their suite, he would be forced to decline.

'Do you have an appointment?' he asked, when she looked at her watch for the fourth time.

'There is *one* thing we could do,' she said.

'Yes?'

'It isn't far. Ten minutes in a taxi.'

'Oh?'

'Do you mind dancing with men?'

'I don't know.' Adam wished he had a poisoned dart and a bamboo tube.

'It's a party given by someone who was very helpful

131

to me. I'd hate it if he knew I was in Paris and didn't go along.'

'Natalie, I'm worried about your health.' Adam finished his Armagnac and put his glass on the floor. It was necessary to squint to look at Natalie, which made it all the more likely that he would fall asleep where he sat. He did not want to appear useless or cowardly.

'Well, I really have to go,' he heard her say. 'Adam?'

Adam tried to make a noise, any noise. His eyes were closed, now. He opened them a little bit when he felt Natalie trying to lift him out of his chair. He struggled to his feet and was aided up the staircase, through the study, up the next staircase, and onto the bed. Natalie helped him undress, and gave him a glass of water. He could feel himself smiling like a groggy child.

'This is nice,' he said, reaching out for her and waving in empty space. He heard the light switch being turned off, then he heard the bedroom door clicking shut. He was alone.

Adam awoke some hours later to the sound of giggles. He opened one of his eyes and made out two shapes in the doorway, silhouetted by the light in the other room. The door opened wider, revealing the shapes to be Natalie and someone very like her, tiptoeing half-nakedly towards him. Through the odours of his own sleep and overindulgence, Adam smelled chlorine.

'Adam, wake up,' Natalie whispered. 'You have *got* to come for a swim upstairs. We had to bribe the night manager to let us in, and we'll have to be very quiet. Come on, Adam, you will be rejuvenated.'

She turned on a mirror light on one of the dressing tables.

'This is my friend, Clara,' Natalie said. Adam opened his other eye. 'Isn't Clara beautiful?'

'Yes she is,' said Adam, into his pillow. 'How do you

132

do, Clara.' He extended a hand, which Clara danced over to shake.

'Clara wants to be an actress, like me,' said Natalie, still whispering.

'She has every chance,' said Adam. 'Good luck to you, Clara.'

Clara remained mute, but stood up straight to pose her body as if for a photograph.

'I've already called downstairs for champagne,' said Natalie. 'Come along, it's just one flight of stairs and you will feel so much better. We can eat breakfast there, too. I told you, I've made a deal with the night manager.'

Without waiting for the reply that Adam could not decide upon, Natalie tore off the bedclothes that covered him. She pulled at one of his wrists. Clara pulled at his other wrist. Adam followed.

The trio held hands as they padded down the hotel corridor. They crouched down, much as Adam and Natalie had done in Didi's château, as if trying to avoid sniper fire. Adam's head felt as if he had dived from a great height into the ocean with a ball and chain attached to his ankle. They trotted up the stairs, closer to the chlorine smell, and into a swimming pool area enclosed by glass. Paris surrounded them. The ceiling was decorated very much like the *Layenfette* tapestry, with minstrels and pennants and hunting dogs and at least one burning village. A tall, green-jacketed waiter looked up from the champagne bottle he had been opening with a cloth napkin, and nodded solemnly. He was a professional, totally unflappable, but he could not prevent the bottle from popping.

Adam, Natalie and Clara entered the pool in a single splash. The room was an echo chamber, and they surfaced into the sound of their own shouts. Because the swimming pool was raised five feet from the surrounding tiled floor, they could paddle to one side, lean their elbows on the railing, and take in a view of Paris identical to the one from Serge's penthouse. And, speaking of Serge, there he was on his own roof, wearing a sunset-orange bathrobe, raising his glass. The waiter brought their champagne over to the edge of the pool, so that they could return Serge's toast.

'Does he recognize us?' Adam asked.

'Of course he does,' said Natalie. 'I saw him just ten minutes ago. I told him we would be coming over here.'

'You were back in his flat?'

'That's where we went for a swim just now.'

'But when you returned, you wore very little clothing, to say the least,' said Adam, unthinkingly, hearing the answer to this riddle even as he posed it. 'Don't tell me,' he said. 'You just trotted along the Parisian streets.'

'It wasn't far,' said Clara. 'And we had towels.' These were the first words she had spoken. To Adam's sophisticated ear she sounded like a Scandinavian who had grown up in Greece and been briefly educated at a French school. Beautiful she may have been, but she was not Adam's type. She had mean, calculating eyes. Not a trace of humour issued from her posed facial expression. It occurred to Adam at this point that only under the most special circumstances would he not be charged with ruinous lust for someone like Clara; by paying so much attention to him, Natalie had set a new standard by which women who happened to go swimming naked with him in hotel pools could be judged. Adam turned to Natalie.

'Old Serge is a good chap,' he said.

'He's a lot of fun, especially at night. He works hard during the day, and then he entertains.'

'But we had lunch with him only this afternoon.'

'That was work,' said Natalie. 'He was visualizing.'

'I see.'

'He liked you, by the way. He said to tell you so.'

'Is that right?'

'Yes. He said I was in good hands.'

Adam put his hands around Natalie's waist, and twisted around so that he faced her with the back of his neck resting on the edge of the pool. Clara drew closer, her eyes still on the rooftop across the way. The waiter placed the champagne bottle within reach, and left through a staff door. Adam anchored himself by his feet on the sloping wall of the pool, and hooked Natalie's legs over his thighs. He stroked her back underwater, and she held on to his hair.

'Where is he?' asked Clara. This was a question Adam could not understand.

'He'll be here,' said Natalie. For Adam's benefit, she added, 'She means her boyfriend. He was right behind us, but he didn't dare come out in the street. He must have gone back for a robe, or his clothes. Don't worry, Clara, he'll be here.'

'Who is he?' Adam asked.

'You'll know him when you see him,' said Natalie.

Adam assumed that they were about to be joined by Bruno L, and stole a glance at Clara to determine if she had been one of Bruno's girls at Serge's lunch party. He had not drawn a conclusion before the entrance of the man Clara had been expecting: Bruno it wasn't.

Adam recognized the man right away, even though he burst through the double doors and dived into the pool at a run. Adam's brain photographed the naked man in mid-flight, and there was no mistaking him. Adam felt a kind of fever coming on. He was used to meeting well-known people, on a reasonable level, but the man who had just dived into the swimming pool was of another category altogether. He was a leading member of the small group Adam had come to think of as the new aristocracy. These people were every bit as wealthy, frivolous and impotent as their predecessors

135

in history, but they had turned society on its head: they were *actors*. The actor in question surfaced on the far side of the pool and waved cheerfully. He took a deep breath, then swam underwater for two lengths. He emerged at the point where he had originally entered. He waved again, and grinned in a way with which millions were familiar.

Adam was ashamed by how much he knew about this man. He knew that he had been born in poverty in rural Illinois, that he had suffered up to five months of poverty in New York before being discovered, and that he had lived since the age of twenty-one in Los Angeles, California, as a maverick, multimillionaire, womanizing, award-winning, much-married, childless, difficult *actor*.

'Hey, Nat,' said the prodigy.

Clara swam over to him.

'Hey yourself,' said Natalie. 'Meet Adam.'

'Yo, Adam,' said the star.

'How do you do,' said Adam.

Clara dived beneath the surface and did something that made the famous actor smile again. He was pale but dark-haired. Too much flesh hung from his arms. He had not shaved in days. A green tattoo stained his right shoulder. At some point during his running dive he had dropped a packet of cigarettes and a lighter. He stretched out to retrieve them from the tiled side of the pool, and began to smoke even before Clara resurfaced.

Adam remembered more of the actor's biography, information he wished he didn't know. The actor's father had been murdered, which helped the actor's career at a time when he needed publicity. All of the actor's wives had been actresses, but these marriages had not survived the premières of the films on which they had met and collaborated. The actor was legally childless, but newspapers reported with some

136

regularity on the bastards who pretended to his fortune. He was very much like a pope, Adam reflected, except that he was taken seriously.

'Yo, Adam. What about it?' said the star.

Adam considered this question carefully. It was so important to appear nonchalant. The star's question amounted to a greeting, followed by what was most likely a colloquial interrogative phrase meaning simply, 'How are you?', or, perhaps, 'Isn't this fun, then?'

'Yes,' said Adam.

'You better believe it,' said the star.

Clara bobbed to the surface, but not before Adam had congratulated himself on having conversed smoothly with someone who, had he lived in Britain, would have been the forty-eighth richest man in the country. She kissed the star noisily, as if she were eating a peach.

Natalie leaned over and kissed the ear lobe on the side of Adam's head that was farthest from the star and Clara.

'We have to leave,' she whispered. 'Don't make me stay with this guy.'

'Which guy?'

Natalie named the star.

'But we were becoming such great friends,' said Adam.

'They're going to want a ride down south,' said Natalie. 'Your car doesn't have room.'

'What, room for *him*?'

'I think we ought to go by ourselves, and I think we ought to go now. We'll see him there, I'm sure.'

'We ought to get some sleep. Don't worry about them. We'll sleep, we'll drive—'

Natalie bit Adam's ear. 'We have to go *now*.'

'Let's go now,' said Adam. 'We'll drive away. This swim has done me a world of good.'

It was easy to make excuses and leave the swimming

pool, as Adam and Natalie merely had to pretend to be going back to their room to do what Clara and the star had already begun to do in the swimming pool.

'Later, Nat. Later, Adam,' said the star.

Adam and Natalie walked naked down the corridor, down the stairs, and into their unlocked suite. They were packed and dressed in seconds. They took the lift down to the lobby, which was manned by the night manager Natalie had bribed or seduced earlier. Natalie preceded Adam through the revolving doors into the street. It was very much in the front of Adam's mind that their night of amusement at the Somerset was going to cost Serge a fortune, when an expensive voice came from behind: *'Monsieur? S'il vous plaît?'*

Adam froze. The front door revolved before him. Natalie waited in the freedom of the street. Adam knew what Natalie would have done in these circumstances, but he could not help himself. His reflexes were too ingrained. He turned, put down his bag and Natalie's, and walked to the desk.

Without quite saying that he considered Adam to be a cheque-dodger, the night manager pressed a button on his computer keyboard and a printer spat out a page of numbers. He handed the page over to Adam, who patted his pockets as if he were used to wearing glasses. As Natalie looked on from outside, Adam scanned the piece of paper and located a grand total, which contained commas and decimal points. With the smile of a petro-potentate paying cash for a yacht, Adam reached into his jacket for his wallet. From this he extracted his only credit card, which seemed to squirm between his fingers like a shrimp above boiling water. This much-abused credit card had a history of misbehaviour that had resulted in Adam's bank manager calling him 'Mate', 'Boyyo', and, recently, 'You.'

Adam's bank manager, Benjamin Friend, had started

out with some respect for his young solicitor client. At the beginning of Adam's debt, when the debt was an amoeba, Benjamin had spoken of it in terms of 'our' debt, and what 'we' were going to do about it. Then the amoeba divided, and divided again. It was now squarely 'your' debt, and 'you' were going to do something about it. 'Listen, you,' Benjamin had said, in a bullying tone of voice that did not for a moment allow blame for having permitted Adam's overdraft in the first place. 'You are going to solve this problem. Do we understand each other, mate?'

Adam handed over his squirming credit card. The natty man behind the desk held it gingerly between thumb and forefinger as he ran its magnetic strip through a machine that was likely to light up its screen with warnings: *Do not betray your alarm! Summon the gendarmes!* Adam leaned on the desk and looked at his fingernails. He was torn between the two possible results of this transaction: rejection would cause embarrassment and delay; acceptance would ruin him. The sum he had seen on the night manager's piece of paper would effectively double his overdraft. It was an amount of money that Adam could have lived on in London for many weeks.

Adam and the manager waited for the machine to reach its verdict. Natalie was no longer visible through the glass doors. The manager made tiny, nervous movements with his lips and fingers, indicating to Adam that he had his doubts about *monsieur*'s solvency. When the machine at last delivered its grudging approval, the manager inspected this information as if he might invoke his right of veto. When he handed Adam a slip to sign, he watched closely. Adam took his receipt, and thanked the manager like a condemned man tipping his executioner. He folded the receipt and put it in his wallet. He returned his wallet to his jacket pocket, where it rested sickly against his beating heart. He walked manfully towards the door, cursing Serge in the foulest language he knew.

Outside, Adam nodded good morning to a street sweeper, thinking that technically he now had fewer assets than this proud government employee. He walked around the corner to his car, and found Natalie waiting there tapping her fingers on the soft top.

'No trouble with the bill,' said Adam, wishing to stress right away that he, not Serge, had paid. He still held out the hope that he might somehow be reimbursed. He unlocked his venerable car, put the top down, and helped Natalie into her seat. She was asleep before he had started the engine. He made the observation that it was typical of someone with so much energy that she would sleep only when in motion, when she was *getting* somewhere.

It was a pleasure, despite his exhaustion, to drive through deserted streets in the centre of Paris. He did not know the city well, and yet it was all familiar to him. With Natalie gorgeously asleep in the passenger seat, he drove in a haphazard manner in a southerly direction. Near the outskirts of the city, and without waking Natalie, he stopped at a street market to buy bread, butter, cheese and fruit. Thinking of his passenger, he also bought four bottles of wine. He was grateful to have brought along far too much cash, because it was possible that after what it had just been through, his card might already have expired in his pocket. Natalie did not open her eyes, even when Adam hit the open road and the wind lashed her drying hair into her face.

It was time for Adam to begin to worry about the impression his parents would make. He would have to stop along the way and warn them of his arrival, and to prepare them to meet his future wife – not that he would dream of presenting Natalie that way, but such a sudden visit would not be interpreted otherwise. His mother would be ecstatic and emotional; his father would be covetous. Adam did not doubt that Natalie would play along, but he dreaded to think what she would make of the old Ambassador and his wife of thirty-six years.

A most unpleasant and incurable streak of pedantry ran through the Ambassador's character. He asked questions of people only to correct their replies. He considered himself to be erudite, and downright learned in several fields. He could not imagine that it was possible to address a topic subjectively, so that any discussion with him always ended in bitter, one-sided argument. His stubbornness had been known to reduce women and children to tears, as when stating categorically that someone's favourite writer was a plagiarist, that a beloved painter was a fraud, that a cherished musician had no business on the stage.

If politics was one of the worst topics to raise in polite company, it was singularly murderous to do so around the Ambassador. Adam had been taught a valuable lesson about life by listening to his father, who knew as much as anyone about the world stage, going off on irrational tangents or spouting untenable, preposterous views on anything from the Common Agricultural Policy to the wisdom of exploiting the natural resources of Antarctica. Adam had learned that to be armed with facts was not to be guaranteed sound judgement. He had also learned that it was bad manners to hold strong opinions in public, unless they were accompanied by a sense of humour, which the Ambassador lacked. He only laughed when he felt he had scored a particularly devastating point in private debate. He did not smile sympathetically, he smiled with scorn. Whatever pleasures he had derived from life must have been shallow indeed, and linked to promotion at work.

Adam's mother had married young, and had probably spent much of her life regretting the decision. Adam guessed that she had been a vivacious, anti-intellectual girl, interested in horses and parties and her many siblings. Once shackled to the boorish Ambassador, she never complained; this was one aspect of Adam's family life that saddened him. It was frustrating not to be able to tell if her smile were as phoney as it looked, if her consistent defence of her husband were a matter of high principle rather than obsequiousness, or if she really gave a damn about anything anymore. Adam wondered if he ought to ask.

During his brief acquaintance with Natalie, he had been given little time to think. Now, as the sun rose over France, he thought. Glancing over and sizing up his passenger, he still felt some of what had come over him on the night of Norman and Didi's wedding. He caught himself being moved by the small acts of friendliness Natalie sprinkled in between her hectic and rather nerve-racking way of going about things: the way she had seized him as her date, whether or not she had been put up to the job by her friend Didi; the way she tried to put him at ease in front of her friends; the way she held his hand on top of the café table. It was not enough for Adam to dismiss her as a *free spirit*, a category of person he did not approve of for reasons of law and order. She genuinely seemed to have the ability to jump to the conclusion that she liked someone, and to carry on from there. There was a vulnerability about such a gift that Adam found endearing, as if it had suddenly become his job to see to it that Natalie trusted only the right people. Perhaps he would be her lawyer, after all.

In the meantime, logistics. He pulled into a motorway petrol station, bought a key ring in order to get change, and made his calls on a public telephone at the back of the building. First he rang his flat in London, and activated his answering machine. This proved to contain more than twenty messages from people who normally paid little attention to him. One after the other, the messages said the same thing: *Impossible* that we haven't got together more often; *do* ring us as soon as you return. Three or four messages of this type were played into Adam's ear before he understood the reason: rumour had already reached everyone about his tryst with Natalie. This flood of interest, and its explanation, fascinated and excited Adam. How *useful*, really, to have a famous girlfriend.

Next, Adam dialled his parents' number in Antibes. His mother answered, which was normal. Adam had only to dip a toe into the matter of his being accompanied by a woman, for his mother to become breathless and almost tearful. She would have to make arrangements. Dinner at home was impossible. The Ambassador was out of sorts, but this news would cheer him up no end. What to wear?

Having given his mother an approximate time of arrival, he hung up and dialled Dick McDavis.

'Dick, Adam.'

'You bloody . . .'

This time Adam's excuse was that, having retreated to Paris from the marauding French farmers, he had encountered a mysterious Englishman calling himself Victor Emanuel Somerset, who bore a striking resemblance to a certain missing viscount. Was Dick interested in this man's affairs? Yes. Was it worth Adam's time to explore the matter further? Well of *course* it was, you bloody . . .

Adam replaced the receiver, visited the men's room

to comb his hair, then came out and walked around the building to his car. There he found Natalie, happily eating a piece of buttered baguette and drinking red wine out of the bottle.

'You know,' shouted Natalie, once they had regained the autoroute, 'I could have used some education!'

Adam nodded.

'I don't know anything. My parents thought education was bourgeois. They taught us at home, or tried to.'

'You speak – what, four languages?'

'And I can't write in any of them.'

'You're not a writer, you're an actress.'

'An *actress*! Who would have guessed?'

'I bet if I'd known you five years ago I would have predicted it.'

'Five years ago I was still working for my mother. I was "The Face of FD".'

'I know, I've seen the pictures.'

'Was I adorable, or what?'

'You were adorable.'

'Mother's business is collapsing, by the way.'

'Is it? I hadn't heard.' Adam had heard.

'It's true. And my father hasn't written a word in seven years. Do you know that all the words he has published in his life wouldn't fill the front page of a newspaper?'

'Very select words. And successful.'

'You wouldn't think either of my parents was successful, if you saw them. They're glum and resigned. It's my father's fault, really. My theory is that he isn't fit for his job, and never has been. He sort of dressed up like a poet and expected the rest to follow automatically. Even I know it doesn't work that way.'

'But it did work.'

'Funny world.'

'Your mother sounds like the talented one. Illustrator, designer, mogul.'

'Yes, but where's the pleasure? I promise you, she still thinks of herself as the muse and helpmate of my father. She thinks of *him* as the productive one. All he does is sit in the darkness of his studio, or outside in the sun – with his special notebooks he has sent over from Finland, and his special pen that belonged to George Tybor, the poet – not putting pen to paper. If he had filled just *one* of those notebooks in his life, he might be a happier man. He's a bit of a drinker, too, but even that is a pose.'

Natalie gulped red wine from the bottle and handed it to Adam. He pretended to take a sip, for the sake of appearances.

'We ought to drop by and see my parents, you know,' Natalie continued. 'It's only fair, since we're seeing yours. This is turning out to be a wonderfully old-fashioned courtship, don't you think?'

'It is indeed. Where are your parents?'

Natalie looked at her watch. 'They ought to be in Ilani, this month. They have a little house by the sea.'

'I'm sorry, I don't know where that is.'

'It's in Italy, just over the border. It's on our way.'

'On our way? On our way where?'

Natalie covered her mouth with her palm. 'Oh,' she said, 'I can't believe I forgot to tell you. Last night Serge found inspiration. His vision is complete. We're going to Yugoslavia.'

Adam felt his car swerve slightly. 'There is no such thing as Yugoslavia.'

'You know what I mean. The Dalmatian coast. Serge needs to film in the ruins of Dubrovnik.'

'*Does* he, now?'

'Apparently he spent many happy holidays there with his wife, and it breaks his heart to think of the town under fire. It's safe enough, he says. The war is miles away. Also his budget isn't what it ought to be, even though Claude – you remember Claude – is involved, and accommodation is very cheap at the moment. You can imagine that from a publicity standpoint, Croatia is—'

'I get the picture,' said Adam.

'I think it's a wonderful idea, and that Serge is a genius.'

'Does your contract say you have to speak that way about him?'

'I'm serious, Adam. You mustn't be so cynical. OK, it seems odd that a man who has produced so little ought to be so well rewarded, and considered a genius. But look at my father. It's the same sort of thing, only Serge actually does make films. You'll see.'

'You wouldn't by any chance be thinking that you needed a driver all the way to Dubrovnik?'

'I don't want you to go out of your way,' said Natalie, moving closer to Adam and placing a hand on his thigh. 'You must have important things to do. Didi told me that you're going great guns, at work.'

'Oh, yes.'

'Is it true that you're going to take over the firm?'

'Is that what Didi said?'

'Not in so many words. She did give that impression. You know how she is. She thinks she's being generous.'

'She certainly is being generous, in this case. Listen, Natalie, I really should explain. I work at a third-rate firm run by a very gung-ho husband and wife team. There is no room for me at the top, such as it is. I may have been right to join, when it was run by a wonderful man, now a friend of mine. But I made a mistake staying on. I was greedy, I suppose, or over-ambitious, or—' what Adam said next sounded like a profound, exuberant confession, because he had to shout it at the

146

top of his lungs over the rushing wind, '—or maybe I was just afraid of the first eleven!'

After explaining to Natalie that this was a sporting metaphor, Adam went on to describe his life in London in as much frank detail as he dared, consistent with wanting her to continue liking him. He told her what long hours he worked and explained that much of his socializing took place among clients. He worked for money, and had begun to wonder if there were any other goal to which he could aspire. He said this in a way that did not betray the fact that one night's hotel bill had transformed his credit card into a liability that hung heavily in his jacket pocket, and was probably hot to the touch.

'If I were you, I would quit,' said Natalie, once Adam had finished describing his daily life.

'No,' Adam corrected her. 'If you were *you* you would quit. If you were *me*, you would crawl along and hope for lightning to strike.' He cringed as he failed to stop himself from saying this. Natalie would think he saw her as a way out of his rut.

'Well, look around,' said Natalie, gesturing at the panorama around them. 'It's a big country now, Europe. You wouldn't be the first Englishman to flee to the Continent.'

'I'm not an Englishman.'

'Oh, yes you are.'

This comment pleased Adam. It was one thing to come from a featureless country no-one gave a second thought to, but to bear that onus without actually having lived there was too much. If he were truthful, he would have said that he wished to be English.

Natalie, who had grown up in Morocco, Libya, the Middle East, Scotland, Portugal, France, Italy, England and Malta, could afford to look upon the new Europe as her stamping ground. To Adam, despite his roots, it

147

was still an impenetrable place. It was a place of bribes and corruption, of splashy food and clothes, of nudity and wantonness, of wars that Britain kept having to sort out. Adam did not think any of that would change. It was not just a desire to contradict his father – the Ambassador was naturally a keen European – that made Adam isolationist. He felt like a small fish, and he wanted to remain in a small pond.

It did not sound pretentious when Natalie replied, when asked where she felt she belonged, 'Right here is fine,' nor was hers simply a youthful optimism. She would ricochet here and there in this rich new world, and Adam did not doubt that she would prosper in the short run. She certainly didn't seem to find it a problem paying her hotel bills.

Everyone in France was already on holiday, so the roads leading south were clear. Natalie slept much of the way, and they reached Antibes in time for a late lunch. Adam assured Natalie that they would be welcome to stay at his parents' flat, making sure to warn her that she ought not to expect too much in the way of luxury. He made it sound as if his parents, though wealthy, eschewed the frills they could easily afford. Natalie said she didn't mind if they had to sleep on the beach.

After lunch, Adam hired a small sailboat and took Natalie out for a sea view of the mansions on the coast. He was so exhausted that it actually occurred to him that he might suffer a heart attack, but he persevered. They had an argument, aboard the sailboat, when Natalie accused Adam of turning up his nose at people who did not live in mansions on the Côte d'Azur. His rebuttal was rather lame – it had to do with individual accomplishment, the rewards of generations labouring for the common weal, the value of mansions *qua* mansions – and only proved that what Natalie had said was true. This made Adam angry, and he accused Natalie of living in a utopian world where she could afford never to make value judgements, never to worry about who her friends were, never to lie in bed wondering what people thought of her.

'My, my,' said Natalie conclusively, from her lofty position in the bow. 'Aren't we touchy.'

At precisely eight-thirty, Adam rang the doorbell in the lobby of his parents' modern apartment building. His mother's voice replied joyfully that she and the Ambassador could not be more pleased to hear that their son and his new friend had arrived. Adam and Natalie entered the lift, the interior of which looked as if it had frequently been repainted against graffiti. They ascended to the fourth floor of twelve, and disembarked into a long, brightly lighted corridor. This corridor was decorated like a shoddy hotel; its petrochemical carpet squeaked under foot. Adam did not look at Natalie as he strode down to the far end of the building.

Adam had been to this flat on perhaps twenty occasions. He hated it. He did not like its odour, its ambience, its *purpose*. Why, after all, would a retired couple wish to live high above a coach station just out of walking distance from the coast people spent their last pennies visiting on holiday? It seemed to Adam that one should either live in the middle of such a place, or not at all.

'Hello, *Mother*,' he said, when the door opened. He kissed her and hugged her and patted her on the back. If he was not mistaken she had shrunk, vertically speaking. He could see his father loitering in the background, but he concentrated on his mother long enough to allow Natalie through the door. His mother had gone only slightly overboard in her rushed preparations for the evening: hair, freshly dyed and coiffed by her

149

faithful Thomàs; dress, the one she would have worn in Stockholm had her husband ever won the Nobel Peace Prize; jewellery, her mother's; teeth, in.

'This is Natalie.'

'I would have recognized her,' said Adam's mother. Adam suddenly remembered that his mother was the sort of person who secretly read the kind of magazines in which Natalie had recently appeared. She shook Natalie's hand with her usual formality, but used the opportunity to pull her farther inside the flat, as if Natalie might have been considering flight. 'And this is my husband,' she said, dragging Natalie over to the Ambassador, who still stood in the shadows of the gloomy flat. The Ambassador stepped forward, wearing the sort of old fashioned, double-breasted, I-used-to-be-somebody suit he favoured even in summer.

'We're underdressed,' said Natalie, stating the obvious.

'Nonsense,' said Adam's mother, adjusting her diamond bracelet.

Natalie shook hands with the Ambassador. Adam had to admit that his father looked robust, for a man in his mid-seventies. His stern expression was the same as always, but even he was unable to cast disapproval on Natalie. He held her hand for a long time, the way Adam hated, and said twice how charmed he was. The tension and emotion in the room was exactly the same as it would have been had Adam and Natalie come home to announce that they were already married. When Adam shook his father's hand, he was forced to endure a meaningful look.

They sat down in the more formal of the two living rooms, a room where Adam had once knocked a valuable vase off a table when trying to sneak into his bedroom late at night. The room contained everything of value that remained in his small family's possession

– except of course for the vase, which had gone to Heaven. The choice of drinks was sherry or nothing, so four glasses of sherry were raised to toast Adam and Natalie's happily-ever-after. Adam used all that remained of his energy to keep the conversation superficial, and to thwart his father's every attempt to deliver a monologue on whatever issue of the day had captured his imagination.

He hadn't spoken to his parents in three months, so it was perfectly natural when his mother asked how everything was going back in London. He did not reply that he hated his job; that he was in debt; that he saw no avenues open to him save cat-burglary; that his friends were getting married and disappearing into an unreachable nether world; that he considered himself a failure whose only mission left in life was to conceal that fact from the charming, beautiful girl beaming lovingly at his side. What he said was, 'Couldn't be better.'

'And Natalie?' asked Adam's mother. Adam steeled himself. He was not familiar enough with Natalie's manners to know if she would say something embarrassing, perhaps along the lines of being terribly sorry but it was a mistake to have come.

'*Well*,' said Natalie, leaning back in her chair and crossing her legs. 'I have to say that Adam here has been a *rock*. These last few months have been awfully busy for me, and I'm quite inexperienced, so it is a relief to have Adam looking out for me. I think we make quite a team, don't you, Adam?'

'Speaking as your lawyer, yes I do.'

'He makes me very happy,' added Natalie, a sentence carrying a sufficiently erotic overtone to cause the Ambassador to raise one of his white eyebrows.

'I'm about to shoot a film,' said Natalie, as if it weren't her first one, 'and I'm hoping Adam will come along.'

151

'I would probably get in the way,' said Adam, before Natalie could tell his parents which brutal war zone Serge had selected to match his *vision*.

It was as he said this that Adam noticed a newspaper open and folded to an inside page. It was a British paper, of the very lowest order, and the photograph on display was of himself and Natalie entering the Somerset Hotel. Adam's right hand was raised like a seasoned, much-harassed celebrity, and his other hand protectively guided Natalie by the elbow towards the door.

'Yes, *look*,' said Adam's mother, noticing Adam's alarm. 'Did you ever think you could be in the news-paper, darling? And described as a "dashing mystery companion", no less? My word.'

'That was awfully fast,' said Adam, imagining film processing, transmission, layout, printing and trans-portation. He also wondered if Dick McDavis would notice the photograph – for this, characteristically, was Dick McDavis's daily paper.

Natalie picked up the newspaper. 'That isn't fair,' she said. 'Adam looks better than I do.'

The Ambassador spoke, in his harshly accented English: 'Are you *terribly* famous, Natalie?'

'Oh, not really at all,' she replied. 'This sort of thing is a matter of public relations. The space would have been reserved in advance, possibly paid for. Someone would have told the photographers where I was going to be. If they had known Adam was going to be with me, they would have given his name – and probably mentioned you, Mr Ambassador.'

Christ, thought Adam. She is *good* at this. Adam's father sat up straighter in his chair, and nearly smiled. 'I don't know about *that*,' he said.

Adam wanted an explanation as to how this par-ticular newspaper had found its way into his parents' home. Judging by the messages he had collected on his answering machine in London, it was likely that a grapevine had been involved. Someone in England who just *happened* to glance at a copy of this *filthy* rag while chatting with a friend at the local newsagent, would have thought it so *amusing* to inform Adam's mother. Adam's mother would have taken a taxi to the centre of Antibes and scoured the tourist shops for English newspapers. The decision whether or not to display the photograph would have been an agonizing one.

'I think it is right that you have tried to remain anonymous, Adam,' said his mother, seriously. She could not conceal her pride. 'It must be so *trying*, Natalie, to live in the public eye as you do.'

'I'm afraid one has to be realistic,' Natalie said. 'Without publicity, it would be impossible for me to pursue my career. It is a business that feeds on little else *but* publicity. I try to think of film directors as my employers. They wouldn't be too pleased if their actresses were invisible recluses, now would they?'

Natalie did have an amazing knack for ingenuous self-aggrandizement. Adam could see that both of his parents were under the impression that they were receiving a veteran actress, respected in her industry, and with a rational head on her shoulders to boot. She had them in her thrall, as she told them about Didi's wedding, about the fireworks, about Serge and his penthouse, about the famous Somerset swimming pool. She did not mention that their son had footed the bill.

Physical beauty went an awfully long way, Adam reflected. Natalie could afford to be relaxed in any company. Adam had noticed that her appearance seemed to change with the light or the time of day. Now she looked aristocratic, as if she belonged seated in his parents' spurious Louis XVI chair, as if she always drank a miniature glass of sherry in the evening – just the one – and as if nothing came more naturally to her than being presented to an ex-ambassador and his wife as a prospective daughter-in-law. She had both of Adam's parents salivating at the prospect, even though the word 'actress' would normally have drawn sneers and derision in their household. It touched Adam that they seemed to take it for granted that their son was worthy of such an extraordinary girl.

'I hope you don't mind,' said Adam's mother at last, 'but at such short notice my husband and I thought it would be a good idea to dine out. There's a place we know of that is supposed to be frightfully good. It's for you younger crowd – *chic*, is what it is – but I don't think they play any awful music.'

Outside, a car and driver awaited them. This was new in Adam's experience since the day his father's tenure as ambassador came to an end. Adam's parents sat in back with Natalie between them, while Adam sat next to the driver. The restaurant proved not to be in Antibes at all, but in Cannes, which gave Natalie plenty of time to work her charm. Adam faced forwards, trying not to fall asleep, listening to Natalie's solicitous banter. He found that he was sunburned from their afternoon sail, and this added to his exhaustion. He was too weak to turn around and participate in the spirited conversation going on behind him. Natalie showed herself either to be the actress Serge hoped she would be, or she was sincerely interested in Adam's mother's shopping routine, the Ambassador's golf handicap, and their mutual plans for an additional potted plant on the balcony. Natalie told compressed stories about her own parents along the same lines – one of which, having to do with her mother's efforts to interest her father in the cultivation of tomatoes, actually caused the Ambassador to laugh.

Adam pressed his temple against the cool car window and saw some of his usual haunts pass by. He remembered girls, mostly, and that feeling of impossible good fortune when they put a hand in the small of his back before leaving the last club of the night. It had to be said that most of these experiences had taken place in the company of Norman, or one of his ilk, when Adam had been able to pass himself off as an English gentleman. Still, the memories were delicious.

Cannes looked fine. Adam tried to imagine Natalie there, on an even more crowded evening, tripping up red-carpeted stairs through shocks of camera flashes. He imagined her giving interviews in perfect English, French, Spanish and Portuguese, laughing off comparisons with previously exploited starlets, maintaining that she was in the business for the long haul.

With two daring and illegal manoeuvres, the driver managed to reach the front door of the restaurant. Adam did not recognize its name; predictably, Natalie said she had dined there not three weeks ago, and she gave her approval. As the Ambassador and his wife went ahead to stake their claim to a reservation, Natalie held back, put her hand in the small of Adam's back, and said, 'I *love* your parents.'

Adam had learned that Natalie was no stranger to sarcasm, but once again he found himself believing her to be sincere. He shrugged his shoulders, took her hand, and entered the restaurant behind his parents. He was amazed that they had chosen this place, which revealed itself immediately to be the fashionable spot of the summer. This Adam ascertained by the number of hands that shot up in recognition of Natalie, who blew kisses in return but indicated with hand gestures that she was enjoying a private night out. One of the hands in the air belonged to the unspeakably gigantic star who had shared their swimming pool earlier in the day. He had no doubt slept late into the afternoon and flown in on a private jet. Adam was used to being out of his depth, but not so *continuously*. He knew now that in his snobbery and disdain he had underestimated Natalie. She was really, really well known. American icons waved to her in restaurants, swam with her in swimming pools – Adam's *parents* had heard of her.

Now Adam began to sweat. He didn't really mind being hauled around Europe on a beautiful girl's whim, but now he could not look at Natalie without somewhat deeper emotions than he was used to poking their way to the surface. He had already spent more time in her company than with his previous girlfriend, and that liaison had lasted two months. He liked Natalie, and he trusted her. Anyone who could reduce his father to a giggling child in the course of a single car ride deserved his full attention.

They were seated. Natalie performed the unprecedented act of taking responsibility for ordering the wine. Wine was one of the things Adam's father thought he knew all about, and it was part of his social repertoire to order, reject, order again, then give his approval to wines with unusual names. Adam had never seen his father relinquish this right of adjudication. Natalie ordered two bottles of the house red. Once again, the Ambassador found her delightful. He did one other thing to set the evening apart from any other in Adam's memory: he reached out a stiff arm, his shoulders quaking with laughter, and patted his son on the back.

A side-benefit of Natalie's sparkling presence was that Adam began to get along with his parents in a relaxed, adult way. His mother looked more youthful than he had seen her in ten years. She seemed pleased with herself for having taken the risk of booking a table at a young people's restaurant. She basked in the attention they received from those of their fellow diners who could not contain their curiosity. She showed open affection for her husband, occasionally touching his sleeve in appreciation of something he had said. The Ambassador did not lecture, he conversed. After two glasses of wine, he made an emotional toast to Adam and Natalie's happiness, then a separate toast to Natalie alone, citing her beauty, her wit, her transparent love for his son. Adam expected that at any moment there would be a toast to their future offspring.

'Of course, we're going to visit my parents tomorrow,' said Natalie, warming to her role.

'Have you never met them, Adam?' asked the Ambassador.

'No, not yet. I'm looking forward to it.'

'They sound *divine*,' said Adam's mother. 'I think we must have one of your father's books at home, don't we, darling?'

'Of course we do,' said the Ambassador, who had no idea.

'My parents are going to love Adam. I don't think they know what a respectable man I'm bringing home. They have lived in fear for years.'

Adam's mother had noticed the inconceivably famous American actor at his isolated table in the corner.

'My word,' she said. 'Do you know who that is?'

Adam had been waiting for this opportunity. 'We had a swim together last night in Paris, actually. Would you like to meet him, Mother? I could introduce you. The girl is named Clara. She's his girlfriend of the moment.'

'Oh, never, no. I wouldn't know what to say. He is *marvellous*. And such a nice, natural looking man. He seems like a nice man, don't you think so, darling?'

Adam's father looked over his shoulder without turning around. 'Charming,' he said. 'Yes, very nice man.'

'He's an animal,' said Natalie, with feeling. 'Some

157

stories I could tell – well, not in polite company.' Natalie put one elbow on the table and leaned conspiratorially towards Adam's parents. They leaned towards her.

'Tell,' they said.

Natalie scowled. 'Let's just say that our friend over there is unused to having his advances rebuffed. For some reason he thought he was instrumental in getting me my first role—' she made this sound as if it had happened years ago, '—and he expected to be repaid for the favour.'

This sounded natural enough to Adam.

'The swine,' said Adam's parents.

'The thing is, it is very tempting. He has so much money, you think that if you're in the same room with him for twenty minutes you're going to become a millionaire by osmosis.'

'Natalie,' said Adam, who wanted his putative spouse not to sound like a prostitute.

'No, it's true. I have to be honest. If you get past the audition and become his girlfriend, you need never work again.'

'*Natalie.*'

'What's the matter with you, Adam? Are you telling me you wouldn't sleep with that guy for a huge amount of money?'

'Me? Sleep with *him*?' He looked over at the star, who ate sloppily and laughed with his mouth full. Adam could not believe he was having this discussion in front of his parents.

'Come on, Adam,' said his father. 'How much?'

Adam thought seriously. 'It's a small amount of money to him, to tell you the truth.'

'You see?' said Natalie. 'In my case it was probably a large amount of money.'

'What are you saying?' said Adam.

'Not what you think. The short version is that I cost his studio a fortune. I gave him a black eye that prevented filming for four days.'

'But wait a minute,' said Adam. 'He was perfectly civil to you last night. You were like old friends, in fact. He called you "Nat".'

'That's the way these things work. He respects me. He says he's never met a woman like me, all that rot.'

'He probably thinks he still has a chance,' said Adam's father, alarmingly. 'Good for you for giving him one,' he added. His English had never been perfect.

Their dinner ended with brandy, over which Adam's father could not resist fifteen minutes of pontification on the subject of Bosnia-Herzegovina. Natalie listened, rapt, while Adam poked himself in the calf with a toothpick to keep himself awake. He thought of the single bed they would be sleeping in back at his parents' flat. He remembered Natalie's skin from the Somerset swimming pool, which seemed days ago.

'That is what no-one understands,' concluded the Ambassador, signing for the bill.

'I'm so glad to hear it from you,' said Natalie, still without a trace of sarcasm. 'And thank you for the loveliest dinner I've had in ages.'

'My dear,' said Adam's father, finishing his expensive signature with a flourish, 'I can't tell you what a pleasure it has been to meet you.'

'Hear, hear,' said Adam's mother. They were one big happy family. 'And please,' she added. 'I want you two to stay out on the town and let the elderly trudge home. Our car is waiting. You must want to touch base with your friend over there,' she said, indicating the tattooed American star on the other side of the restaurant.

Adam stared mesmerically at Natalie, hoping to hypnotize her into declining his mother's liberal advice. He thought that if he had one more drink, one more hour of socializing, he might not survive to drink and socialize another day.

'You're so kind,' said Natalie. 'If we just stay here, I'm sure he'll join us. It will be interesting.'

'That's settled, then,' said Adam's father, handing Adam a spare set of keys to the Antibes flat. 'Don't get up.'

They got up. Natalie was kissed and hugged by both of them. Adam's cheeks were pinched and kissed, his body was hugged, his hair was tousled. His parents loved him and were proud of him. They held their heads high as they left the restaurant. They would say more to each other in the next two hours than they had in the previous two years.

It took the star fifteen seconds to rise from his table and come over to visit Natalie. He was disgustingly inebriated. He smelled drunk. He sat down heavily next to Natalie, after a clumsy stab at patting Adam on the shoulder. Adam tried not to stare at him, not because he was embarrassed to be star-struck, but because the man was so unlike the version of himself Adam had grown sick and tired of seeing on the big screen, on television and in newspapers. His face was pitted and veined. His glassy eyes floated in pools of pink. His growth of beard contained bread crumbs and saliva. Adam glanced back at the star's table, and reckoned all the men standing behind it were bodyguards. Clara ignored him.

'Nat, you look beautiful,' said the star.

'Thanks. You remember Adam?'

'Adam,' he said, slack-mouthed. He reached up to his forehead, and after two attempts he managed to snag a greasy lock of his trademark hair and drag it backwards over his much-pierced right ear. 'How are you, my friend?'

'I'm very well. May I buy you a drink?' Adam felt suave.

'No you may *not*,' said the star, bobbing his head back and forth, imitating Adam's accent. 'I have taken the liberty, the liberty of ordering a drink for you and for Nat and for me. Because we are going to have a party. Aren't we going to have a party, Nat?'

'That's possible,' said Natalie.

'Now Adam,' said the star. He had caught Adam looking over his shoulder at the table where Clara sat alone against a backdrop of bodyguards. '*Hey*,' he said, sounding exactly like one of the characters he was paid millions to portray. '*Look* at me when I'm talking to you.'

Adam looked at him.

'Those were your folks?'

'They were my parents, yes.'

'I wish I had parents like that,' said the star gloomily, snapping his fingers in the air above his head. A waiter promptly arrived with a tray bearing at least seven different types of alcoholic beverage. 'Take what you want,' said the star.

'Nothing for me,' said Adam.

'Nor me,' said Natalie.

'Oh,' said the star. 'Oh. Yes. Right.'

There was a pause, as the star collected his thoughts and poured himself five fingers from the closest bottle to hand.

'Listen to me, Adam,' he said, moving his head about to keep his eyes centred in their sockets. 'I just have a question, one question for you.'

'I'm listening,' said Adam, who had never felt so sober in his life, if only by comparison.

'Are you fucking Natalie?' asked the star.

'I beg your pardon, sir?'

'You heard me.'

161

'I know I *heard* you,' said Adam, sitting tall in his chair. 'I was politely pretending I hadn't. Don't you *dare* speak to me that way.'

'Are you fucking kidding me?' asked the smiling star, who owned five mansions.

'I am not kidding you. If you continue to use that sort of language you aren't welcome at my table.'

The star looked at Natalie. 'Is he fucking kidding me?'

'Leave,' said Adam, clearly and firmly. 'Get up and go.'

The star chuckled, and extended his hand. 'I love you, man. I fucking love you. Oops!' he said. 'There goes my fucking mouth again.'

'Don't you "man" me,' said Adam, ignoring his hand. 'Go back to your men and leave us alone.'

'I think I want to fight you, man,' said the star. 'You can't be tougher than Natalie.'

'That's fine,' said Adam. 'We'll go out to the pier and I'll throw you into the sea.'

'Woah,' said the multimillionaire, putting up his hands in mock surrender. 'I think he's serious, Nat.'

Seconds later, they were outside. The bodyguards followed at a safe distance, as if they knew their employer needed this sort of release in order to keep his craft on an even keel. Clara had stayed inside the restaurant. Natalie remained at Adam's side, but said nothing. Adam felt powerful and righteous. The star limped and swerved. He was shorter than Adam by five inches, and older by fifteen years.

'Do you want me to do this?' Adam asked Natalie. 'I'm trying to think of your career.'

Natalie might have answered, but was interrupted by several flashes from photographers who had been staking out the restaurant entrance. The bodyguards swiftly had them scurrying for the safety of their cars.

'I just wanted to know if you were fucking Natalie,

man,' said the star. 'I don't mean to pry, or anything.'

'That's enough,' said Adam.

'Hey, look,' said the star, as they reached the closest dock. He stumbled forward and stopped inches away from Adam, and reached out to stroke his lapel.

'That's enough,' Adam said again. 'Don't touch me.'

'I was only going to apologize,' said the star. 'You poor fuck. Do you know who you're talking to?'

'Yes,' said Adam, grasping the fingers of the star's right hand and twisting them sideways and backwards in a way that was most painful to his victim. The star was now helpless. He naturally followed the direction in which his hand and wrist were twisted, which was the easiest way of preventing his arm from being broken. This led him to a wide space between two power yachts, and the oily water that separated them. Adam let go of his hand, for which the star began to show gratitude. Then Adam thumped him squarely on the forehead with the base of his palm, sending the star over the edge of the dock and into the water. Two of the bodyguards dived in after him, while a third pinned Adam's arms behind his back. He did not struggle. He did not look at Natalie. He felt only a great surge of pleasure in his chest and arms. He was only dimly aware of the photographers' flashes from fifty metres away.

Adam relaxed, and the bodyguard let him go. The bodyguard, now that Adam could see him, was a balding, muscle-bound American wearing an expensive suit and a look of impatience with his boss. For a moment Adam thought he was going to apologize for the star's behaviour, but instead he told Adam to stay where he was until he found out whether the star wished to 'press charges'.

'I'm a lawyer,' said Adam. 'There were witnesses. It was a duel.'

163

'Duelling is illegal,' said the surprisingly well-spoken ape. 'Let's just see if the man's injured.'

The man wasn't injured. If anything, his swim had sobered him. He was pulled aboard one of the empty, anchored yachts, then helped to the dock. The cameras flashed from closer than before. The star approached Adam with his arms outstretched, palms up.

'I fucking love this guy,' he said, going for a wet hug. Adam side-stepped him. 'I want you to be my guests tonight,' he said, naming his hotel. 'Come on, Nat, tell your boyfriend it's fine. We'll say hello to the gang.'

Natalie came up to Adam and whispered that it would be a good idea to go along.

'All right,' said Adam, to the star. 'We ought to shake hands first.'

They did so, with the star remarking on how old-fashioned Adam was. Then, to his bodyguards, 'I fucking love this guy.'

A series of linked suites on the top floor of the star's hotel was the venue for that night's party. It proved to be the star's forty-sixth birthday − a landmark he invested with great importance because his father had been murdered at the same age. Adam was made to feel welcome, because he was greeted by name by Serge and Claude and Bruno L. It was interesting to observe Serge in the presence of the big star and other American notables. His aura was considerably reduced. He was forced to play up the intertwined tragedies of his life and art.

The Americans were, by and large, an impressive lot of confident, energetic men and women. Adam was by no means the only lawyer on hand. They were happy to chat with Adam, while Natalie circulated and raised her profile. With the extreme exception of the big star, the Americans were abstemious, polite and stimulating.

They looked like people who got a great deal done every day. There did not appear to be a single Briton in the room.

Adam had been revivified by his altercation with the ill-behaved star. He circulated easily. It occurred to him that a hundred years ago this party would have been made up of aristocrats and European industrial tycoons. The industrial tycoons had survived, in the form of American entertainment moguls; but the aristocrats, poor dears, had been replaced by actors and personalities. Adam had seen the limousines parked outside, the chauffeurs drinking coffee together by the water, the bodyguards comparing notes on security, the paparazzi marking their territory with cigarette ends.

A man whose name Adam recognized engaged him in conversation on the subject of children. His third wife had recently given birth to his fifth child. She was quite young, the man implied. He, on the other hand, was too old for that life. Where was she now? Well, on the ranch in Wyoming, as far as the man could remember. Adam continued to chat with the man, who was a power-broker worth almost as much as the big star, while watching Natalie's progress over his shoulder. He hoped he hadn't alienated her by punching the star into the harbour. It was so hard to tell what was correct behaviour in this crowd.

Adam could see the star, who had changed into dry clothes, pointing him out to his friends and throwing back his head in mirth. He wondered if the madman he had knocked into the harbour behaved appallingly because he was an untouchably wealthy film actor, or if he was an untouchably wealthy film actor because he behaved appallingly. Adam could just imagine what he was saying now, as Natalie joined him and took part in the laughter – perhaps defending her chivalrous escort, perhaps not. Clara was at the star's side as well, looking vulpine and rather evil. Others orbited the star, and fell in closer when an opportunity presented itself. Some of these others were men, brightly dressed, buffed to a shine, who made their designs on Natalie as obvious as if they had handcuffed her wrists and marched her to the door.

Adam was fully aware how much money mattered. He knew that the thrice-married man standing in front of him – whose conversation was monotonous and self-centred, who could not even keep a toupee free of dandruff, who was obese in a way that highlighted his broad navel through his polo shirt – would soon leave the party with one or other of its beautiful young girls on his arm. It crossed Adam's mind that he ought to make a discreet exit before one of the handsome young somebodies made Natalie an offer.

It was helpful that the four people Adam had spoken to were so entirely wrapped up in their own lives and work that he was never asked where he fitted into the equation. Because he was a nobody, he was able to distinguish with ease between those who were on the make, looking to improve their status through transparent exaggeration of their achievements, and those who were self-confident enough, like the power-broker, to chat meaninglessly about their being too old to raise new families.

'I mean, my God,' said the power-broker, probably for the fiftieth time that day, 'my oldest *son* is older than my wife.'

Adam wanted to throw him into the harbour, too.

'Sorry, someone's waving at me,' Adam said, pointing over the power-broker's shoulder. When the power-broker turned around to see that it was the big star, his eyes widened at Adam as if he should have recognized him sooner. 'Come along,' said Adam casually, patting the power-broker on the shoulder. Adam led the way across the room.

'This fucking guy,' said the star, taking Adam's sleeve and pulling him into the centre of the group. 'I *love* this fucking guy.' To prove how much he meant this, the star reached up, grabbed Adam's head, and kissed him noisily on the temple.

Adam had already made the firm decision that he would forego *any* amount of money, adulation and power not to have this man's personality and intellect. He wiped his temple with his sleeve, and tried to laugh with the others in a way that showed his superior disdain for the uncouth star.

Far from having latched on to a somebody, Natalie eagerly came to Adam's side and hooked his elbow with her arm.

'I met Adam's parents for the first time tonight,' she said. 'They're divine.' She introduced Adam to the group, and made him feel that all of these people had come to the suite in his honour. She retold the story of Didi's wedding, without mentioning that she had met Adam there for the first time forty-eight hours ago. The people Adam had just been introduced to were all Americans, all young, all successful. He recognized three or four of them. The one who interested him most was an angry looking black man who said nothing to anyone, who did not smile, and who wore a heavy overcoat and hat. He had an undeniable presence, but he was an inscrutable wall of ill-temper. Adam said hello and shook the man's hand, which was dry and did not squeeze back.

'You don't look like you're having a very good time,' Adam said.

The man turned his head to look Adam in the eye. 'I'm thinking,' he said.

It was always dangerous to ask the identity of people

who might possibly be known to billions, but Adam's policy was to adopt an attitude of ingenuousness. 'Are you in the film business too?' he asked.

'No,' he replied, in a deep voice.

Adam paused for ten seconds, still looking at the man, then said, 'You're not very forthcoming.'

'No,' said the man.

Adam did not wish to try to knock this fellow into the harbour, so he did not point out that it was rude of him not to contribute more to the conversation, when Adam was making such an effort. 'Should I guess what it is you do for a living? . . . I'm sorry, I didn't hear your name.'

'Charles,' said the man.

'I'm Adam,' said Adam, shaking his dry, limp hand again.

Charles was exactly Adam's height, and they were positioned just the right way in the group so that they stood facing each other, staring each other straight in the face. Rarely had Adam seen features set in such a mask of disdain. He looked to be in his early thirties, he had a broad face and a thick neck, and when he had deigned to speak Adam had detected between his lips the glint of a gold tooth.

Charles was still unwilling to volunteer information, so Adam pressed on. 'These are friends of yours?' he asked.

'Some of them.'

'And are you in France on business, or pleasure?'

'Not pleasure.'

'I can see that,' said Adam, smiling.

Charles scowled.

'Now, if I guessed that you were in some way involved in the media, would I be a million miles away?'

Charles squinted. 'You know who I am,' he said. 'Don't pretend you don't. I hate that.'

'I'm not pretending,' said Adam. He was affronted. 'I have no idea who you are.' It was hard to say this without sounding rude, and Adam tried to keep his voice down.

Charles told Adam who he was, in one terse sentence naming the internationally famous recording artists he produced. Adam took a deep breath and apologized for not having known. 'That's OK,' said Charles. 'I guess you're not in the business.'

'No, I'm not.'

'Well, who are you, then?'

'I'm with Natalie,' Adam said, nodding his head in her direction.

'Oh yeah? You wouldn't be the one who got our friend wet on his birthday, would you?'

'I'm afraid so.'

'You're that guy?'

'Yes, I'm that guy.'

Charles's lips separated in a huge, gold and white smile. 'Good for you, man.'

Full of satisfaction at having made a new friend out of such unpromising material, Adam drew Natalie into the conversation. She knew Charles. His mask fell in her presence, and he proved to be a soft-spoken musician and sound-engineer who had turned his talented friends into serious business concerns. Adam had made the decision to get to know him better, when a short, slender, Italian-looking man wearing a bright-green jump suit came up to his side and said, 'Monsieur Gosse?'

'Yes?'

'Someone demands you at the telephone.'

Adam had the presence of mind not to say, in front of everyone, that no-one in the world knew where he was. He followed the elfin Italian into an adjoining suite, and from there into an unoccupied bedroom.

'May I bring you a drink? An ashtray? Anything?' said the Italian, who had accessorized his bright-green jump suit with white ballet slippers and an unflattering codpiece.

Adam held his hand over the telephone mouthpiece. 'No, thank you very much. I just wanted to ask you, though. How did you recognize me?'

The Italian clasped his hands behind his back and stood on point. 'He said to look for the handsome Belgian.' With that backhanded compliment, the leprechaun was gone.

'Hello?' Adam said into the phone.

'Adam, wonderful. Guess who?'

'Let's see, Norman. Who could you possibly be?'

'Got it in one.'

'How the devil did you find me?'

'For one thing, I saw you in the bloody newspaper. I recognized the Somerset. I rang them. They didn't know where you had gone, but they had a guest who did know. A girl named Clara?'

'Right.'

'So I called your parents, assuming you would visit them while you were in the neighbourhood. I'm afraid I had to wake your father. He gave me the number of the restaurant. The restaurant said that if you weren't in gaol you would be at this hotel. The hotel said you would be at a big party. And there you are, Adam, you great Lothario. You idol of mortal men. You bloody *swine*, Adam. What have you *done*?'

'I don't know what you mean.'

'You've done this on purpose, haven't you. You waited until the *moment* I got married before swanning off on the binge of the century with the only girl of my dreams. I *hate* you.'

'I take it you're not in Argentina, if you saw the newspaper.'

'You are correct. I am spending my honeymoon without my wife in a flat in Chelsea that is full of temptations.'

'Where is Didi?'

'Didi, I'm afraid, is in Thailand.'

'All alone?'

'She took Marina with her. I gave her the most brilliant idea, that she ought to look at fabrics and things out there and become some sort of decorator, you know.'

'Didi? Are you mad?'

'Well, the girl needs an occupation.'

'That's *before* they marry noblemen, Norman.'

'*Is* it? What a frightful *faux pas*, then.'

'And what about your honeymoon?'

'Cancelled. Medical emergency. Pain in the left testicle, that sort of thing. Told her I didn't want her around for the diagnosis, shame to waste the tickets. I'll be shipshape in no time.'

'I just want to say one more thing, Norman, even though I have fulfilled my responsibilities as best man.'

'Yes?'

'It's a favour I have to ask, actually.'

'Go on.'

'Could you please, *please* not hurt Didi's feelings by infecting a lot of girls and having one of them complain to her?'

'That seems like a simple favour,' said Norman. Adam could visualize him blowing on his fingertips. 'Now you do me one.'

'We'll see.'

'Tell me everything. I have to know what I'm missing.'

'I'm a gentleman, Norman. Unlike some gentlemen I could mention.'

'Don't give me that. Whose party is it?'

Adam told him.

'You *must* be joking.'

'It's the truth. If you pick up the paper tomorrow you might see us together. We had a fight and I boxed him into the harbour.'

'I can't believe what I'm hearing.'

'The other news is that I presented her to my parents this evening.'

'Her? *Natalie?*'

'Yes.'

'Oh, Lord. What did she make of them?'

'Her impressions are immaterial. The point is my parents have given their approval.'

'What are you saying?' Norman sounded panicked.

Adam continued casually. It was a novel experience to hear real envy in Norman's voice. 'We're visiting Natalie's parents in Ilani tomorrow.'

'Where the hell is that?'

'A little place in Italy. Just over the border, you know.'

'I'm on my way,' said Norman. 'I can't let you marry Natalie without one last shot at her.'

Adam felt a depth of feeling and protectiveness for Natalie out of all proportion to his exposure to her. 'Don't you *ever* speak about her that way again,' he said.

'My, my,' Norman wheezed. Adam could hear him blowing cigarette smoke into the telephone. 'Aren't you the doting fiancé.'

'I'm not her fiancé. I'm her friend.'

'I'm so moved, Adam. I'm rethinking my whole life view.'

'Say what you like, Norman. We're just trying to have a good time.'

'Think how differently things might have turned out,' said Norman, on his third night of marriage. 'Didi was kind enough to reveal to me that you made the most

172

touching proposal of marriage to her not so long ago. "Sweet", she called it.'

'You are such a—'

'And now, Adam, do you know what I wish? I am starting to wish she had said yes. I could have been *your* best man, you could be in Thailand with Didi, and I could be rubbing elbows with Hollywood in Cannes and eloping with the beauteous Natalie. Life isn't fair, my friend.'

Adam was able to keep his temper because it was clear to him that Norman had already played his own life true to the form of his class and personality: Apparently he didn't see why, if he were supposed to have an empty, loveless marriage, he ought not to have it right away.

'Look, I have to go, Norman. It sounds as if you have everything perfectly under control as usual.'

'But I'm *lonely*, Adam. Please entertain me. I'm afraid to leave this flat lest I misbehave.'

'Good luck to you, then,' said Adam. 'I'm off to carouse.'

Adam put down the phone and sighed. Norman was not the only one of his friends whose most endearing characteristic, that of the lovable scoundrel, had not aged well; in Norman's case it had aged to putrefaction.

It no longer surprised Adam that he should find himself sweating in a large hot tub at three o'clock in the morning, in the company of Natalie, the star, Clara, Charles, the power-broker, Serge, Claude, Bruno, Bruno's girls, and several other girls whose naked feet he had touched with his own, but to whom he had not yet been properly introduced. Some of the party had openly taken substances that Adam's newspaper and magazine reading had told him were passé. Natalie stuck to champagne.

173

Adam had the palest, but still the most attractive male body in the tub. The star, while sinewy and tanned, was scarred with tattoos and other wounds. Charles's torso was doughy and grey. Serge's stomach had grown in such a way that when he sat up straight against the wall of the tub, a channel of water separated his chest from the dome of his belly. The power-broker had a sunken, jaundiced torso. Claude, like the star only more so, was covered in crude tattoos. Bruno had a boy's body plus ugly, flared hips. The girls were all so young that comparisons were senseless.

The star dominated the conversation, although it was impossible to understand a word he said through his droning, post-dental-surgery undertone. He mumbled anyway, if his performances were anything to go by, but now he was drunk in a way that Adam had observed only in the company of his most alcoholic friends. The star would speak unintelligibly for several minutes, while everyone else sipped their drinks, stroked their girlfriends' inner thighs, or stared steamily into space. The star would run out of nouns and verbs, and silence would descend on the hot tub. Another member of the group needed only to open his mouth to speak for the star to stutter into his gargled incoherence once again. The birthday-boy's guests found themselves testing this phenomenon: waiting for him to grind to a halt; deliberately leaving his silence undisturbed for a minute or more; making a bid to speak; watching the star put his uncooperative mouth into gear again, summarizing what he supposed they were going to say. This reflex occurred with iron regularity, and entertained the gang for more than an hour.

Adam chatted with Natalie in whispers during the star's extended spells of babbling. She surprised him by expressing her thanks for accidentally arranging her invitation to this select birthday party. Adam said it was nothing. She said that far from being nothing, this party had resulted in introductions she might have spent years arranging on her own. Her gratitude clashed with Adam's previous impression, which was one of a girl who let life wash over her, and took her breaks where she could find them. Now she revealed a healthy, calculating side to her character: she had recognized a favour. It was a deep thought, by Adam's standards, but he drew a comparison between Norman's envy and Natalie's appreciation: both now looked up to him, for different reasons. Adam drained a glass of champagne, leaned back so that everyone in the tub would see his body surfacing, sleek as the back of a porpoise, and felt extremely good about himself. He was loved and admired.

'Adam?' came a voice. 'Adam?'

He opened his eyes, with some effort and discomfort. One of his eyes opened more easily than the other, but even that eye seemed clouded over by a film of wax. He had recognized Natalie's voice, and as his better eye came into focus he recognized the costume of the diminutive Italian in ballet shoes.

'Have a beer,' said Natalie's voice. Evidently beer was the least poisonous liquid available in the combined suites of the star's hotel rooms. 'There are strawberries and cream, too.'

Adam soon discovered that he had been mistaken to assume, as he had done on regaining consciousness, that he was safely in hospital. He was still up to his nipples in the hot tub, along with everyone else. Adam took a cold bottle of beer from the Italian, and thanked him by splashing his free hand in the hot, bubbling water. He sat up and smiled at the others, as if he fainted all the time. He hooked an arm around Natalie's waist and drew her deeper under water next to him.

Serge, smoking a cigar and drinking cognac, had begun to beg the star to appear in his film. He had a new *vision*. The star showed that he liked the vision by frothing at the mouth. The power-broker pointed out to Serge that he was unlikely to be able to meet the star's minimum fee, even if he was backed by the French government. Serge said he *was* backed by the French government, and that price was no object where art was concerned. Bruno interrupted to ask if the film role under discussion weren't already his. Serge looked furiously at Bruno and told him to mind his own business. The power-broker began to look nervous. The trilingual girls on either side of him, who were almost certainly prostitutes, thought they were witnessing cinematic history. The discussion might well have gone on, and cinematic history been made, had the star not splashed face-first into the hot tub, unconscious. He was removed by two of the bodyguards Adam had seen down at the harbour, who appeared magically from behind a curtain of steam. The star, regaining consciousness, was held up by his armpits and gently led away. Clara, emerging glossily from the tub and wrapping a towel around her waist, followed behind with sober, Machiavellian footsteps.

The thrice-married power-broker, perhaps remarking to himself that the girls next to him were younger than his oldest son, took a towel and wrapped it around his waist underwater. With his modesty intact, he left the tub and gestured for the unwilling girls to follow him; they did so.

Bruno and his girls, still excited and full of stimulants, rushed off to their room to carry on.

Claude snored.

Charles heaved his big body out of the tub, and in his deep voice bade everyone good night. In doing so, he made a handgun out of his thumb and forefinger, and shot it at Adam. He accompanied this gesture with a golden grin.

'I have always rather liked this hotel,' said Serge, who slid over to be close to Natalie. The roiling water was not clear enough for Adam to see what Serge was doing with his hands. 'My dear, you are so beautiful. Don't you think we have had a wonderful time tonight, Natalie?' For some reason, Serge spoke in English. Adam thought that it might be for his own benefit, that it was a warning to clear off while the conquering giant of artistic film took care of business. 'I came to this hotel often in the Sixties, with my wife, Mireille,' said Serge, invoking the name of the holiest saint in his canon. He raised one of his hands out of the water and used it to draw a strand of Natalie's hair away from her moist forehead. Adam sat not three feet from Serge, on Natalie's other side, and felt an uncommon power in his right arm – the same right arm that had toppled the star some hours ago.

'Natalie. There are some things I must say to you,' said Serge. The word 'unctuous' popped into Adam's mind for the first time since university. Serge put a thumbnail to his mouth, like a grieving widower at the edge of an open grave. 'I think of you so often. Ever since we met, when it seemed destiny . . . you have been in my thoughts and in my dreams.' He had submerged his stomach. The water lapped against spring-like curls of grey hair on his brown chest. 'This is a time in your life, now, Natalie,' continued the genius, 'that I understand only too well. I have seen it so often. It is impossible for you to see yourself as clearly as I see you. You are a girl, you know. Just a girl. The woman, only I can see. Do you trust me?'

'Yes,' Natalie replied. She was under contract.

Adam felt invisible, but full of rage. He moved away from Natalie so that their thighs no longer touched. In doing so, he touched thighs with Claude, who extended a beefy arm and put it around Adam's shoulder. Claude snored, belched, sneezed, coughed and farted all at the same time, which made a sound Adam had never heard before.

'I am so glad,' said Serge. 'Do you know how much I have waited and longed for you?' he asked, rhetorically. 'Before I ever laid eyes on you, you were in my mind,' he said, mystically, stroking her right collar bone with his index finger, lowering it to the level of the water between her breasts. He carefully swabbed two droplets from her flesh, then put his finger in his mouth. He sucked on his finger, holding Natalie's gaze. He removed his finger from his mouth, and let his hand drop into the water between his legs.

Adam was amazed at the license of the artistic world. In his line of work, to talk to an employee in this way was likely to result in a law suit. Office affairs had to be conducted like Cold War espionage, with the parties gently probing each other for a matter of months before agreeing to meet in secret; either that, or alcohol worked its magic at a party and the couple would succumb to instinct. Serge's form of attempted seduction was utterly out of bounds.

'Can you see that I am falling in love with you?' said Serge, switching to French. Adam could see from the angle of Serge's arm that he was stroking Natalie's abdomen, and inching higher.

'That I can see,' said Natalie. Relaxed and smiling, she lifted her toes out of the water. 'I also understand that you must,' she added. 'I don't know you very well, but I think I can see that you need to feel this strongly for your vision to become reality.'

'You understand!' cried Serge. He leaned over and buried his head in Natalie's neck, below her jaw.

Natalie put an arm around Serge and hugged him,

then stroked the bristles of white hair on the back of his head. Adam, in Claude's sleeping embrace, was dismayed – that is, until Natalie turned and winked at him. Adam shook his head and mouthed the word, 'Careful.' Natalie shrugged her shoulders without actually moving them.

Serge was kissing Natalie's neck now, and openly fondling her. He was so involved in what he was doing that he did not notice when Natalie failed to stifle a yawn; he may have mistaken it for a sob of pleasure. Serge looked up from his business and saw Adam wallowing beneath Claude's heavy arm. This made him smile. His world made sense.

'Oh, Natalie,' he said, in French. Her name sounded better pronounced that way. 'How I have longed for this moment.'

Adam thought about how long he had longed for that moment, too.

'We aren't alone,' said Natalie.

'They don't mind.'

'I do,' she said.

'Come to my room. It is downstairs. Oh, Natalie.'

'I won't come to your room.'

'What?'

Adam, the lawyer, could hear her argument coming a mile off.

'It isn't right, Serge. Your vision would only suffer as a consequence. We must be strong,' said Natalie. Adam giggled through his nose at the obviousness of her defence, and at the likelihood of its success. 'You have spent far too long imagining a world,' she continued. 'I may be a part of that world, but until it exists, until you have captured it for eternity, we mustn't do anything to jeopardize your vision. I think I love you, Serge,' she added, with a politician's break in her voice, 'but nothing is worth putting your work at risk. It wouldn't be you who would falter, of course. I would be the one to be overwhelmed, and I would not live up to your expectations. I know you agree.'

Serge wept into Natalie's brown cleavage. Natalie looked over at Adam and mouthed the word, 'Wanker.'

When Serge had recovered enough for the diminutive Italian to help him downstairs to his room, Adam disengaged himself from Claude and moved back to Natalie's side.

'I could hear what you were going to say before you said it. You were perfect.'

'I'm new to this,' said Natalie, frowning seriously. 'It's so hard to know where to draw the line. I want this job, you know. It may be my only day in the sun.'

'Don't be silly. Still, you were right to string him along.'

'I didn't *string him along*. How dare you.'

'I think you know what I mean. He had to be placated. You couldn't very well emasculate him, and on the other hand you couldn't – well, I suppose you couldn't.'

'Nothing happened,' Natalie insisted. 'You don't know what you're saying. What you saw was just an artist's show of affection. He's under a great deal of pressure. He has to reach out. He must get to know virtual strangers, like me, in order to fit them into his scheme. I don't blame him at all for what he did – and you can't discount all of that champagne. Everyone here was emotional.'

'Please, Natalie. I didn't mean to accuse you of anything. I just told you I thought you handled him perfectly.'

'You make me sound so calculating. That is not the way I am. I want to try to do the best I can, and let everyone else be dishonest. Did you see those other girls, tonight?'

'I saw them.'

'They're whores, Adam.'

'It isn't a nice word.'

'But you know it's true.'

'Yes.'

'I'm not a whore.'

'Of course you're not.'

'So don't make me feel like one.'

Adam did not want to kiss Natalie so soon after Serge
had done so. In any case, Natalie had no time for that:
they were due for lunch at her parents' house in Italy.
They dressed and went downstairs to the reception
desk, where they told a woman that a large Frenchman
was asleep in the hot tub, and should not be allowed to
drown. Adam was not asked to pay for the star's hotel
suites.

'I'll need to buy some clothes, if we're going to go any
farther,' Adam said, in the taxi to Antibes.

'Me too. We can go shopping in Monte Carlo.'

'Don't we always?'

Natalie asked the driver for a piece of paper and a
pen, so she could write a note thanking Adam's parents
for dinner. When they arrived in Antibes it was just six
o'clock, and Adam put the note and the spare keys in
his parents' letter box. He had paid for the taxi.

Behind the wheel of his car, headed towards Nice,
Adam felt more like a passenger than a driver. Natalie
slept, of course, leaving Adam to grip the wheel with
white knuckles and sing Christmas carols to himself to
keep awake. The roads were not empty for long, as all
of France made for the beaches. It was a hot, hazy
morning. Adam drove slowly along the coast. His car
was perfect for the weather and the setting. Pedestrians
stopped walking to look at the car and its glamorous
occupants. Natalie slept, but as she wore dark glasses

she appeared to onlookers to be merely blasé. Adam put on his white driver's cap, and felt like a god.

He did not often allow himself to wonder why he had decided to buy an expensive car, because to do so made him feel stupid. He did not like to be reminded that he was the kind of man who would inflict a nearly mortal financial wound upon himself for the sake of appearances and as a sop to some primeval desire for destructive speed. He knew nothing about automobile mechanics, and it was his ill-fortune to have fallen in love with a car that, no matter how beautiful to the eye, had a way of stopping for reasons of such subtlety that only the most expensive hands could tease her back to life. Adam had learned the names of parts he considered unnecessary, as he and his bank manager sat down to agree formulae for raising the money to pay for them. There was nothing quite so frustrating as the kind of impasse Adam experienced three or four times a year: showered, shaved, dressed to the nines, flat locked, wine bottle or flowers in hand, bounding round the corner to the cripplingly expensive garage, into the driver's seat, top down, key in the ignition . . . and the beautiful car responding with the sigh of a pubescent girl in love.

Adam therefore tried to take what satisfaction he could on the coastal drive past Nice, for which his car was presumably made. He preferred the winding, hilly drive to the hypnotic motorway not just for aesthetic reasons, but because it kept his body moving and his eyes open. He had reached a point of exhaustion that he had not experienced since a sleep-deprivation project for which he had volunteered at university. He had spent one of his holidays being kept awake – first by conversation, then by coffee, then by amphetamines, finally by being dragged around the room by his armpits by two tall men who smelled. He had begged the scientists to let him go home after only twenty-four hours of the experiment, but they reminded him that he had signed a document handing over his human rights for as long as he remained awake. He could not prove that his desire to leave was not an interesting symptom of his tiredness, so he was kept there and tortured for four days.

By the time Adam nosed his albatross into Monte Carlo, the shops were open and the streets were crowded with tourists. He found a parking space, which made him feel better than he had in a long time. Natalie took off her dark glasses, blinked in the sunlight, and smiled. She seemed only to have two gears: deep sleep and frenetic wakefulness.

'That one's for the boys, this one's for the girls,' she said, pointing out two nearby shops. 'See you in ten minutes?'

She loped away, leaving Adam to put the top up and lock his car. He entered the shop, zombie-like, and bought two white shirts like Bruno L's, a pair of loose white trousers like Claude's, and only just managed to stop himself from buying a pair of espadrilles like Serge's. Because he was now the sort of man who casually popped into Monte Carlo in his sports car for no particular reason, he also bought a fine leather belt, a wallet, a handkerchief, a fountain pen and an alarm clock. He handed over his credit card with both hands, as if expecting to be handcuffed. The credit card was run, screaming in pain, through the shop's magnetic decoder. The cash register coughed out a receipt, and Adam signed. The deeper he went into Europe, he thought, the farther this card would go.

Adam transferred his money and documents to his new wallet. He put on one of his new shirts and his new trousers. He stuffed his new handkerchief into his jacket pocket. He looped his new belt around his waist. The shopkeeper gave him a bag for his old possessions, and Adam strode out into the street a new and even more bankrupt fellow.

Natalie waited for him next to the car, with a man. The man looked like the shopkeeper Adam had just done business with, but was merely similar. Natalie wore a sun dress and sandals that made Adam weak. The man wanted Adam to pay for them.

'I'm terribly sorry, Adam,' Natalie said. 'But could you just do this? Last time I had any cash was for the taxi to Didi's wedding. You look terrific, by the way.'

'Sure, of course,' said Adam, brandishing his new wallet. 'Here are the keys to the car. I'll be right back.'

Compared with what Adam had spent on himself, Natalie's dress and sandals seemed like a bargain. His credit card no longer cried out as it was processed. He noticed that two women who worked in the shop went out of their way to get a look at the man who possessed such a car and such a woman. He continued to feel like a god.

Adam returned to his car to find Natalie sitting in the driver's seat, sunning herself in her new dress.

'I thought I'd drive,' she said. 'You need some sleep, I'm sure.'

No-one else had ever driven Adam's car. He did not pause too long before agreeing to her suggestion, but he could not prevent his face from drooping as he sat for the first time in the passenger seat.

'It's better, really,' said Natalie. 'I know the way.'

'That's fine. Carry on. Don't expect too much of her.'

Natalie drove beautifully. The road turned when she did. She seemed to get a pleasure out of the car that Adam was too preoccupied with its innards and its expense to appreciate. She did not drive recklessly, as Adam had supposed she would, but with care and good humour. She had an impressive store of French and

Italian imprecations to leave trailing in the wind when she passed lesser vehicles driven by inferior drivers. She sang the *Internationale*, right fist raised, as they swooped through Monegasque hills and beat it to the Italian border. At the frontier, she only just slowed down enough to deliver a rich-European wave to un-manned customs checkpoints. This was her territory, and it stretched from the Bosporus to County Kerry – with some spots of unpleasantness in between, as usual.

Despite his nationality and his new clothes, Adam would never be a European like Natalie – his English upbringing would see to that. It seemed to have come about that England was more distinct from Europe than even the fringe countries that aspired one day to join the fold. Adam knew the reasons for this, and was not dispirited: It was enough consolation to have been born at a time when he had not been required to spend most of his youth in danger of being killed by Germans, which was more than any of his male ancestors could have said.

When Natalie announced that they were half an hour from her parents' Italian house, Adam decided it was time to ask her if she had ever brought home a man before.

'Only . . . four times,' Natalie said, counting on the steering wheel with her left hand.

'Four times?'

'Is that too many?'

'It's too many. It's crying wolf.'

'You'll see that things aren't too formal, with my parents. I could have brought home a seventy-year-old woman, and said I was going to marry her.'

Adam was still not used to these conversational pirouettes around the subject of their own potential marriage.

'What were the other men like?'

'Too suitable, for my father's liking. Scary for my mother. I was awfully young, the first time I brought a man home. That was when my parents lived in Malta. I was nineteen years old, and the man was someone older and well known.'

'Well known in a good way?'

'Well known in good and bad ways. It was the bad ways they were worried about in their own house, no matter how well known he was. They're not like your parents, though, Adam. They're from that other side, the self-consciously artistic type. It's just as embarrassing for their kids as the strict version, believe me. Even when I was nineteen, they made a show of putting me and the well-known Lothario in the same room together. "We don't want you sneaking around," my father would say. "Would anyone like to get high?"'

'Mortifying.'

'You bet.'

'What about the three others?'

'Let's see. There was Scrubby Digs, the musician, whom they pretended to adore. Once, at their Paris flat, I brought home Alphonse Robert, and you can just imagine.'

'I'm afraid I don't know who Alphonse Robert is.'

'Well, then you can't imagine. I think my father was terrified that I'd come over all Establishment. That was the first genuine Marriage Fright, but they had no idea how much I didn't care about him.'

'But he was your boyfriend?'

'Not like *you*, Adam. It was more of a sexual thing.'

'Ah.'

'And the most recent one was a really nice man, an Algerian.'

'What?'

186

'You're not supposed to be surprised by that, these days.'

'The hell I'm not. What do you mean an Algerian?'

'A man from Algeria. He was a friend when I was a little girl, and we got back in touch.'

'Is he a businessman? A diplomat? An artist?'

'No, none of those. He runs a little bar in Marseilles.'

'Natalie. Isn't that pushing things a bit far? What did your parents make of him?'

'To tell you the truth, they didn't like him one bit. He had become a small-time criminal, so they were disappointed in him.'

'That's a very wide selection of suitors, Natalie. What will they think of me?'

Natalie looked at him and smiled. 'My mother is going to eat . . . you . . . *up*.'

'And your father?'

'You know, Adam, my father has a very narrow band of moods. I'd recommend not trying to kiss up to him, to be frank. He can't stand that. If he engages you in conversation, don't mention anything having to do with Britain. He feels betrayed by his country.'

'What have they done now?'

'They have neglected his work. It used to make him feel superior, when he did well in Europe, but deep down he always wanted to be recognized at home. It got worse and worse. Now he broods about it, and won't have Englishmen in the house.'

'Have you warned them that I'm coming?'

'No. I guess I didn't really have a chance. But it will be very relaxed. My brothers might be around, too. We can be a happy family, if my father takes his little pills.'

'Listen, Natalie,' said Adam. 'Do you mind if we stop somewhere along the way for a glass of wine?'

'I know a place.'

They stopped at a village restaurant in the hills, and sat in the garden in the shade of cypress trees and mimosa. A young man who knew Natalie brought them an unmarked bottle of white wine and a plate of olives. Natalie looked at home in this setting.

Adam contrasted this peaceful scene with his life in London, and despaired. The pressure of a working life in a big city had become a relentless onslaught on his sensibilities. He told Natalie how seldom he thought he used the parts of his brain and personality he had grown to like and trust; how the most routine socializing seemed like an ordeal; how he rarely awoke feeling any enthusiasm for the day ahead.

Natalie humoured him through his complaints, then changed the topic of conversation back to her family.

'There's one other embarrassing thing,' she said. 'My father has fixated on a little matter that we all have to skirt around.'

'Yes?'

'He thinks his oldest son, my younger brother Tom, might not be . . . the marrying type. He sometimes asks guests – he might even ask you – if they don't think poor Tom's a bit of a "swish", or whatever word he uses. For a poet, he's awfully down on them.'

'How am I supposed to reply?'

'You're supposed to express horror at the idea in general, and of Tom's being that way in particular. Drop your glass, or something. Laugh out loud. Slap him on the back like a grizzly bear and tell him how preposterous a suggestion he has made.'

'That ought to do it?'

'It will put his mind at rest for an hour or so.'

They had a bottle of wine to finish, and plenty of time to do so.

*　　*　　*

Natalie's parents lived not beside the sea, but high above it. Their house was reached by a pitted road winding up a scrubby hillside where shade was in short supply. It was not a place Adam would have chosen to live, but the house itself raised his spirits: a broad, three-storey white villa with a substantial terrace built along three sides of the top floor. It was not an old house, and it had been built for entertaining. The dry, sloping land surrounding the house lacked substantial foliage, save the potted palms that alternated between sun-bleached statuary around the swimming pool.

Natalie stopped the car and pointed out her father, who was seated alone at a picnic table in the sunshine, not writing. Her mother emerged onto the terrace and waved hello. Her brothers, reclining by the swimming pool and listening to music, had not noticed their sister's arrival. There was no sign of lunch.

Feeling like a trespasser, Adam got out of the car and followed Natalie over to the picnic table. Natalie's father, who wore a paint-stained work shirt and blue jeans, stood up to greet his daughter with a warm hug and a kiss on top of her head. His thin, sandy hair curled artistically at the collar, the grey parts framing a narrow, red face. His sharp blue eyes looked to have been interrupted in the throes of creative inspiration, though the worn notebook in front of him was blank. He extended a hand for Adam to shake, as Natalie introduced him with exactly the tone of voice a girlfriend would use if keen to impress.

'How do you do, sir,' said Adam, with a potential-son-in-law's nod of the head.

'You're English,' said Natalie's father, in the same way Adam's father might say, 'You're German.'

'No sir,' said Adam. 'I'm Belgian.'

'Oh, fine, then. Call me George.'

'It's a pleasure to meet you, George,' said Adam, who

had learned that the discomfort of having to address one's elders by their Christian names was best met head on.

'And you. I wish we had known you were coming.'

'I didn't know myself, until last night.'

George was awfully relaxed, Adam thought, for a father who had just met yet another young man who was presumably enjoying the favours of his only daughter.

Natalie's mother emerged from the house and glided youthfully to her daughter's side. She was the source of Natalie's looks. Adam had to assume that the clothes she wore were of her own design, for he had never seen anyone wearing anything quite like them: skin-tight blue leggings that flared abruptly one inch above her matching sandals, an embroidered white shirt rather like a Filipino *barong*, and a faded leather choker around her neck. She wore her greying hair girlishly, in a pony tail. Her appearance had not been cosmetically altered, and Adam was reminded of the importance of bone structure. She had a smoker's mouth, and she gave an immediate impression of total competence.

She spoke French to Natalie, then greeted Adam in English. He found her to be flirtatious, as Natalie had indicated her mother might be, while not being coy in the least. Adam had no difficulty calling her Françoise.

'This is such a surprise,' she said. 'If you had only told me, Natalie. You should have done, you know, and then we could have prepared a special lunch. As it is I will just have to see what Marie and Bernard can throw together.' People with servants had such fun, Adam thought. 'Meanwhile, both of you please sit down and have a drink.'

This was music to Adam's newly alcoholic ears. He sat down across from Natalie's father, who closed his empty notebook as if to conceal its tinderbox literary contents. He did not look in the slightest put out to have had his afternoon of not writing interrupted by the appearance of a stranger who might prove to be a close relative for the rest of his life.

'I don't speak French, you know,' said Natalie's father. 'Not a bloody word. I've lived in French-speaking countries for – well just let me think. I've lived in French-speaking countries for approximately twenty-five years. I learned a little Arabic, a little Spanish, you know. Some Portuguese. But French sticks in my craw.'

Adam saw how much Natalie's father enjoyed employing this last phrase, and how he glanced at his notebook as if he had lost for ever the opportunity to write it down.

'My French isn't very good, either,' said Adam. 'It was put to the test at a friend's wedding on Saturday. I was best man, you see. The *garçon d'honneur.*'

'Didi's wedding, wasn't it?' asked Natalie's father.

'That's right.'

'I remember her as a little girl. She visited here once, with her father. Didi married a friend of yours?'

'Yes.' Adam told Natalie's father Norman's full name.

'Poor Didi,' he said. 'If you don't mind my saying so.'

'I don't mind. I know exactly what you mean.'

An elderly couple who could only be Marie and Bernard came out of the house bearing heavy trays of food and drink. Adam could not believe such a feast had been organized since his arrival. Hoping that he did not appear too eager, he stood up to help unload wobbly bottles and heavy platters. Marie and Bernard looked eighty years old each, but unused to assistance. The food they had brought was marvellous. There was a clay pitcher of iced water, a bowl of spiced olives, two bottles of white wine and two bottles of red, a platter of meats decorated with hot peppers, sausages, beets, one raw carrot, a tomato-and-onion salad sprinkled with parsley and drowned in vinaigrette, halved avocados with a lemon near by, three small loaves of French bread, butter, salt, pepper, radishes, spinach salad, a bowl of walnuts, silverware, linen napkins and sturdy glasses.

'Thanks, Marie,' said Natalie's father, who looked upon this banquet with the same level of appreciation as Adam would have devoted to a pint of bitter back home. 'Alert the boys, will you Bernard?'

Bernard limped along a brick path to the swimming pool, and turned off the boys' music. Only now did Adam notice that both of Natalie's brothers were naked. They put on shorts and shirts before coming over to be introduced.

Adam was pleased to see that they did not appear to be jaded by introductions to Natalie's boyfriends. The older son, Tom – who was so obviously what his father feared he would be that Adam had to make an effort not to mention the fact aloud on meeting him – was a soulful, put-upon-looking young man of twenty-three. Seeing him together with his father, it saddened Adam to contemplate what the future held in store. Eddie, the youngest, was as attractive as his brother but even more reserved. He was the one Natalie had said wanted to emulate his father's career, and by the look of his tan he had written every bit as little as the old man in recent months. The boys sat down to eat without making much fuss about Adam, except that Tom admired Adam's new shirt.

Conversation turned immediately to Natalie's film. Her family had seen the newspapers, despite their efforts to avoid the gutter press. The photograph of Natalie and Adam together outside the Somerset Hotel had been brought to their attention. Natalie's mother asserted her objection to film *tout court*, and raised the issue of what she called Serge's 'paedophilia' as one reason why a girl might want to steer clear of him. Natalie's father asked about money, without quite doing so. Tom asked about the big star. Eddie said he thought all of modern culture had 'dissolved into a miasma', a remark that stopped Adam's fork on the way to his mouth. Natalie replied to all of their questions with the same lofty remarks she used to keep the press both interested and at bay. It must have been a shock to her parents and siblings to see her transformed into a world-famous actress, when she had not yet acted; more so, perhaps, to see her apparently attached to a London-based Belgian solicitor.

'Do you read?' asked Natalie's father. Adam had enough of his wits about him to know that this was not a simple, yes-or-no question.

'Yes,' he replied, regardless.

'Then you will be aware of the brouhaha surrounding my own contractual difficulties? I never did have proper legal advice in London. They always assumed I was some airy-fairy artiste ripe for a fleecing.' He looked at his notebook again.

'I'm sorry to hear that.'

Every member of George's family made simultaneous, unsuccessful attempts to change the subject.

'Have some more wine, Adam, and tell me about the law.'

Adam held out his glass to be refilled. Natalie's family looked at him. Marie and Bernard continued to ferry food from the house to the picnic table.

'I'm afraid I've already bored Natalie with that,' he said. 'Scintillating, it ain't.'

'I meant the law, as it pertains specifically to me,' said Natalie's father. He went on to explain his plight, which sounded to Adam like the simple case of a British publisher quite understandably – and legally – refusing payments that had been contingent on the submission of written material. If Natalie's father had been a McDavis client, Adam would not have hesitated in suggesting that he climb down off his pedestal and jot a few English words in his notebook.

'You have every right to be annoyed,' he said, instead. Out of the corner of his eye, he saw Natalie's mother smile. 'It is one of the frustrations of my job that I deal with people who care only for rules, for small print. They do not have a larger view,' Adam continued, implying that George did. 'I would have to read your contract, but it strikes me that these people are perfectly capable of making life difficult for you – and I can't imagine anything more counterproductive than that, when dealing with a poet. It is poetry you owe them?' asked Adam, innocently, stressing the word *owe*.

'No, a story. Françoise thought she might want to get back into the illustration game. She's quite good at birds – aren't you, darling? I thought a bird story, for children.'

Adam wanted to say that a bird story didn't sound too difficult.

'It's hard not to be influenced by the war,' said George, gesturing with a piece of bread as if the war were just over the hill.

'Which war would that be? A current war?'

'Yes, of course,' George said. 'You know, Tybor once told me . . .'

A collective sigh issued from George's family, but it did not prevent him from continuing with a favourite literary anecdote. Adam had never met a real writer before, so he tried to concentrate and analyse the story. It proved to be exactly as self-serving as any story someone like Norman's father might tell, in that its elements of glory or pathos reflected favourably on the teller. It also assumed a knowledge of his own works

194

on the part of the listener, the way Norman's father would assume familiarity with the doorman of the Carlton Club. The story ended with the information that a key figure in one of Tybor's best-loved poems was based on George himself, a character portrayed as tortured and doomed because Tybor was *jealous*.

'You do know Tybor, don't you?' he asked.

'Yes,' Adam replied, not quite truthfully. Tybor was five letters of the alphabet arranged in Adam's mind in a way that triggered the word 'poet'. Adam was a member of a generation that ceased reading literature when their academic advancement no longer depended on doing so. He was not bothered by this, and had always preferred to spend what little free time he had going out with and seducing girls. He would read later, if it were absolutely necessary to pass the time.

George told another story, giving Adam time to recline in his chair and take a good look at Natalie's family. They all appeared to be healthy and proud of each other. From what Adam knew of their lives, he doubted that it was possible to have had a much more comfortable, stimulating time of it. Adam had learned that people like Natalie's father were almost invariably unbalanced in some way, but there was no outward evidence to indicate the divisive influences of incest or other abuse at work. Françoise was composed and patient, and gave every impression of being devoted to George. The boys were well-behaved, uncompetitive, only slightly in awe of their older sister. Tom, the one who was going to have the roughest ride, managed to combine effeminacy with an athletic build and a confident smile. Eddie, who would have to climb over the molehill of his father's literary reputation, was quieter and more anxious. He covered his mouth when he laughed.

'Adam has been such a good sport,' said Natalie,

retrieving the conversation from the gravitational pull of her father's ego. 'I'm afraid I'm making him miss several days' work.'

'That shouldn't be a problem,' said Adam, suavely, thinking he had probably been sacked *in absentia* by now.

'We have to call someone in London,' said Natalie. 'There may be an item in the paper. You won't believe what Adam did last night.'

For a moment Adam could not remember what it was he had done. When Natalie told her family the story, it was as if he heard it for the first time. Young Eddie loved this tale, and said he wished he'd been there. Veins stood out on the great poet's neck as he laughed with his mouth closed over a mouthful of wine. Adam thought that if he had only known that a bit of physical violence would make him popular, he would have started as a boy.

'Adam,' said Françoise, with perfect manners, 'I hope your parents are well.'

'Yes, wonderful. Natalie and I had dinner with them last night, in Cannes. My father can be somewhat severe, but Natalie melted him.' At this point, Natalie reached over and held Adam's hand on top of the table. Adam felt the blood and the wine and the food all rushing to his cheeks. He could not believe the goodwill all around him. Soon there would be a siesta, and a special room in the big white villa. Adam felt terrific, though weak with fatigue.

'You know I have heard of your father,' said the impeccable Françoise. 'In fact I even saw him, in Rome, nearly twenty years ago. He certainly looked like an ambassador.'

Adam knew Françoise was at least exaggerating, probably lying outright, and he didn't care. He had come to think of insincerity as a hallmark of excellent breeding. It was clear to him that Natalie had called ahead, that the Ambassador had been researched; Adam had reached a level of self-awareness where this duplicity was as plain to him as the hot sun in the sky overhead.

'Yes,' Adam said. 'He always had that look.'

'I think he is terribly handsome,' said Natalie. 'He is old-fashioned and he has wonderful manners. He kissed my hand, Mum.'

Françoise put the back of her hand to her head and swooned.

Adam could see by the way he giggled that young Eddie wanted to say something. His older brother nudged him in the ribs and said, 'Don't.'

'I have to,' said Eddie.

'Please, Eddie, don't,' said Tom.

Eddie said, 'I suppose you two are going to set a date, now? You might as well tell us and get it over with. The suspense is unbearable.'

Adam was eager to hear the answer to Eddie's question.

'Eddie, that's not what you ought to be asking,' said Françoise. She added a further warning in French.

'Sorry, Adam,' said Tom.

'Don't worry,' Adam said. 'Natalie will explain.'

Natalie put down her fork, swallowed, and beamed at her family. She took Adam's hand again. Adam shook his head bashfully.

'How do you know we aren't already married?' Natalie asked her family. 'These things happen all the time.'

'We would have seen it in the paper,' Eddie said.

'You only see what I want you to see,' said Natalie. 'I'm a puppeteer.'

Françoise stopped smiling and lit a cigarette. George took his napkin out of his lap and put it on the table.

'You aren't wearing a ring,' said Tom.

'I wouldn't, would I, if I were trying to keep it a secret from the press?'

'I don't think this is quite fair to Adam, darling,' said Françoise. 'Just tell us, if there is something to tell.'

Natalie squeezed Adam's hand, and said, 'We were thinking of eloping, but we thought that wouldn't be fair to you, or to his parents. Isn't that right, Adam?'

'That's right, yes.' Now that Adam had begun to feel like a pawn in a subtle family chess game, he decided to say as little as possible and agree with Natalie when necessary. His first impression had been all wrong. These people were lying to each other. It was a family coming apart at the seams. Adam worried that he had lost his touch, where social observation was concerned. In the event, he was not required to equivocate much longer: Marie and Bernard methodically cleared the table; the boys went back to the swimming pool; Françoise said she had to make some phone calls; and George, exhausted from his day's non-work, went upstairs to take a nap.

'So,' said Natalie, once they were alone. 'I think that went very well, don't you?'

PART THREE

MARRIAGE

Adam and Natalie lay side by side on their freshly made bed. They had opened the tall French doors leading to the terrace, so the hot afternoon sun filled the white, airy room. Natalie spoke into a portable telephone, which rang every time she turned it off; a single call to her agent had opened the floodgates, and there was much for her to discover. Adam had taken off only his shoes, and felt comfortably European – Latin, even – in his new clothes. He was sleepy, but Natalie's end of several successive conversations kept him awake.

Adam's moment of fame had arrived. His name had been discovered by London journalists, and printed. There were not only photographs, but videotape of his altercation with the gigantic star. It was the time of year when newspapers fell on such a story as if a world leader had been assassinated.

'Luckily,' said Natalie, into the telephone, 'no-one knows where we are. We weren't followed, I made certain of that.'

'They know where we are,' muttered Adam, throbbing with celebrity on his side of the bed. 'I told Norman.'

Natalie covered the phone with her hand. 'Norman won't tell, will he?'

'Norman will tell, believe me. Norman always tells.'

Natalie relayed this information to whoever was on the other end of the line. Public relations were being marshalled back in London. Adam thought he heard a helicopter outside.

'Is there another telephone line?' Adam asked.

There was, so that a few minutes later Adam and Natalie lay side by side again, speaking on different lines.

'Norman, it's Adam.'

Norman made the same noise Adam had heard him make on the golf course having holed a shot from eighty yards out.

'Norman, please. This may be serious.'

'Adam, my best friend. My best *man*.'

'Yes, yes.'

'You are *huge*.'

'I need to know exactly what's going on. I'm cut off, out here. Did you tell anyone where we went?'

'Afraid so, Adam. They pried it out of me, the wily bastards. I thought I was doing you a favour, until they told me what you'd done.'

'What did they say I'd done?'

'It all sounded a bit as if you had a dust-up with the world's biggest movie star, beat him to a pulp, and tossed him over the side of an arms dealer's yacht into the deep blue sea. I don't know if attempted murder was a phrase they used, but grievous bodily harm entered into it somewhere.'

'No charges were pressed,' said Adam, biting his lip. 'It was nothing at all.'

'There's a picture in the evening paper, Adam.' Norman sounded happy. There was very little real excitement in his life. 'I have the picture in front of me. I've also seen some of the footage. They're playing it on the *BBC*, mate.'

'Tell me about the pictures.' Adam was disgusted.

'The one in the paper here is in colour, and it shows you clearly breaking the arm of someone we can't see very well because he's hunched over in agony. He's identified in the caption, and once you know who it is—'

'Is my name mentioned?'

'Yah. Spelled correctly, you'll be glad to know. Inside you are identified as the Ambassador's boy, and you are called "a member of the Euro-jet-set".'

'I am?' Adam cringed.

'Sure. This could be very big for Natalie, you know. Is she aware of what's happening?'

'Yes. She's busy with containment, at the moment.'

'Is that her voice I hear in the background?'

'Yes, it is.'

'Christ, is she luscious. And *Christ*, am I jealous.'

'You've been in the paper quite a lot, Norman.'

'Yah, *getting* thumped. By the *police*. Not like this. You're a bloody hero.'

'I'm so glad you think so, Norman. Now look, I just want to beg you not to say a *word* more. These people are animals, you know. They'll trick you, bribe you, lie to you, blackmail you. Don't say a word.'

'Oh, all right,' said Norman, who sounded disappointed. 'Mum's the word.'

'Thanks. I'll give you the number here, if you absolutely *vow* not to give it to anyone. You can ring me with developments if they're urgent. Don't call just to gossip.'

'It's a promise.'

Adam gave Norman the number of the line he was using, and reminded him that there were several things he could leak to the press that would be far more embarrassing than Adam's minor affray. He said a wary goodbye. He leaned over the side of the bed to put the telephone on the floor, then returned to his mummy-like pose next to Natalie. Listening to her conversation with Jane Wheeler, Adam began to appreciate the magnitude of the fallout from what had seemed an insignificant event. He had to smile when he heard Natalie discussing the likelihood that the star's new feature film, in which he played the sort of person who would never allow himself to be chucked into the sea by a Belgian solicitor, might now be crippled at the box office. It was possible that Adam's simple act of chivalry might cost a Japanese multinational corporation tens of millions of dollars. Californians would lose their jobs. Crowds would not form outside cinemas. The star would be asked about little else as he went about publicizing his movie.

'This is serious,' Natalie said, after finishing her conversation. For once, the telephone did not ring right away.

'Am I in trouble?'

'It depends how much you like having everyone interested in you. If you have any terrible secrets, I suggest you gag anyone who knows them.'

'I don't have any terrible secrets.'

'Well then, if you want a bit of money you could start ringing the papers.'

'I would never do that. I mean . . . what exactly would the papers want?'

'They'd think of the most extreme way of telling the story of what happened, and ask you to sign your name to it.'

'I couldn't possibly.'

'I'm glad, Adam,' said Natalie, smiling. 'You must keep your dignity.'

'We have to look at this in perspective. It's a one-day story, surely?'

'For you, maybe. But there's one big movie star who's not going to hear the end of it. Let's hope he's not the vengeful type. He has a great deal of power, you know.'

Adam saw how coldly Natalie responded to publicity, good or bad, when his only reaction was one of horror. 'I just hope it doesn't reflect badly on you,' he said. 'Will Serge be terribly cross?'

'I can't even guess how Serge will react. It's nothing to do with him, really.'

'I suppose not.'

'Don't worry, Adam. We'll lie low for a couple of days and hope another story comes along.'

'I'll be a footnote in cinematic history. It's a good thing I didn't injure him.'

Natalie frowned. 'Actually,' she said, 'the paper reported that he suffered a concussion and almost drowned.'

'But that isn't true.'

'No, but it's a better story.'

Natalie's telephone rang again, so Adam stared at the ceiling while she listened to the latest news. His limp body pressed heavily into the bedclothes. Natalie's questions indicated a tidal wave of interest sweeping across the Atlantic from America. Reporters had naturally come to the conclusion that a little-known European actress had been seduced away from her nonentity boyfriend by the big movie star, and that the nonentity boyfriend had retaliated in a blind rage. Adam tried to imagine, from the bedroom of a peaceful villa on an Italian hillside, the hundreds of people going about the business of broadcasting this fiction to a slavering world. With a growing sense of embarrassment, and Natalie's calm, shrewd voice in his ears, Adam fell asleep.

'Adam, wake up.'

'Sorry. I didn't mean to—'

'Listen, Adam. Listen to this.'

205

Adam drew himself up on his elbows, and listened. Someone was shouting, outside.

'That's your father,' Adam said.

'Yes. I'm afraid the paparazzi have arrived. They came up the hill on motorcycles, in vans . . . Come outside and look, but keep your head below the railing.'

Adam climbed off the bed, and crawled along the floor next to Natalie. Outside, they raised their heads inches over the balcony wall, and surveyed a chaotic scene of Italian photographers, journalists and cameramen arguing with Natalie's father. His only weapon was an antique-looking golf club, which he held in one hand and swung for emphasis.

'Clear off!' he shouted. 'The police are on their way. *Police!*'

The photographers calmly snapped his picture. The cameramen turned on their lights and rolled film.

'You can't win,' said Natalie. 'Now *this* will be on the news. I hope he doesn't hit any of them.'

'You have enough violent men in your life as it is,' said Adam.

'Come back inside, before they see us.'

They returned to the bed and sat down.

'How long will they stay?' Adam asked.

'Until they get what they've come for. Even if we manage to kick them off the property, they'll set up camp across the way, or along the road down the hill. There's no escape.'

'They were photographing my *car*,' said Adam.

'I know,' said Natalie, soothingly. 'They're beasts.'

'I'm not used to this,' said Adam.

'Why don't I go get us a drink. It will be dark soon enough. We can sit outside and eavesdrop on them.'

'On the journalists?'

'Sure. Don't call them that, though. It gives them too much credit.'

'I hope your father calms down.'

'He wouldn't be doing it if he didn't love it. He likes attention. If he's in the British papers tomorrow, it will make his year.'

'Let's hope they spell his name correctly,' said Adam, sarcastically.

'That's the idea,' Natalie said, in all seriousness.

The police could be heard several minutes before their arrival, whining up the hillside with sirens on maximum volume and strobes flashing in the fading light. Adam and Natalie watched from a corner of the terrace, where they could peek through a trellis of ivy and not be seen or photographed. The police made a grand, dusty entrance to the property, taking out shrubbery, digging up lawn, hooting at paparazzi who were slow to get out of the way. Natalie's father stood his ground on the front steps of the house, shaking his fist and swinging his golf club at the cameras.

Natalie had fetched a bottle of wine and glasses, so she and Adam spent an interesting cocktail hour observing the stand-off below. Adam had never seen an argument erupt so quickly, nor had he ever seen anywhere near the disrespect for authority exhibited by the newsmen. The police were at an immediate disadvantage, for everything they said and did was filmed, recorded and written down. They had to suffer floods of abuse without retaliating. The most aggressive member of the paparazzi was a bearded, long-haired Italian in his twenties with four cameras slung around his neck; unlike most of his confrères, he wore an elegant suit and tie. He had begun to shout at the fascist-looking police even before they had a chance to establish the circumstances of the complaint. Using his hands in just the way Italians were said to do, he spat invective in every direction and spurred on his colleagues to do the same. It was some minutes before the highest ranking officer could make his way to the front steps to interview Natalie's father. Françoise emerged from the house to translate.

Their voices could be heard over the rumble of argument in the background. George clearly stated his desire that the newsmen be herded off his property immediately; the officer asked if the mob might not be thrown a sop of some kind, perhaps a photo-opportunity and a quote or two from the principals. George asked the police officer if he was out of his mind – if he wanted to protect private property, or the careers of an unruly crowd of sociopaths. The police officer said he took George's point, but that there were several freedoms to be kept in mind, not least that of the press, and that in his experience the most tenacious paparazzi could only be driven away with a gesture of compromise. He added that brandishing a golf club was not wise, and it would be confiscated unless George put it away. George said he would put the club away up the police officer's backside, but Françoise elected not to translate this remark.

Tom and Eddie came out onto the terrace thirty yards away from where Adam and Natalie hid. They were photographed hundreds of times in twenty seconds. Questions were shouted up to them. The boys shrugged their shoulders and pretended not to speak Italian.

'I don't like being famous,' Adam whispered.

'It won't last,' Natalie said. 'But you've affected the reputation of one of the most famous people in the whole world. Just imagine what it's like for him.'

'He probably has a wall around his house.'

'We were thinking of building one here.'

Natalie's parents did not live in Ilani year-round. They maintained a house in Malta, a flat in London that Eddie made his permanent residence, an apartment in

Paris and a disused farm in Wiltshire. If they had fallen on hard times, Adam had to wonder what their lives had been like before.

'You have to decide if you want to say something to them,' Natalie said. 'The cop is probably right. They won't leave us alone until they get a quote and a photo.'

'They can go to hell,' said Adam.

'That's a nice thought, but I think you'll find they hold all the cards. If you don't give them a quote, they'll make one up. They'll write such fabulous lies that you'll have to come out and deny them. By then the damage will have been done. You'll only prolong the agony if you stonewall.'

'You sound like such a hardened pro, Natalie.'

'I'm a quick study.'

'You certainly are.'

'Oh, and another thing. If you think the police want to wrap this up in a hurry, you're wrong. They're just members of the public in uniform. They want to see the hero who protected his woman from the big movie star.'

'I'll do whatever you advise,' said Adam. 'I'm out of my depth.' Adam wished he could evaporate.

'I say we let my father have his fun for a while longer, then go out and say hello. Just act naturally, and everything ought to be fine.'

'If that's what you think is right.'

'I do,' said Natalie, moving close to Adam and hugging him sideways. 'After that, we might be alone at last.'

'There's an incentive,' said Adam. 'Pour me another glass of this, and I'll be ready to face the savages.'

While the argument continued to rage outside, Adam rang Dick McDavis.

'Dick, it's Adam Gosse. Look, I'm terribly sorry but—'

'Adam, thank God you rang. We were worried about you.'

'Worried? Is this Dick McDavis?'

'Yes, yes, it's me. Look, is there any help you need? Money?'

'Money? I was ringing to see if you'd sacked me.'

'*Sacked* you? Adam, my good friend. Please, please relax on that front. I understand why you wanted to keep your private life private. I would have done the same. It must be *terribly* difficult to carry on this sort of relationship in secret.'

Adam looked out of the window at the cars and vans and motorcycles. Two men in white overalls had begun to erect a satellite transmitter on an empty patch of lawn. 'You're right about that.'

Dick exhaled noisily down the line, then said, 'I have to say I really admire the way you've balanced your work with this other . . . this other life.'

'What do you mean, Dick?'

'Well, you know. A lesser man might have thrown it all in. Your loyalty is to be commended.'

'I don't know what you're talking about, Dick.'

'Where are you, by the way?'

'We're in Italy, not too far across the border from France.'

'Don't tell me exactly,' said Dick, sounding awed. 'The media will beat it out of me.'

'Too late, I'm afraid. We're surrounded as I speak to you.'

'Now, you just be careful. Take as much time as you need.' This, from the man who had once threatened to sack Adam for leaving work early to see Mr Stephenson in hospital when he had broken his hip in a fall. Adam tried to visit his former boss at home every month, to chat to him about the firm; on these occasions he omitted any mention of its desecration at the hands of Dick and Judy McDavis.

'That's good of you, Dick. I'm not certain what will happen next.'

McDavis's tone turned sour. 'You could have *told* me, you know,' he said.

Adam supposed this meant that if McDavis had known about his employee's glamorous affiliation, he would have required less of him at work. 'I only met her over the weekend,' Adam said, scrupulously honest as always.

McDavis seemed not to hear. 'This is just so big,' he said. 'The telephones have been ringing since noon. I haven't leaked a word.'

'I'm sure you haven't.' This was the first conversation of any length with McDavis in which Adam had not been called a bastard.

'They asked if you were going to marry her, and I didn't say a thing.'

'They asked that?'

'Yes.'

'And you didn't say a thing, Dick?'

'No I didn't,' he said, proudly.

'That's good of you,' said Adam, 'given that you didn't even know I knew her. Which I didn't.'

Once again, Dick missed the point. He could have been drunk. 'Anyway, Adam, *are* you getting married? That's the word here, as I say. You'll be needing a best man, eh? That'll be a switch.'

'I beg your pardon?'

'Well, what with all of your best-manning. That's all I mean. I didn't mean . . .' McDavis ran out of words. Adam thought he could hear his boss squeezing the telephone with both hands, ringing its neck, hoping he wouldn't be disconnected. 'Adam, this is just so good. I wish you all the best. You *are* a good man.

Do tell me if there is anything I can do to help.'

Adam tried to visualize the giant behind these grovelling words. 'I ought to go,' he said.

'Just a moment, Adam. Just a moment. I wanted to ask you. Is she there? Is Natalie there?'

'Well of course she is. It's her parents' house.'

'Is she near by?'

'I'd say so, Dick. She's right here.' Curled between Adam's arms, Natalie looked at him over her shoulder.

'Oh, my God,' said McDavis. 'Is she beautiful?'

'Sure,' said Adam, as if he were chewing gum. 'She's beautiful, all right.'

Holding Natalie's hand, Adam emerged from the house into a lightning storm of camera flashes. A boom microphone swung across the sky and bumped him softly on the temple. He tried to smile. He looked at Natalie, who knew how to adopt a winning expression of gratitude and surprise, as if she hadn't known anyone cared. The newsmen had relaxed, or perhaps they had exhausted themselves arguing with the police. Natalie's parents retreated into the shadows near the front door.

Adam waited for the motor drives to stop whining, then ignored the first questions shouted at him in Italian.

'May I just say a few words first, please?' he asked. 'I will speak in English, if that's all right,' he added, as if fluent Italian were an option available to him. The mob collected itself. A silence waited to be filled. Adam's thoughts moved quickly enough to register the idea that his every word carried the potential of being broadcast into the consciousness of many millions of fellow human beings. A thicket of microphones presented itself to him, sucking sound from the air. Adam cleared his throat.

'I believe I know why you are here,' he said, in his firm English voice. 'I will be happy to answer whatever questions you have, about what I know you will find to be a small matter, if not a complete misunderstanding. I only ask that you show the courtesy to my host, whom I met for the first time only this afternoon, of leaving his property as soon as we have finished speaking to you. I am embarrassed enough to have disturbed his privacy this evening, and I would appreciate your co-operation in that regard.'

The mob snarled impatiently. Adam made out some faces in the camera lights, and reckoned they were not the sort for whom a plea for good manners carried any weight. In any case, Adam had made his request for the benefit of Natalie's father.

The most aggressive paparazzo was the first to ask a question, which sounded to Adam as if it contained a dozen sub-clauses. Natalie waited for him to finish, then turned to Adam. 'Did you have a fight with the star?'

'A tussle, more like.'

'What was it about?'

'A minor, private dispute. We had only just met. I suppose I ought to say I overreacted, but only marginally. I thought he was rude.'

'Did you try to kill him?'

'No. I warned him that I was going to throw him into the water, then I did so.'

'Are you a martial arts expert?'

'No.'

'Did he put up a good fight?'

'None at all, actually.'

'Do you have anything against his films or his acting?'

'No. I am indifferent.'

'Had you been stalking him for long?'

'I was trying to ignore him. *He* stalked *me*.'

'Was the fight over a woman?'

'No.'

'He says it was.'

This was news to Adam. 'That's news to me,' he said.

'He says it was over Natalie.' This question sounded strange, when Natalie translated it herself.

'If he saw it that way, then I have to assume he was very much mistaken.'

Now Natalie was asked her views, so that Adam was left in the dark. Only when a camera crew asked her to repeat her answers in English was Adam enlightened.

'No,' she said, 'we never had any relationship of any kind. We had met only three or four times. I have always admired his work. He is a consummate professional as well as a great artist. I must stress that our relationship has never been romantic, let alone . . .'

Adam began to feel angry. It was galling to have to speak about personal matters to a horde of strangers. What *possible* right did they have to know the answers to questions that their victims might not have resolved for themselves? Natalie seemed happy to go on detailing aspects of her life that Adam would have found difficult to discuss with a fellow lawyer sworn to confidentiality.

'Adam and I are very close,' she said. Adam turned and looked at her. The cameras flashed on his expression of tender devotion. 'I feel very sorry that he has been dragged into this mess. He acted like a gentleman, not realizing what the consequences might be. I hope any of you would have done the same. It was harmless enough – I was there and saw everything. The only difference between this and any little argument is that you are all so interested.'

'Did he visit his victim in the hospital?'

'There was no hospital,' said Natalie. 'We were all good friends afterwards. We went to a party together. Please print the truth.'

The interview returned to Italian for a few minutes, until the only woman in the crowd asked Adam a question in English. By the time he heard the question, he seethed inwardly as he had not done since the last time Dick McDavis had falsely attributed blame to Adam in front of a client.

'Are you going to get married?' was the woman's question. The group went so quiet that Adam could hear spindles whirring in video cameras.

He could not very well answer 'No.' 'Yes' was presumptuous. 'None of your business' was appropriate, but Adam had already learned that instinctive defensive responses played into the newsmen's hands.

'We would very much like to get married,' he heard himself say cautiously, 'if we could just be left alone long enough to get to know each other.'

Those who understood English laughed. Natalie squeezed his hand. More photographs were taken. Natalie's father coughed in the shadows.

Adam and Natalie repaired to the upstairs terrace and reclined in wooden deck chairs. The paparazzi had been seen off; the police had been bribed with wine and olives. Tom and Eddie manned the telephones. Marie brought the publicly engaged couple a bottle of cold champagne and plates of local delicacies. It was cool enough for sweaters, one of which Adam had borrowed from Natalie's suddenly mute father.

'How did I do?' Adam asked.

'Do you want the truth?'

'Yes.'

'You didn't give them what they wanted. They'll have to make it up.'

'What can they possibly say?'

'If I were one of that crew, I would dictate a banner headline to be put over a picture of the two of us, in which you look nervous and confused, and I look innocent: " 'I'm No Murderer': Star Stalker". The

215

short article would go on in that vein, including your denials, ending with your plea not to be sent to the guillotine.'

Adam stretched, and rubbed his neck. The sea seemed closer at night. Ilani blinked at the foot of the hills, while navigation lights twinkled like stars on a black sky of water.

'So, assuming what you predict is what will happen, where does that leave us?'

Natalie pondered this question. Adam had to hold his head when he looked at her. It was hard to imagine that she did not have an exceptional destiny.

'It isn't important at all,' she said. 'There is a parallel world out there.' She gestured at the horizon. 'As Claude says, "zere are ze lookers, and ze lookees." Now that you are a lookee, you simply have to make the best of it. You will be forgotten in a matter of hours.'

'But not you?'

'I'm only *beginning* to learn self-importance,' she said, tossing her head. 'Come on, Adam. Relax.'

'I am relaxed. It's beautiful here.' He wanted to ask her why she liked him so much.

'They are going to print our plans to marry,' she said. 'Do you mind?'

'That was what we were planning, wasn't it?'

'In the depths of one's soul, perhaps.'

Natalie sipped her champagne. Adam ate an olive. They might have discussed their nuptials further, but Eddie and Tom emerged from the shadows to interrupt.

'Sorry,' they said, in unison.

'That's all right,' said Natalie.

The boys arranged themselves on the railing.

'We just thought we ought to tell you,' said Eddie, biting his nails with anxiety, 'that Mum and Dad are making love.'

Adam, Natalie and her brothers were silent for half a

minute, as if they expected to hear evidence confirming this news.

'It's true,' Tom said. 'We saw the whole build-up and everything. It was really strange.'

'Amazing,' said Natalie. 'Next thing we know he'll *write* something.'

Adam saw the mixture of love and suspicion in Natalie's brothers' eyes. He wondered what they could make of their sister's calculated rise. Her superficial success did not bode well for their prospects of conventional employment. There were few advantages to being an only child, but one of them was not having tough acts to follow.

Adam listened as Natalie's brothers quizzed her about the press. They had missed most of the interview because they had been required in the kitchen to calm Marie and Bernard. The couple had fetched an ancient but functioning pair of fowling pieces from a basement closet, and threatened to defend the honour of their employers by firing blindly into the pack of newsmen and police.

Tom took a piece of paper out of his shorts pocket and read out the telephone messages he and his brother had collected.

'Someone named Norman called for you, Adam. He was ever so excited, and wanted you to know that his wife had heard all the news way out in Bangkok. Isn't that amazing?'

'It certainly is.'

'A Jane McDavis also rang. She wanted to assure you that legal representation would be entirely complimentary. Isn't that nice?'

'It certainly is.'

'Natalie, you had several calls: Claude, Serge. *Bruno L*, if you please. A hairstylist in Milan named Sarto. A photographer named David who said you know where he is, and another man who refused to say who he was and wouldn't tell me where he got the number.'

'What did Serge say?'

'He said he had urgent news. They all did. I took down his number. He seems to be in Milan, too.'

'I wonder what he's doing there.'

'You'd better ring him back,' said Tom. 'He sounded upset.'

Natalie sighed. She got up and went into the house with Tom's piece of paper, leaving Adam alone for the first time with his potential brothers-in-law.

Adam clasped his hands behind his neck, looked overhead and noticed a half moon.

'What have I done?' he said. 'I didn't mean to cause such a fuss.'

'I'm sure you didn't,' said Tom.

'I wouldn't worry,' said his younger brother. 'These people thrive on drama.'

'I just don't want to jeopardize Natalie's first job. These offers don't come along every day.'

'She can take care of herself,' said Tom.

Adam sat up straight and addressed the boys man to man. 'It happened exactly as we told you earlier. It was a small thing. I was exhausted and tense, and the man was rude in front of your sister. I think I did the right thing.'

'Don't worry, Adam,' said Tom. 'We think you did the right thing, too. Dad didn't show it, but he was pleased. You scored some points there, I can tell you.'

'I'm not trying to score points.'

'Well,' said Eddie, shyly. 'It doesn't hurt, you know.'

It was odd to feel so much older than a couple of grown men. Adam thought he could see that Tom and Eddie were fascinated by their sister's new beau. They asked him where he lived, and were impressed by the address. They asked about Adam's father, and said they

218

thought ambassadors to the United Kingdom were some of the luckiest people in the world. They wanted to know about Adam's childhood, and he told them the story of his dance with Princess Georgina. They asked if he worked with many famous people, and Adam admitted that the real nature of his employment had been misrepresented in the press.

It was Adam's turn to interview the boys. They seemed not to have the faintest idea what to do with their lives – unless it was to announce to the world that they were writers or designers, then wait. It did seem true that there was very little the boys could do that would effectively improve the quality of their existence. They were like Norman and Didi, in this regard, except that they had even fewer responsibilities. Like Natalie, they assumed lightning would have to strike before their identities could be forged.

With their quick exchange of biographies over, Adam and the boys relaxed and talked of the present.

'I'm just happy to be in such a peaceful spot – now that the crowd has gone away. Natalie and I are exhausted. She needs to rest before filming starts, which could be any day now. Her director operates on impulse. What we need is a night or two of sleep and relaxation, if that's all right with your parents.'

The boys said it would not be a problem, and Tom began to tell Adam about some of the amusements to be found in the area: riding, golf, swimming, a particularly friendly restaurant in the hills—

'Oh, hello, Natalie,' Tom said, interrupted by her return to the terrace. 'What's the news?'

'We have to go,' said Natalie, bluntly. She looked agitated. 'Serge has another *vision*.'

'Oh, no,' said Adam.

'Yes. He's diverted all the crew and equipment, who'd made it nearly to the Croatian border. He's decided that would be too dangerous just at the moment. He's turned everyone back to a town called Sampara. That's on the Adriatic coast of Italy, Adam. It isn't terribly far, but we have to be there at dawn to shoot the first exterior. The crew will work through the night to be ready.'

Adam tried not to show how his body ached, how his patience had worn parchment-thin, how four days and three nights in Natalie's company had wound his frayed romantic sensibilities into a tight ball of physical need.

'That's fine,' he said. 'A drink before we go?'

They left the house without disturbing Natalie's parents, laden with a basket of food from Marie and Bernard's kitchen. Adam drove slowly down the winding drive towards the road to Ilani. Camera flashes burst like sniper-fire from the bushes.

'Don't worry about them,' said Natalie, as a pair of motorcycles appeared in the rearview mirror. 'They know where we're going.'

Natalie navigated until they reached the open road. Adam spoke encouraging words to his car's fragile engine. The half-moon rode along to starboard.

'Music might keep us alert,' said Adam, turning on the radio. Natalie made no reply; she was already asleep.

Adam found a French station, and listened to a news broadcast in which he did not figure. Instead, he heard about war and pestilence. This was entertaining enough, though he thought he could understand why people wanted their war and pestilence spiced now and again with scandal and vice.

Adam thought about class and social standing. The movie star he had dunked in the Mediterranean was a good example of someone who was at once strato-spherically superior and basically beneath a man like Adam. The same was true, less dramatically, of his passenger. It was all very well for people with some semblance of breeding – even transplanted Belgians – to disdain the attention and wealth paid to a lucky minority of entertainers, but a point did seem to have been reached where their power had grown out of all proportion to their contribution. Adam felt his political life-view swerving between fascism and anarchy – then settling, exasperated, on apathy.

Driving slowly in the darkness, his hands loose on the steering wheel, Adam also thought about Natalie's motives. He was a good enough judge of character to know with certainty that she was not playing a game, not toying with him for youthful amusement. Her age was still a problem, though. If she were a student or an aspiring solicitor or Norman's niece, the situation would be entirely different. She would defer to Adam, and learn from him. As things stood with Natalie, Adam was in the position of knowing more about her likely future than she did, but in no position at all to warn her off what he thought she would face. He wished someone had been around to convince him to leave his firm after Mr Stephenson suffered his stroke.

It worried Adam that Natalie had allowed the subject of their theoretical marriage to go so far that the world's press would carry the story the next day, and that her family now took it as fact. He could only explain this by imagining that, to Natalie, marriage was something people like her did several times in their complicated lives, and she might as well get Number One out of the way as soon as she met a man who was not a direct physical threat.

The two paparazzi motorcycles overtook on his left, impatient with his lazy driving. He slowed down even more, and let them disappear around a long curve. He knew he would have to stop and sleep for a few minutes if he wanted to get Natalie to the set on time. He reached over his shoulder and poked around in the picnic basket, and landed on two pickles packed in a small, brown paper bag. He ate both pickles, concentrated on the road, and listened idly to a French song about the way love was sometimes like the fire-bombing of Dresden, sometimes like a solo excursion to the North Pole, sometimes like stepping barefoot on a piece of rotten fruit; the song could not decide, but asked its audience to give love a try anyway.

It was after midnight. Adam found that he enjoyed driving through the darkness of unfamiliar territory, at the boundary of what he considered to be Europe. He imagined the Alps towering weightily over his left shoulder, the boot of wild Italy to his right. There was a great deal of history to ponder, close at hand. He had a beautiful, charismatic girl in his car. He knew how tired he was, but he made sure to think of Roman legions and Hannibal and the Retreat from Caporetto, just to perk himself up. He had been dragged deep into Europe. He had wished for romance and adventure, and sure enough, as in a dream, here were romance and adventure in his passenger seat and under his right foot. He would learn Italian.

It was not a violent crash. Natalie woke up and brushed the hair from her forehead and asked Adam why he had stopped. He said he had stopped because he had driven into a barrier, bounced across the road into non-existent oncoming traffic, and come to rest facing the wrong way in a convenient and possibly life-saving lay-by. He apologized. He got out and inspected his beloved automobile, which was still running but would never forgive him. He had lost one headlamp and several layers of epidermis on the driver's side of the car. When the seriousness of what had happened sank in, he apologized again, in earnest.

'Natalie, I'm truly sorry. I have never, *ever* done that before. Lack of sleep. I'm awake, now.'

'Would you like me to drive?' Natalie asked, unperturbed. She didn't appear to mind that her life and career might have come simultaneously to an end. 'It's all right, Adam. No damage done.'

Adam jumped back into the driver's seat and accelerated into the night. A couple of minutes later Natalie advised him to move over to the right lane.

Adam was both lost and fairly near Natalie's destination when dawn insinuated itself overhead. At various points during the night, with Natalie trustingly asleep at his side, Adam had found himself scaling great heights, coasting back down again to save petrol, stranded at the edge of the sea, nearly driving into a broad estuary, pleading with a petrol-station attendant to speak English, French or Russian. An unexpected tour of central Florence had taken more than an hour to complete, and was one hundred miles off course. He hadn't wanted to wake Natalie, but when she did so of her own accord she sat up, took one look around the fairly nondescript landscape, pointed forty degrees to port, and said, 'That way.'

The sun had still not risen as Adam guided his battered car through the entrance of the minor walled town of Sampara. Natalie had never been there before, but seemed to know instinctively how to negotiate its narrow streets and get to the large, modern hotel where they were to meet the crew. Adam parked the car, kissed his fingertips and pressed them to the steering wheel. He sighed in relief, and slumped against the door.

'I'll just die quietly here,' he said. 'You go on ahead and become a movie star.'

'Don't be silly. Come have a cup of coffee and

something to eat. Serge will be happy to see you.'

'I expect everyone will be ducking out of the way when I try to shake their hands, after all the publicity.'

'Nonsense. They love you.'

After a minute or two getting his legs to move in synch, Adam followed Natalie into the hotel, through the lobby, and out to a conservatory that overlooked a ruined wall and the broad, flat beach beyond. It was characteristic of Natalie's style that she should sleep most of the night in an aimless, crashing sports car, zigzagging its way across Italy, and wake up to arrive exactly on time for an important meeting.

Serge sat imperiously at a long table in a roped-off section of the conservatory. He was joined, Last Supper-like, by half a dozen members of his crew. He leaned across the table to kiss Natalie's hand. He did not ask about her journey – assuming, perhaps, that she had made the trip by helicopter. He shook hands with Adam, then solemnly congratulated the couple on their impending marriage. He had already learned the news from a contact in London, who worried that Natalie's emotional life might threaten the filming of *Te Deum*. Serge dismissed this idea as paranoid, and urged Adam to join the meeting and have a bowl of coffee.

Adam was introduced to Make-up and Wardrobe, who soon left to attend to their business. He was introduced to Lighting-Camera, a cheerful Italian Serge's age who oozed loyalty and competence. He was introduced to Production Manager, a French woman who used a clumsy lorgnette to peer at notes on her clipboard. He was issued a pair of binoculars, and introduced from a distance to three grips laying rails on the beach three hundred yards away.

It all seemed to Adam a very minor operation. For all the talk of movement orders and logistics, this might as well have been the weekend shoot of a student film.

The atmosphere felt informal, and even visionary Serge, dressed like a fisherman, seemed happy to make small talk even as he felt the first contractions of artistic labour.

After a few encouraging words, he dismissed everyone but Adam and Natalie. He opened a folder, extracted a slender manuscript, and turned to the back. Natalie went around to the other side of the table and sat at Serge's elbow as he decided what he wanted from her in the way of performance: she was to gaze wistfully out to sea for as long as he decided was appropriate once filming began; she was then to walk twenty yards up the beach towards the retreating camera, and bitterly mouth the word 'Marcel'. There was no need for sound recording, Serge said. He wanted to direct her aloud. Her one spoken word, and any natural sound-effects Serge deemed appropriate, would have to be dubbed. There would be a large amount of music, Adam gathered – the Schubert they had been forced to listen to in Serge's Parisian penthouse.

That was the end of the meeting. Natalie was sent off to make-up and wardrobe, located in a cabana closer to the beach. Adam and the great director were left alone.

'I love all of my people,' said Serge. He looked emotionally drained. The script under his left hand was stained and torn at the edges. 'I am so eager to begin,' he said, Napoleonically.

Adam did not say what was uppermost in his mind, which was that Serge's production looked amateurish to his untutored eye – childish, almost.

'I don't want to be in the way,' he said, instead. 'I can get a room in the hotel.'

'There is a key at the desk in Natalie's name,' he replied, to Adam's relief. His credit card had been through too much already, thanks to Serge. 'Keep the binoculars, if you want. You will see everything from your balcony.'

Adam thanked the director, taking this as his cue to leave. Serge put up a palm to stop Adam from standing up, and spoke with almost tearful sincerity.

'You do love her?' he asked.

'Natalie?'

Serge squinted. 'Of course, Natalie.'

'Yes, I do,' said Adam, formally. 'I want to make her happy.' He thought this was what he was expected to say.

Serge sighed, perhaps at the thought of having to abandon his traditional two-year cohabitation with his starlets.

'What you did in Cannes,' said Serge. 'You were courageous. And you were correct.'

Adam had no idea what version of events Serge had adopted as fact. 'I'm glad to hear you say that, sir.'

A rind of orange sun appeared on the horizon. Serge looked at his watch, then back out to sea. A photogenic mist still clung to the beach. It would be a sweltering day. Serge would sweat for his art.

'When you are in bed with Natalie,' said Serge, out of nowhere, 'and you hold her very close in your arms?'

'Yes?'

'And you make love to her?'

'Yes?'

'I know you will show her what it is to be a woman.'

'I hope I will,' said Adam, nodding. He saw that Serge had thought he had not heard properly. 'I mean, I hope I *have*.'

'Go, now,' said Serge. 'I must be alone. Natalie will be ready soon.'

'I hope so,' Adam replied, sincerely.

Adam stood. He bowed. He shook hands and wished Serge good luck. The director looked lonely but determined. He gazed out at the rising sun as if experiencing a premonition of doom.

Adam loved the hotel suite almost as much as he had loved his bedroom in Didi's château. He took off his new European clothing and explored, feeling Cro-Magnon, from room to room. He had a hot tub, in case he felt like entertaining Claude, Serge, Bruno L and the gang. He had a living room that gave on to a generous balcony built partly into the ancient Sampara walls. It was an excursion to reach the bedroom, itself equipped with a balcony; this gave on to part of the quaint old town, a vineyard and the grassy bluffs that had built up over the centuries to reclaim the old main road.

Magnetically drawn to the bed, Adam avoided it lest he sleep all day long. He installed himself on the main balcony with his binoculars, a beer from the mini-bar and some of the sausages, bread and mustard Marie and Bernard had packed. He was naked except for his dark glasses and his watch. The morning broke warm and humid. A flimsy mist still bode well for creative filming.

He raised his binoculars with weary arms, and focused on Serge's men. They had finished laying the rails and erecting the camera on its dolly. They smoked cigarettes, and appeared to be arguing. One of them produced a thermos of coffee. There were already two equipment vans on the scene, and soon a jeep arrived bearing the director and his closest assistants. It really did seem very unprofessional, Adam thought. He had always imagined that in Hollywood there would be hundreds of people milling about, and police to guard the set.

It was as Adam thought this, and leaned out on tiptoe to get a better look at Serge's arrival, that he noticed he was being photographed from the broken town walls across the way. The paparazzi had found him. He made what he hoped was an obscene gesture in Italian, and returned to the bedroom for his trousers. Adam was angry. So, he thought, the jackals want more. Their pictures of him might serve, if they weren't preoccupied with photographs of dead bodies from any of the various wars available to them, or other titillating ephemera.

Adam returned to the balcony and waved angrily at the two photographers, trying to shoo them away. They photographed him. He looked around to make sure there were no other hotel guests within earshot, then shouted at the paparazzi to leave him alone. They photographed him some more. He tried a new tack, which was to stand erect and smile warmly at them. They photographed this pose, and several others, before they were appeased. They waved thank-you as they departed.

Down on the beach, Serge stood apart from his crew and visualized. The camera dolly was tested on its rails. A junior member of the crew stood at Natalie's spot while the cameraman and a focus puller, sitting side by side on the dolly, organized the shot. Adam thought film-making looked awfully easy.

Ten minutes later, Natalie emerged from the cabana, accompanied by Make-up and Wardrobe. She had been dressed in a costume that was probably not unfamiliar to her: a low-cut, short black dress. It must have helped the make-up and hair people that Natalie had not slept in a proper bed for days now, because she was clearly meant to look like someone who had stayed up all night after a party and suffered some sort of romantic setback. She carried a pair of black stilettos in one hand, picking her way across the deep sand on thin, tanned legs. It was difficult for Adam to believe that this exceptionally beautiful girl — no matter how vulgarly attired — was someone close to him not only in fact, but in the eyes of a greedy world.

Adam tried to imagine what Natalie could be feeling as she bravely took to her mark. Here it was at last, her début in the world's most glamorous job. Serge spoke to her, using his hands, and she nodded gamely. Did she know her motivation? Was she sufficiently steeped in her character? It was so quiet, for something so important to be happening.

A last dusting of make-up was applied to Natalie's chin and forehead. Bits of her hair were tugged this way and that. A man positioned a reflector to highlight her features. A clapper board was snapped in front of the camera, and Natalie began to *act*.

Serge directed her aloud, waving his arms balletically, like a conductor, presumably narrating her character's emotions so that they could play across her face like shadows. After a long, long time – which was probably no more than a minute and a half – Serge instructed Natalie to turn and walk towards the camera, which was then pulled along its rails by two intent young men. After ten paces, Adam saw her spit the word 'Marcel' and toss her head in disgust. She walked more quickly, with determined gait. Serge exhorted her to stride angrily towards him, and out of the frame.

'Cut,' said Serge, or its French equivalent. Everyone rushed back to their original positions, while Serge had a private word with his leading lady.

Adam thought he knew a thing or two about film-making, and fully expected Natalie and the crew to spend days perfecting this scene. It surprised him, therefore, when the subsequent take, identical to the first, was applauded by Serge, a gesture that signalled the end to the morning's filming. Natalie returned to the cabana, and the crew began to dismantle their equipment. Serge took a stroll alone down the beach.

Adam felt let down. That was European art film? No tantrums, no walking off the set, no nudity, no *catering*?

He wanted to have an open mind, and a generous disposition towards the art form of his age, but what he had just seen filled him with doubt. It was too easy. An emotion had been created for the screen in less time than it would take for a proper actress to muster tears.

In his state of exhaustion he thought he might be getting somewhere in his analysis of modern culture, but there was an annoying amount of noise coming from somewhere behind the hotel – noise of machinery and construction. What could the humble denizens of Sampara be working at so early in the morning? Adam ate some more of his sausage and bread. He finished his beer, and ached for sleep. If the racket didn't cease he would have to change hotels. Who did they think he was, to carry on this way when he needed his rest?

Adam went back into his suite, turned right at the hot tub, turned left at the dressing room, turned left again at the bedroom, and went out to the other balcony. What he saw explained the noise, and dashed his recent notions about Serge and the film business in general. During the hour he had spent watching Natalie's acting début on the beach, a large number of Serge's employees – using cranes, lorries, lumber and paint – had gone some way towards constructing a convincing replica of Dubrovnik's round tower.

On his way through the bedroom back to the east balcony, Adam lay down and slept for twelve hours.

'It's almost time for dinner,' said Natalie, sitting at the dressing table, brushing her hair. She still wore the black dress she had been issued by Wardrobe.

Adam struggled to collect himself, to pin down the date and time, to remember where he was.

'Could you please come over here and lie down?' he asked. Actually, it was an order.

230

Natalie took off her shoes and reclined fragrantly next to him. Adam told her that he had watched her performance from the balcony, and suggested that hers might have been the smoothest, most professional début in the history of film acting.

'I wouldn't be at all surprised,' said Natalie. 'We spent all afternoon filming me walking up a steep street in the middle of town. They've almost finished building the big tower.'

'So I heard.'

'For three hours, they filmed Bruno getting out of a taxi. His trousers were too tight, then too loose, then his hair went crazy – he blamed salt air and the heat – then there were technical problems, and light, and cigarette breaks for the crew. I'm learning a lot, Adam.'

'I'm sure you are.'

'At lunch we had a lecture from Serge about the mood and meaning of this picture. We were told about "the nature of Christ", which was illuminating. We were played some Purcell and Handel, for atmosphere.'

'Interesting. Is Serge really a genius, then?'

'Decide for yourself,' said Natalie. 'They're screening his last film for the crew and cast tonight. I had to admit I'd never even heard of it – Serge found that endearing and gave me a fatherly hug.'

Adam turned on his side and placed his palm on Natalie's stomach, which he knew in advance was a paranormal way of making the telephone ring.

'Hello?' said Natalie. 'Didi, my goodness,' she said, switching to French. 'Aren't you in Bangkok? How did you find me?'

Adam fell on to his back and listened to Natalie's end of the conversation. He thought that with each passing moment he was more likely to make a scene. He moved his lips and shook his head sarcastically from side to side, imitating the mouse-like noises that leaked between the receiver and Natalie's ear. It was hard to listen to Didi's chirpy exclamations without recalling the last time he had seen her alone – at four o'clock in the morning exactly one year ago. He had escorted her to the taxi stand outside a hotel near his flat, having just proposed marriage. This proposal followed one of the most inspired dates Adam had ever organized, including a profoundly meaningful union in bed. When Didi laughed at his utterly sincere proposal – covering her mouth when she sensed her cruelty, but unable to stop herself – Adam went into the kitchen to make coffee, and wept.

This was shame, not sadness. His face burned and his hands clenched. He wanted to take a carving knife, go back into the drawing room and slice his own head off in front of Didi. He wanted to hold out his severed head and place it in her lap before he collapsed. Rethinking this plan of action, he decided instead to bring her coffee and pretend nothing so apocalyptic had entered his mind. When he saw her, pulling on her stockings and still laughing, he thought he realized how objectively hideous she was. Her Medusa hair, unkempt from four or five hours of hard-earned ecstasy; her too-deep tan; her evil mouth.

'I hope you're not too upset,' Didi said, in her disgusting accent.

'What gave you that idea?' said Adam, his face twitching, coffee cups rattling as he removed them from a tray and tried to put them down on his only table.

They did not drink the coffee. Adam helped Didi on with her coat, opened the door for her, and escorted her outside. On the way to the taxi rank, Didi said, 'I wouldn't worry, Adam. You're going to have a very enjoyable life.'

'People have to be thick to enjoy life,' Adam replied.

*   *   *

'Didi says hello,' said Natalie. 'It's amazing how easy we are to track down.'

Adam told her about the paparazzi outside, and that nude pictures of him were likely to appear in the world's newspapers.

'Lucky world,' said Natalie.

As Adam turned again to lie on his side next to Natalie, it was difficult not to feel like a character in one of Serge's films – if Adam guessed correctly how they looked and behaved. All he needed now was emotionally charged music soaring overhead, and nicotine on his breath.

During the past couple of days, Adam had become intimidated by the prospect of this moment. It was the great director himself, who presumably knew vastly more than Adam about such things, who had said he expected Natalie to be shown what it was to be a woman. Adam felt underqualified in this regard, and furthermore he judged by Natalie's hectic schedule of constant interruption that there wouldn't be enough time to show her what it was to be anything but a source of his own increasingly acute frustration.

Anyway, he kissed her neck. The telephone did not ring. He kissed her mouth, and still the telephone did not ring. Natalie reciprocated in various lovely ways, and even *then* the telephone did not ring. Adam began to believe that the telephone would never ring as, with a surge of shooting anticipation, he kissed Natalie's collar bones above her costume dress.

A knock came on the door.

'Enter!' Natalie cried, over Adam's shoulder.

Footsteps could be heard on the carpet outside, then Bruno L poked his head into the bedroom. He looked ravishing.

'Hi Nat, hi Adam,' he gleamed. 'Can you believe it? They sent *me* to fetch you all. There must be a hundred of us working here, and they send *me*. Anyway, chow time.'

Evidently the entire hotel and one other besides had been booked for the crew and cast. The restaurant and conservatory tables had been arranged like a prison mess, so that everyone faced a projection screen. Adam sat between Natalie and one of Bruno L's girls – not the one he had called a miserable whore. They were allowed to eat and get quite drunk before Serge stood up to introduce his most recent film. Made six years previously, *Antonine* told the story of a printer's apprentice working in pre-war Lyon who falls in love with the daughter of a wealthy restaurateur. They marry, are ostracized by the girl's family, and move to Paris to have a fabulous time during the Nazi occupation. The girl loses a baby and goes insane. The boy shows an interest in film.

Adam inwardly rolled his eyes as he heard the plot summary, and tried to find a comfortable position in his chair so that he might doze off when it all became too refined and artistic. The projector at the back of the conservatory clicked into action. Credits scrolled forebodingly over stunning images of Lyon, taken from a helicopter nosing low over the Rhône and the Saône. A sort of music unfamiliar to Adam, which was soon credited to Brahms, gave the images universal significance – or so it seemed to Adam who, despite all the reservations an envy of successful artists can generate, found himself physically and intellectually caught up in the story Serge's film had to show and tell.

The printer's apprentice was an immediately likeable fellow. Adam poured everyone within his reach another glass of wine as the winsome youth went cheerfully about his business, graceful under the random abuse of his brutish employer. Adam thought of Dick McDavis.

Then there was the girl with whom the apprentice immediately fell in love, who looked like a more rounded, rural version of Natalie. Adam wanted her to take off all of her clothes. Their falling in love was sweet, dangerous and believable. Their flight to Paris took a lot of guts, for a pair of young, inexperienced provincials. Their lovemaking, once the Nazis marched in, was impressive for its spiritual content. The couple's refusal to join the Resistance – on the grounds that they wanted to be left alone to enjoy each other, Nazis or no Nazis – reeked of credibility. The girl's descent into madness, explored with ample Christian allusion and allegory, was heartbreakingly real.

Adam had never enjoyed a film so much. When the girl lost her mind, and her young husband had to take her to the château sanatorium (having stolen and sold the diamond brooch of a Nazi officer's wife), Adam thought he would burst into tears. The crew applauded. Serge took a bow. He waited for the ovation to end, then explained that he had shown the film for one reason, and one reason only: It was perfect. His people should work to attain the standard of what they had just seen. Serge's ego was big enough for everyone in the room. His charisma seemed to shine through the dense cigarette smoke, as the film projector had done, and to form a halo behind his head. Adam was impressed.

'It was wonderful,' said Adam, his face close to Natalie's. 'I had no idea. I should never have doubted.'

'I did say he was a genius.'

'Can he do it again? Are you going to be a star, like that other girl?'

'That *other girl*,' said Natalie, her head lowered beneath Adam's jaw, 'lived with Serge for two years in Paris. She grew impatient, I believe the story goes. She had an affair with a musician. She never worked again, despite tacky comebacks.'

'So this would not be a blueprint for your . . . trajectory.'

'*Non*,' said Natalie.

Serge wanted to make another toast, a toast to his cast. He had never worked with any of them before. In particular, Serge had to say, he wished to single out the young, inexperienced girl everyone had seen doing such a terrific job on her first day of filming. To Natalie, he said, and to Natalie's marriage.

All glasses were raised in Adam and Natalie's direction. The couple returned the toast. They kissed, for the benefit of the boisterous crew. When that was done, Bruno's girl gave Adam an inordinately erotic kiss, and for the hell of it he kissed her back. It ran through his mind that he was starting to behave like Norman. Coffee was served, more cigarettes were smoked, and the room became noisy. The glass doors at the back of the conservatory were slid open, and some of the cast and crew strolled outside with their coffee or brandy. Slow, Latin music was piped in for the benefit of those who wished to dance. The moon was out, the air was calm, and the tower of Dubrovnik loomed over the hotel walls.

Adam recalled guiltily that his parents would have heard increasingly lurid or romantic reports of their son's activities, so he excused himself to ring them. He did so from his suite – where he would not have minded living for a year or more, just to make sure he liked it as much as he thought he did.

'Yes, what *is* it?' his mother said, which was not her customary telephone manner.

Adam identified himself.

'Oh, I'm *so* sorry. It's just that the telephone has been ringing every half hour – at all hours. Are you all right, darling? Where are you?'

'I'm in Italy. I don't really remember the name of the town. I met Natalie's parents . . . yes, charming. Drove all night to reach this place, where Natalie is filming.'

'It sounds wonderful. Exciting.'

'I hope you haven't been too upset by the things in the papers. Have you seen them?'

Adam's mother hesitated. '*Glanced* at some of them, I suppose, yes.'

'It's just the silly season, Mother. They'll print anything at all. Don't believe the ugly parts. We're absolutely fine.'

'It was so lovely to see you,' she said, evidently unconcerned by the press reports. 'And Natalie is such a dear.'

'She liked you, too.'

'I don't want to be a *mother* about this, darling, but some of the things we have . . . *glanced* at suggest that you two might be getting married. I hope you know how much it would mean to me – to both of us – if we were allowed just a *glimpse* of the proceedings?'

'Of course I know that. Nothing firm is planned.'

'No? Oh, that's fine. One paper said it was more of a *fait accompli*.'

'Hardly. We'll just have to see.'

'Your father wants to say a word, Adam. Please keep in touch, darling.'

'I will.'

Adam's father had never sounded so pleased. He was a different man. He wanted to know all about Natalie's parents, about their house in Ilani, their other residences, their politics. He said he couldn't wait to meet them. He noted that they were practically neighbours. He said he had located an old copy of *Army Ants*, and found it riveting. He repeated his wife's reminder that, as a rule, parents liked to attend their children's weddings. He expressed an interest in

237

Adam's brief description of the technicalities of film production. He offered Adam money. He said 'Well *done*,' four times, the fourth time in signing off.

Adam brushed his teeth, and went back downstairs.

The scene in the restaurant had deteriorated into revelry. Adam could not immediately locate Natalie in the crowd. Everyone looked exhausted, but their cast-party mood looked as if it would keep them going for some time. Adam ran into Claude, who had spent most of the day supervising the construction of the tower. He said he had just bought a house near by, so enchanted was he with the region's topography and inhabitants. He was thinking of selling his house in St Germain-en-Laye, but the house in Trouville would always be the place he went to unwind and be alone with his thoughts. Adam agreed that this was a sound policy – one he followed himself, in fact: he wouldn't dream of giving up his pied-à-terre in London, for example. Too right, Claude said.

Adam found that he spoke French perfectly, even colloquially. He guessed that this transformation had occurred by osmosis. Bruno's girl, whom Adam had kissed after Serge's toast to the soon-to-be-married couple's happiness, remarked that Adam was self-assured; she found this trait lacking in most men. Adam, falling in love with Bruno's girl, excused himself to look for his fiancée.

On the way, he fell in with a group of tough, cynical young Frenchmen who were plebeian members of Serge's crew. Their congratulations and bonhomie filled Adam's heart with a love for the common man that he had never known before. They gossiped easily about logistical problems Serge had faced in trying to film in Dubrovnik, and asserted that it had been their influence, rather than Serge's artistic inspiration, that had resulted in the wholesale move to Sampara. Art was one thing, they said; champagne on tap was another.

It was then that Adam spied Natalie outside the conservatory, in the moonlight, hanging lightly by both hands from Bruno L's neck. While some primitive instinct caused Adam to fly into an immediate combination of rage, jealousy and panic, he had to remind himself that in Natalie's circles it was not easy to distinguish between a passionate, amorous embrace and a casual greeting. He rubbed his temples and shielded his eyes, so that it would not be obvious that he was staring. He continued to chat with grip, set-builder and clapper-loader alike, while continuing to search his mind for reasons to explain Natalie's treachery. They could be rehearsing, he thought, as she reached up and admiringly stroked Bruno's lustrous hair. When she stopped doing that, Serge was not long in appearing at Natalie's elbow, perhaps to ask if she had recently been made to feel like a woman.

Actors, thought Adam. Public opinion held – as had Adam until now, for the sake of his moral self-preservation – that actors were the most egotistical, over-indulged members of modern society. Their well-known self-regard, luckily enough, was mitigated by the likelihood that they would get their just deserts and fade into obscurity before being psychologically prepared for oblivion. Adam thought these things, before reminding himself that the very qualities that had resulted in Natalie's becoming an actress – beauty, an outgoing nature and a sense of adventure – had been what drew him to her from the moment they met. So far, having met only one, he had not known an actress he didn't like.

Natalie caught Adam's eye, and waved to him. Adam excused himself from his new friends, and went outside. It was a warm, peaceful night. He approached her with his usual confident gait, slipped his arm around her waist, and kissed her above her ear; at the same time, in two relaxed, fluid motions, he shook hands with Serge and Bruno. Adam told the director how much he had loved *Antonine*, and how strongly he had identified with its protagonist. Serge looked sincerely appreciative of Adam's praise.

'Natalie's been telling us a bit about her life,' said Bruno. 'Isn't it incredible?'

Knowing how much stock people took in world travel and exotic modes of living, Adam had to agree. 'I was very lucky to meet her parents not long ago,' he said, to emphasize his closeness to the starlet. He did not mention that it was only yesterday. 'They certainly have lived interesting lives.'

Natalie, so alluring in her coquette's costume that Adam felt a knot in his abdomen, announced that Serge had come up with another brilliant idea. She wanted to know what Adam thought of it.

'Tell me the brilliant idea, then,' Adam said.

'Well, there's a wedding scene in the film. It's an exterior, informal thing – Serge,' she said bashfully. 'I don't want to speak for you. Tell Adam your idea.'

Serge folded his arms across his chest, over his round belly. He pursed his lips like a chess player having second thoughts about a move. His bald head, brown as a conker, wrinkled in thought.

'Yes,' he said at last. 'I have this idea. There is a wedding scene, very simple. It is scheduled tomorrow afternoon.'

'Serge keeps to a rigorous filming schedule,' said Bruno, articulately and sycophantically. 'Like Hitler's trains,' he added, with an unhappy transposition of dictators.

'Very brief, very simple,' Serge continued. He

switched to French: 'I was married in Dubrovnik. This is not something I have told anyone before now. I wish it to remain a secret between us. Do not tell the man standing next to you.' He meant Bruno. 'I have told Natalie because I love her and I want her to be as happy as I was when I was married to Mireille, thirty-eight years ago this week. I said to her that we will have the authorities of the town acting as themselves, and while they are there – with your permission, but it would be beautiful and significant – the two of you could be married in reality. Do you understand?'

'I understand,' said Adam, not looking at Natalie. His solicitor's mind had an objection or two. He pointed these out in a flat tone of voice, citing birth certificates, length-of-stay, potential religious conflicts, and other matters he would have to research to be certain about. 'So I admire the concept,' he concluded, 'but I doubt if it would be legal on such short notice.'

'Come now, Adam,' said Serge, in English again. 'This is *Italy*, my boy.' He rubbed his thumb and index finger together.

'Isn't that a romantic idea?' asked Natalie, referring not to bribery, but to a spur-of-the-moment wedding in a mock-up of Dubrovnik.

'I don't know if I have the right clothes,' said Adam. His legs had begun to tremble in the way he remembered they often did after the first skiing run of the season.

'Wardrobe,' said Bruno, helpfully. 'We're about the same size.'

'Are you marrying Natalie in the film?' Adam asked the American.

'No,' he replied. 'Well, sort of.'

'He is a ghost,' said Serge, as if that explained matters to a real-life groom.

'I'm a *ghost*? That wasn't in my script.'

241

'I excuse myself,' said Serge. 'There have been alterations.'

'This is the strangest conversation I have ever had,' said Adam.

Natalie stroked his back and laughed. 'You poor man,' she said. 'Come along, now. We'll have a little talk.'

'Of course,' said Serge. 'Go.'

'A *ghost*?' Bruno repeated, as Adam and Natalie headed for the beach.

Hand in hand, Adam and Natalie strolled along the beach in the moonlight. A stray dog joined them, wet and curious, then splashed away through the stagnant shallows of the Adriatic. Behind the hotel, Serge's nearly completed tower – only inches thick, according to the men Adam had met at the party – looked ancient and mighty in orange floodlights.

Adam tried not to watch himself, lest he burst out laughing at his loose European clothes, his windblown hair, his fashionable growth of beard, his fabulous girlfriend, his friends in the film industry, the Italian sand underfoot.

'An unusual day,' said Natalie.

'Yes,' said Adam. 'I got some sleep.'

'Are you having a good time? Is everyone being nice to you?'

'Sure. They've planned my wedding, haven't they?'

Natalie stopped walking and faced him. 'You don't have to take that too seriously, if you don't want to.'

'Don't I?'

'It is a nice idea, though.'

'What, the idea of Serge's plans, or the idea of getting married?'

'Both,' Natalie said, leaning against Adam's chest.

She felt young. Adam hugged her as reassuringly as he could, then cleared his throat to speak.

'Natalie,' he said, 'I think I ought to ask you something.'

She looked up at him, with her famous eyes. 'Yes?'

'Could you tell me . . . could you tell me why you like me so much?' Adam had been wondering this for some time now.

'I could ask you the same question,' Natalie said.

'I would have thought the answer was obvious. Everyone likes you.'

'Everyone likes you, too,' Natalie said.

'Something occurred to me during dinner,' said Adam, formally. He was unused to voicing his emotions. 'I was thinking about some of the things we have been through recently – well, they would have to be recently, I suppose.' Adam did not say them aloud, but he was thinking of little gestures, like holding his hand on top of the table, or making his parents think he was a super chap.

'You've been . . . friendly,' he said. It was the only word he could think of. 'What I want to say is that it occurred to me, just in the last hour, that you're the best friend I've ever had.'

'What a terrible thought,' said Natalie.

They began to stroll again, back in the direction of the hotel. The music was louder now, and the almost entirely male crew milled about the terrace under lanterns, not dancing.

'It was right here,' said Natalie, pointing down at the sand. 'This is where I became immortal.'

They looked at the sand together. Adam thought he should say something by the way of congratulation.

'I think your secret is you don't take it too seriously,' he said. 'Imagine if you were worried about everything, every step of the way. You would be paralysed.'

Natalie sniffed. 'If you don't think I'm serious, Adam,' she said, 'then you haven't been paying attention.'

*   *   *

'When I was a little girl, in Portugal,' Natalie said, 'a friend of my mother's got me alone and gave me some advice I have never forgotten. She was French, and had known my mother all her life. She seemed grand-motherly, but of course today I know she was in her mid-thirties. She had married a French businessman, she had two young children – they're friends of mine, today. Her life was as comfortable as can be. She lived in a big house with a tennis court, and a swimming pool. Her husband made a lot of money. He was conservative, religious, handsome, devoted – to the extent that his mistresses were not paraded about – and solid. He was like a smaller version of Didi's father. Her hair had begun to go grey, and it suited her. She was tall and thin, and she was the best tennis player in her social circle. She beat the men. She was proud of her children, both boys, and intended to raise them in the mould of their father. Every summer they went somewhere beautiful for two months – often to wherever we were staying, because she got on so well with my mother. Her husband joined us for half the time. One day, after giving me a tennis lesson, she sat down on the lawn with me and said she wanted to give me another lesson, this time about "being a woman". You can imagine what I thought she was going to say. I was only eight or nine years old, and I thought she was jumping the gun. Her children were playing badminton not far away, in perfect whites. Her husband sat by the swimming pool, reading a fat book about war. The servants were laying a long table and bringing out so much food it makes me guilty to remember. Anyone would have thought this was as happy as people could be. Safe, prosperous, loving, healthy. She said to me, "Make sure of only one thing, Natalie. Make sure you have an *interesting life.*" I don't suppose she expected me to be

244

listening – much less that I would remember what she said for ever. But it was the contrast between our surroundings and her sad, resigned tone of voice that shocked me. When I went back to school in Paris – it was one of the years we were allowed to go to school – I used to terrify my little friends with my new philosophy. "Make sure you have an *interesting life*," I told them. If they became delinquents, it was probably my fault.'

'What happened to your mother's friend?'

'Nothing changed. When her children left home, she began to talk about going into business, as my mother had done. She thought for a couple of years about what that business might be, then she died of a stroke. Everyone was so sad.'

It was Adam's turn to tell a story. 'When I was a little boy, living in London,' he said, 'my mother once disappeared for six weeks. You can imagine how difficult this was for the Ambassador. There was no suggestion of foul play, because my mother had left a convincing note saying she had gone away to think things over. She didn't say where she had gone. My father was understandably embarrassed. There was talk of hiring a lookalike to cover for my mother at official gatherings. I was only dimly aware of what was going on, but I knew more than my father thought I did. My nanny told me everything she knew. Imagine what it must have been like for my father. Think of the balance between worry and anger. He must have been afraid to inform his superiors in Brussels. He decided to hire a private detective, rather than to make an international incident out of what he must have known was a personal matter. The detective, retired from the world-famous Belgian army, spent all of five days not finding my mother before he gave up. She had taken a suitcase

245

of clothes, and plenty of cash. It was determined that she had not travelled by air. The detective was able to rule out any visits to her English relatives. She had simply disappeared. For the first week, the Ambassador told people she was ill. For the next two weeks, he told people she was seriously, seriously ill. For a further two weeks he said she had gone to the United States for treatment. You can see that he was digging a deep hole for himself, lying that way. If she failed to return, he would have to answer to his government. He began to cancel appoint ments. He paid even less attention to me than usual, and spent hours in the library staring at an antique globe. The last week of my mother's absence, I really thought he was going to shoot himself. Not out of grief or guilt, you understand, but embarrassment. He had aged ten years. He was pale and distracted. He walked with a stoop. People had started to talk. He put out the word that *he* was ill, so he didn't have to continue appearing alone at dinners. If Belgium were a real country, diplomatic relations might have suffered. History might have been changed.

'When my mother came home it was very odd. She arrived by taxi, at exactly the time she knew I would be ready to go to school. She kissed me on the cheek as she always did, walked me and my nanny to the car, and without another word she entered the house. I was not privy to my parents' reunion. The episode was never mentioned again.'

'Where do you think she had gone?'

'My guess,' said Adam, 'is that she was trying to have an interesting life.'

Because they were kissing publicly on the beach, it was inevitable that there would be catcalls from the most inebriated members of the crew on the terrace. Adam and Natalie waved in acknowledgement, continued kissing briefly, then returned to the party. Natalie danced with Serge, to warm applause. Bruno's girls danced together, betraying an erotic professionalism. Some of the crew members danced with each other, drinks aloft.

The party began to thin after midnight, because there was work to do early in the morning. Bruno had overindulged in something, and had to be carried away; his girls went along. Serge retired alone. The homosexual members of the crew paired off as best they could. Adam and Natalie, further bonded by their brief exchange of autobiography, took what food and drink they could from the leftovers on the terrace, and ascended to their suite.

They spent time on their food and drink. The conversation flowed. They floated together in the hot tub. Whenever the telephone rang, as it continued to do until past two o'clock in the morning despite instructions at the front desk that they should not be disturbed, Adam answered it and told whoever it was that the starlet needed to rest before her wedding. Even Norman was not allowed more than a minute before being disconnected, during which time he informed Adam that he had rushed out into the night to buy the papers, and at least one morning tabloid carried a nude photograph of him with the word 'Hero' obscuring the part of him that was illegal to print.

It was a revelation for Adam to go to bed for the first time with someone he actually knew rather well. Perhaps for this reason, it began as a lazy, almost nostalgic affair. They spoke of marriage. Adam had been loath to probe Natalie's opinion too deeply, even though he had made up his own mind. She seemed to like the idea in principle, but was not so starry-eyed that she failed to take publicity into account. Serge's *Te Deum* amounted to a desperate comeback attempt, no matter how loftily people spoke of his *oeuvre*. It was hard enough to draw attention to a serious film without missing opportunities to get members of its cast into the newspapers. With Adam already in the news, it might not be such a bad idea to strike while he was hot.

Adam asked if Natalie didn't think that something as important as marriage ought to be considered on other grounds than profitability to Serge. Natalie replied that they had been through all of the normal stages of courtship – including audiences with both sets of parents and Adam's potential brothers-in-law – and she saw no reason why bonuses ought not to be taken into account.

At this stage in their discussion, Adam had thought it proper to point out that he had no money at all. He reminded her of the Somerset hotel bill, and explained to her what it had meant to his lack of solvency. He said he understood why most of the world's cultures adhered to formal or informal rules of dowry. Natalie replied that money was not romantic. Adam said he could not agree more, but that in the case of hotels, air fare, delicious food and wine, romance had to be paid for somehow.

Adam tried to stress his unsuitability by saying that he was the poorest person he knew, and always had been. There was such a thing as relative poverty. He might have lived well all of his life, for one reason or another, but he could not recall a social occasion since university where it had not occurred to him that everyone else had money, and he did not. In a way it was unfortunate, he said, that he had been allowed to develop sophisticated tastes, and to take refined modern living for granted, without having been supplied with the funds necessary to purchase them. Natalie found this boring, and said they had better things to do than talk about money.

Adam had his pride, and worried that someone in Natalie's line of work would be accustomed to rarefied lovemaking practices of a kind he could only guess at, but probably not supply. Her delicious young body, now that he held it properly in his arms, was as taut as a bowstring and seemed to require more from him than he could possibly provide. He began to think his fears were misplaced when Natalie effectively took control and ravished him. When he was not crying out in pain, which Natalie misinterpreted as ecstasy, he listened with some alarm to the actress's histrionics; he could not believe these rather grotesque noises were necessary, or even sincere. She got so carried away that Adam horrified himself by wanting to slap her face. In a reversal of traditional roles, Natalie achieved some sort of cosmic climax, pushed Adam away and fell asleep.

Adam went into the bathroom and looked at himself in the mirror. He was not one to judge such things qualitatively, but what he had just been through had been shockingly unpleasant. He recalled some of the things Natalie had hissed into his ear as she appeared to lose control of her limbs, and he was embarrassed. Adam sat down on the toilet and held his head in his hands.

At six o'clock, Natalie opened her eyes and smiled. Adam hoped she couldn't tell by his expression, or by the force with which he held her, how deeply he had been thinking while she slept. He asked her if she felt ready for her big day. She replied that she thought so, but that first she had to satisfy her animal desires. Adam winced.

It was eight o'clock when Adam, showered and shaved, escorted Natalie downstairs. He placed her in the care of the production manager, who drove her away from the hotel in a white van. Adam sipped a cup of coffee by himself in the conservatory, awaiting instructions.

He was soon joined by one of Bruno's girls – the one with whom he had fallen in love for a few seconds the night before. Then Bruno himself appeared, looking less perfect than usual but still alarmingly handsome. These were Adam's new friends.

Bruno said he wasn't required on the set until noon, and that he had half a mind to spend the morning buying a house in the neighbourhood. Claude had done so the previous day, after all, and there did seem to be several quite private villas available with adequate views of the sea. He wished he had brought his gym. He missed his trainer. He had begun to read English poetry. Bruno could talk and talk.

Claude came into the conservatory bearing copies of Adam's coverage in the London press, transmitted to the hotel by a helpful clippings service. With all the insouciance a private man could muster when faced with his total public exposure, Adam glanced at the items like a punter checking a racing form.

'It's not so bad,' he said, as if there were anything in his life to date with which to compare the experience of being laid bare in tabloid newspapers. 'It appears that I am a Hollywood agent, with a long-standing grudge against this particularly powerful movie star.'

'*Aren't you?*' asked Bruno.

Adam read some more of the copy. One paper portrayed him as being on the run from Interpol. Another claimed he had demanded diplomatic immunity from the French authorities. A quality paper, in one hundred words, reported the Cannes skirmish more accurately than Adam himself could have done under hypnosis; it was not an interesting story. A middle-brow paper carried a photograph of Adam's father posing formally with Winston Churchill. In general, Adam was characterized as a wayward playboy. The star was seen to have been taken by surprise by a deranged fan. He had returned to Los Angeles for medical and psychiatric treatment, having abandoned his European round of publicity. His people had issued a statement remarking on the increasingly violent masses, from whom men like the star had to be protected by state police or the military; the French government was implicitly blamed for this particular infringement of the star's human rights. The star himself was said to harbour no resentment towards the French Interior Ministry, and had found it in his heart to forgive his crazed attacker.

'*Cool, hein?*' said Claude.

'*Oui,*' Adam replied. '*Cool.*'

Adam wondered how many of his friends would adorn their bathroom walls with framed pages of his disgrace. He recalled that on his own bathroom wall hung a similar photograph of Norman, emerging bleary-eyed from the Old Bailey. He tried to decide which was more embarrassing – to be caught naked on the balcony of a European starlet's hotel suite, or caught red-handed trying to bribe a creditor with heroin. This comparison put his predicament in perspective.

Bruno's girl had inspected the photograph with some care. 'You are an Adonis,' she declared.

Adam had to shake his head in wonder at this woman. Here it was, his supposed wedding day, and with a single remark Bruno's girl had made him want to run away with her. Twelve hours ago she had carried off the same feat simply by calling him self-assured. Adam pitied any man on whom she set her sights in earnest.

'Do you work out?' asked Bruno, who wore a white T-shirt to show off his not-so-exemplary physique.

'No,' Adam replied, bluntly, hoping this would cause

Bruno to rethink the years he had wasted in his private gym.

Bruno's girl, who had breasts like cricket balls, moved closer to Adam and touched her downy forearm against his. 'Are you going to marry Natalie today?' she asked. 'That's what Bruno says. She is so beautiful. And so talented.'

'We'll see,' Adam said.

'You are an amazing, amazing man,' said Bruno's girl.

Bruno was angry because his bodyguards had been held up at the airport. He blamed racism. Adam thought he detected resentment on Bruno's part that he had been separated from his bodyguards for nearly two days, and yet he hadn't been kidnapped or murdered yet.

Claude asked if Adam felt nervous.

'No,' he replied. This was the truth. 'I feel like another cup of coffee.'

'The waiter is hiding,' said Bruno. 'I'll go find him.'

'Serge is in a funny mood,' said Claude, confidentially, once Bruno had rounded the corner and gone inside the restaurant.

'Is he? In what way?' Adam enjoyed conversing in his new-found French, which seemed to work even in the morning.

'He woke me at six o'clock, and took me outside to stand with him in the little square we've built. I thought he looked depressed. It was bringing back too many difficult memories for him. He misses his wife very much.'

'Does he never visit her?'

'Every month I think, yes. But he misses his *wife*, not the woman he visits.'

'Have you met her?'

'No. I understand she is a tiny old lady now, who does not speak.'

'How ghastly.'

Claude undid his ponytail and splayed his thin blond hair on his shoulders. This angelic look was out of place atop such a big, rough man. He looked vulnerable and sensitive.

'I hope Serge doesn't have a breakdown,' Claude said. 'It happened last time, you know.'

'Did it? But the film seemed perfect. I loved it, by the way.'

'It took two years, eighteen months of which poor Serge spent in his swimming pool in Paris. You've seen it?'

'Yes.'

'He chained himself down there at the bottom of the pool, sucking on his air tank. People thought he would kill himself. His skin, always it was looking like a prune.'

'He seems to have made a full recovery.'

'Oh, yes. This was years ago, before I knew him. But he is a profound man, and what I saw early this morning distressed me.' It struck Adam that he had begun to like Claude, as he tended to like all those who worked hard for a living.

When Bruno returned, personally bearing a single cup of coffee for Adam, Claude put a finger to his lips and said, 'Do not dispirit the actor.' Adam and Bruno's girl indicated that they understood: Bruno must be kept in the dark. Perhaps it was nothing, anyway, and Serge would summon the nerve to stare down his ghosts.

Adam thanked Bruno for the coffee. Bruno smiled in the celebrated way he had, and Adam was reminded of a film he had seen in which Bruno played a tennis professional who was dragged into the violent machinations of the narcotics underworld. Now that Bruno had been so nice to him, Adam considered his new friend to be a first-rate film actor. Adam had *believed* that a millionaire sportsman would take time out from

253

sleeping with beautiful girls and sunning himself by his Florida swimming pool in order to be raked by automatic weapons fire for a period of weeks. Adam was sorry that Bruno had been arrested for statutory rape.

Bruno looked at his watch – the one that cost three-quarters of Adam's annual salary.

'I really ought to get ready,' he said, uncertainly, as if he weren't entirely sure what preparation for acting entailed. 'I suppose I should go to my room and . . . concentrate. My men will be here before long.' This meant his bodyguards. 'I can send them to buy a house. Do you think that's a good idea, Adam?'

'It does seem that you will be spending more time in Europe,' said Adam. 'Do you ski?'

'Yes, I ski.'

'Well, then. That's a short journey away.' Adam stopped himself from giving further rational property advice, when he remembered that the point of Bruno's purchase was merely to luxuriate in impetuosity. It was a strange way for a man in his early twenties to live, but it was real.

Bruno's girl thought the villa was an excellent idea. She also suggested that a particular model of four-wheel-drive vehicle would be necessary to negotiate the rough terrain. Bruno made a mental note to buy one, then excused himself. His girl went with him. Claude suggested that Adam accompany him to the set. He mentioned that he already owned the special four-wheel-drive vehicle Bruno's girl had said she wanted. Claude said he might give it to her.

Their drive to the set lasted twenty seconds or so, including the time it took Adam to admire Claude's wheels. Workmen still laboured frantically to construct an authentic Croatian atmosphere. The scene was nothing like the previous day's miniature operation. The area was crowded with vans and trucks and driven-looking human beings carrying unlikely objects. The focus of their attention seemed to be a stone fountain, artificially weathered and distressed, and a section of crumbling wall cleverly built of wood and painted styrofoam. To Adam's eye it looked like an appropriate setting for an execution by firing squad. Claude assured him this was a replica of the spot where Serge and Mireille had been married, alfresco.

Adam put on his dark glasses. The sun had risen on another cloudless, hazy day. He recognized several faces from the previous night's party, and he admired their resilience. Claude left to attend to important matters inside a small inn, where he had set up an office; this left Adam free to roam about, feeling in the way.

Serge ran a tight set. No-one was unoccupied. Tourists and villagers were kept behind wooden barriers. When Adam walked in front of them, he was photographed. A German woman beckoned him over and asked for his autograph. When he wrote his name in her address book, she looked at his signature and beamed with delight.

'I'm not in the film,' he said to her, in English. 'I'm nobody.'

'Nobody?'

'I'm afraid so,' said Adam. He leaned down and crossed under the barrier to her side. He stood next to her, just another tourist, and sensed her embarrassment as if it were an odour. Her husband said something in German that sounded as if it meant, 'I told you so, you silly, stupid woman.'

Adam squeezed out of the crowd and circled round the back of the fake tower. Tourists from the one hotel not taken over by Serge's company had begun to trickle down to the beach. Adam bought a glass of orange juice from a pretty street-vendor who wore a bikini under her loose blue apron, and a white visor. She was so pretty, in fact, that Adam wanted to advise her to try her luck in the fast, interesting world around the corner. She could sleep with Serge that afternoon and, in the director's current mood, marry him by sundown.

'What's your name?' Adam asked the girl, in French, trying on his new charisma.

'Anna-Maria,' she replied, in all the world's languages.

'That's a beautiful name,' he said. He had never spoken this way before. He leaned sleazily on the girl's sticky counter. 'My name is Adam.'

The girl smiled. She cut an orange in two.

Adam leaned close to her. 'Do you have a boyfriend, Anna-Maria?' He listened carefully to his own voice. He was without guilt, in the certainty that a pretty girl like Anna-Maria spent most of her day fending off unpleasant men of all nationalities.

'No, I don't have a boyfriend.'

'I'm with the film people, over there,' said Adam. 'Have you been watching them?'

'I'm not interested,' said Anna-Maria.

'You wouldn't like to meet them? You could be in the movies, you know. A star.'

As Adam heard himself say this, he had to wonder at how naturally it had come to him to use fabricated power, even as an experiment.

Anna-Maria looked up at him from beneath her visor. 'You're serious?' she said.

She believed him. Her expression was so trusting and pure that Adam was quick to retreat.

'I'm serious that you're beautiful, and could be a star,' he said. 'But I'm not in the business. I'm engaged to one of the actresses.'

'Congratulations,' she said, not in the least deflated.

'Thanks,' said Adam. He finished his juice, and placed the plastic cup on the counter. 'Goodbye, then, Anna-Maria,' he said, turning to leave.

'Adam,' said Anna-Maria, in English this time, only slightly accented.

'Yes?'

'Your French sounds pretty awful, you know.'

Adam found a souvenir shop that sold some of the previous day's British tabloids, then sat on a bench to read about himself. He ripped out a page that carried a photograph of him and Natalie outside her parents' house. He did not look entirely deranged. He carefully folded the page and inserted it in his jacket pocket. He remained seated on the bench for half an hour, waiting to be recognized by passers-by. When this did not happen, he continued his stroll.

Sampara was not an attractive town, and probably never had been. Its crumbly, narrow streets spoke to Adam not of quaintness, but of cholera. Mass tourism could debase a plague pit, and Sampara had not been spared its comprehensive vandalism. No vulgarity had been spared in ensuring the town's aesthetic suicide. Serge's ambitious set would presumably remain standing for a few years, and attract future waves of visitors if the film became a success.

Adam caught his reflection in the window of a shop that sold useless pieces of plastic and cheap photographic equipment, and noticed that he had lost weight. He looked almost slight, almost Italian. He had been transformed into a European man. A sun-lightened wave had appeared in his hair.

The streets were full of brightly dressed people, half of them small children. National stereotypes screamed from their faces and attitudes. Those omnipresent, obsidian men in tribal costume rattled drums and thrust leather belts or carved animals at the tourists walking by; Adam could not have been alone in wondering how supply and demand could account for their number, when no-one ever seemed to purchase one of their pitiable trinkets.

With other such shallow thoughts in his still quite relaxed mind, Adam reached the top of a steep incline. Here the town abruptly ended. From that high vantage point he could look down the coast to an enclave of villas of the type Claude had bought and Bruno coveted. Lucky people, Adam thought. At a low moment he had once paced off the distance from one wall of his London flat to the other, practising this until, like a prisoner, he could do so with his eyes closed: twelve small steps, right turn, through the door, six small steps, window overlooking someone else's beautiful garden.

Adam started back down the hill. He took off his jacket and slung it over his shoulder, and felt himself moving his hips in an un-British way. In his European clothing and with his lack of touristic accoutrements, he could have been a prosperous young villa-owner walking into town to visit his aged mother. His body felt loose, healthy and inexplicably rested.

Near the bottom of the hill, Adam encountered a small crowd gathered at one of the crude wooden barricades, on the other side of the artificial square from the place he had signed his autograph for the overeager German tourist. He noticed the entrance of a small inn with a leafy terrace on the first floor, and decided to watch the proceedings from there. He entered, and a woman dressed as a matronly inn-proprietor immediately addressed him in Italian. He found to his surprise that he was able to say to her in her own language that he would like to eat some food and drink some wine on her terrace. She said nothing could be more normal.

He climbed the stairs, went through a small restaurant, and emerged into the hot sunlight. There were three tables on the terrace, two of which were unoccupied; at the third sat two young tourists, two men, whose Swedish nationality was evident even before their somewhat absurd-sounding voices were audible. Adam could see how much they envied his European demeanour and sophistication. They drank soft drinks, and wore clothing of an athletic orientation, of the kind a pole vaulter might wear before stripping down for his jump.

In the square, an assistant director barked instructions through a loud-hailer, telling the crowd that they were welcome to watch, but would be severely punished if they made the slightest noise or flashed their cameras. Another assistant was recruited to repeat this warning in Japanese. There were pockets of argument here and there, one possibly having to do with the removal of an ancient tree that presumptuously cast its shadow on part of the styrofoam wall. A separate group was made up of a dozen extras, some of them real people, who were demanding to be told their motivation.

Adam was brought an unmarked litre-bottle of red wine and a plate of tomato-and-onion salad by a plain young woman wearing blue jeans and a too-tight tube-top. She paused and asked Adam if he knew anything about the film. In an Italian he felt certain he ought not to know, but using mainly nouns, proper names and hand gestures, Adam conveyed to the woman the importance of the moment. The Swedes were mightily impressed. A black cat came out of the restaurant and rubbed its body obscenely against Adam's shins. He felt like someone who had made a great deal of money, illicitly.

The waitress leaned buxomly over the railing to get a better view. She recognized Bruno L, who had stepped at that moment from a small caravan. His smile could be seen even at a distance, like the sun-glint off an assassin's rifle. He wore a blue, spangled suit and a white bow tie. His hair appeared to have been dusted with silver. Adam remembered that the script had been rewritten so that Bruno played a ghost. The waitress remarked upon how beautiful he was. Adam had to tell her that he was Bruno's friend.

The waitress turned her star-struck eyes on Adam, and almost lost her footing.

'You are a friend of his?'

'*Si*,' said Adam, in perfect Italian.

'You could introduce me?'

'*Si*.'

'I would die,' said the waitress.

'He has a girlfriend,' Adam warned, partly in English.

'Oh of course he does,' said the waitress, still in Italian. 'I'd just want to touch him once.'

'Why would you want to touch him?'

'Oh, well, because he is . . . who he is.'

The waitress became quite flustered as she tried to respond to Adam's question. When he pressed her, she seemed not to have the slightest idea why the sight of a famous man had made her exclaim to a stranger that she wanted to touch another stranger. Adam thought this might explain Bruno's absent bodyguards: if happy, gentle waitresses wanted to touch him, then surely mankind could supply her opposite, who wanted to harm him.

Bruno looked exposed as he approached the fountain in the middle of Serge's square. He tried to lean casually against it, then found how insubstantial it was. He was waved away by a pair of men who were trying to arrange for water to spout from its centre. He put his hands in his pockets and walked with studied casualness towards the styrofoam wall, which he might have knocked over had two more of Serge's hands not warned him away. As a last resort he fell in with the extras, who offered him cigarettes that he chose to decline.

Adam did not have the Italian to point out to the waitress how tiresome her idol's job was in practice. He tried to make this obvious by yawning and sipping his wine and not paying any attention to Bruno at all. Still, she clung to the railing and could not take her eyes off the actor. Adam seethed with anti-American self-righteousness, but only briefly; his primary emotion was embarrassment.

The production manager noticed Adam on the terrace, and waved. Adam waved back, like a Pope. The waitress turned and looked at Adam, then asked if there were anything she could do for him.

'Not for now,' said Adam, in English. This reinforced his international reputation, especially where his Swedish neighbours were concerned.

An English couple appeared on the terrace, and seated themselves at the third table. They were identifiable as English as easily as a mountain might be known to be snow-capped: on sight and unquestionably. The woman, in her early forties, her buttocks only just accommodated between the arms of her chair, seemed distressed by her surroundings and blamed them on her weedy, sunburned husband. Adam went through a mental checklist of their likely region, class, education and employment; he would have bet his car on his conclusions.

They were not happy to be in Sampara. The woman made it obvious to anyone in her vicinity who spoke English that her level of cultural refinement demanded more from a visit to Italy than a sub-par lunch in a tourist resort. She required authenticity. She was not like the others, the sheep, the sun-seekers. She knew people who had written *books* about Italy. Adam had by now pinned down her London postal code, if not the exact street. Her husband, icily calm, gestured towards the square and remarked that it might be of some anthropological interest to take in an hour or so of a film's genesis. His wife wasn't sure, until she picked out Bruno L among the extras near the styrofoam wall. She could not conceal her excitement, hard as she tried. She abandoned any pretence of sophistication, any superior knowledge of Italy. She had seen a film star in the flesh. Adam could hear her report to her friends: 'No, actually, he's quite *charming*. Nothing at all like his reputation, of course. Really as friendly as can be.'

Now Natalie emerged into the square from a humble van. The sight of her caused Adam some distress. He thought he might find it difficult to use body language or Italian innuendo to make it clear to the waitress and the Swedish eavesdroppers and the English tourists that this was the woman he had spent the night with and was scheduled to marry. The waitress named Natalie aloud, which was disconcerting. The two Swedes made primitive noises. The English couple muttered something under their collective breath. Natalie wore what must have been Serge's idea of a wedding dress suitable to the memory of a child bride who had grown up to go insane. This was a figure-hugging, bright white affair, probably elastic, that ended above the knee. She wore a miniature spray of white flowers in her hair. She carried a pair of white shoes in one hand, and was barefoot. She was attended by three women identically dressed in black leather skirts and black leather jackets.

Adam sipped his wine in a worldly way, and prodded a slice of tomato with his fork. The waitress managed to pry herself from whatever fantasy involving Bruno she had worked up, and went over to ask the English couple what they wanted. The woman ordered in broken Italian. When the waitress went back inside the restaurant, the woman remarked to her husband how sweet she had been.

A stripped-down jeep, possibly of military origin, had delivered Serge to his set. He was a fat ball of energy. He fell into agitated conversation with his cameraman, then scuttled over to Bruno and the extras for some final instructions. Everyone seemed to know what was required, and a scene gradually arranged itself between the fountain and the wall. The camera, still affixed to its dolly, waited to capture a performance. Natalie stood patiently in the shade of the tree that Serge's men had been convinced not to cut down.

Adam looked at Natalie, and swallowed. Love, or its close approximation, was strong stuff. He thought how easily he might have been married to Didi right now, but for her farsightedness. He was more conscious than most people of life's unceasing bifurcations, each leading to a route that would constitute a final biography. These occurred with nauseating regularity in the young, who were lucky enough usually to be oblivious of their significance. Adam had not yet abandoned all of his ambitions, but most had been whittled away by time or circumstance. Someone like Natalie – so pretty and brave down in the square, ready to put her back to the wall and face the camera – was at a stage where decisions presented themselves almost constantly; at her age she could afford to seize apparently random opportunities and hope for the best. Someone would take care of her.

Serge had lost his temper with a young man whose job seemed to be to throw a chicken into the camera's field of view. It was rather shocking to see Serge shouting and kicking at the dust underfoot and having to be restrained by an assistant director from flying at the culprit's throat. Adam thought this was a bit more like the birth of art than what he had seen so far, but he could see why Claude had been worried. The hapless crew member was sent away, his crime unexplained to onlookers. Serge was brought a glass of iced water, and Claude made an effort to calm him down. Almost everyone carried a telephone, which caused an unnatural chirruping in the birdless square.

Bruno and another actor were the first to be filmed. They stood against the wall, smoking and looking at their watches. Bruno emoted so successfully that Adam was able to place his character as the ghost of a departed lover spectrally realizing his dream of a marriage made impossible by his untimely death in a street fight. During the subsequent repetitions of this scene, in which Bruno had to say perhaps twenty words, Adam tried to make eye contact with Natalie. When he succeeded, and she waved joyfully up at him, Adam's fellow diners suddenly went quiet.

'My fiancée,' Adam said, when Natalie returned her attention to the action in front of the camera. 'I mustn't get in the way.'

He could see the English woman streaking back through the remarks she had made in the last half hour, searching for reasons to be retroactively embarrassed. She had taken Adam for a local.

It was wonderful to observe the almost unbearable tedium of film-making. The level of job satisfaction seemed to grow in reverse order of hierarchy. The most junior grip had more constructive and distracting things to do than his immediate superior, and so on up to the actors, whose job required above all the ability to stand still for long periods when hot and thirsty.

Serge was angry again. Perhaps he had made a psychological error in attempting to film a climactic wedding scene so early in the shooting schedule. He kicked at the ground again, and shouted at the crowd behind the barrier. He verbally abused his sound man, and only just stopped himself from kicking him. Claude had to intervene again. Serge calmed himself, looked up at the sun, looked at his watch, called for action.

It was Natalie's turn. Evidently she was to come running down a narrow, cobbled street, late for her wedding, and express relief that her boyfriend had waited for her. She was to ignore Bruno, who was a ghost, and marry the other chap. It was heartbreaking.

The scene was rehearsed four times before film was expended. Adam was impressed with his girlfriend's acting. Natalie ran down the street in a way that suggested that the audience was already intimately familiar with her naked body, which it would be by the time Serge finished with her. Adam's personal familiarity was infinite, so he was perhaps more receptive to her subtle clues.

Natalie ran down the street again. She stopped, pushed her hair out of her face, smiled, ran again towards her lover. Serge clapped his hands. Natalie sighed with pleasure and relief, and fell into her fellow actor's arms. Bruno pouted, still in character.

The extras were called in. Natalie retreated to the shade and looked up at Adam. She hopped up on her toes and waved. Adam raised his glass to her. His neighbours on the terrace stared at him in awe.

The filming dragged on. The crowds swelled. Serge appeared to become cramped or annoyed, and enlisted the services of local police to push back the onlookers. Adam finished his wine, and a main course of veal. The Swedish men departed. They were replaced by a middle-aged French couple who were connoisseurs of Serge's work, and therefore rapt.

From what he could overhear of their conversation,

they were both doctors. They had a high opinion of their own cultural taste. They rated Serge – though they disapproved of his private life, which they considered pretentious. When they noticed Natalie – now kissing the French actor as Bruno hovered ghost-like in the background, weeping with an ecstatic combination of love and grief – they presumed aloud that she was Serge's latest muse and lover. Adam cleared his throat, and came close to correcting them.

Adam ordered coffee, and paid the waitress for his meal using his forlorn credit card. He took the folded piece of newspaper out of his pocket, and read about himself again. He didn't sound so bad. He sounded like someone who had made his way in the world.

'Excuse me,' said the waitress.

Adam looked up to see the waitress – and behind her the English and French couples – looking at him as if he had fainted and only barely been revived.

'Yes?'

'Someone wants you, there. Look.' The waitress pointed over the railing at the square.

Adam sat up straight and looked down, where Serge himself was gesturing up at him. He waved one hand impatiently, and stamped his foot. Adam indicated that he would be right down.

'Sorry,' said Adam, to his audience of five. 'I'm on.'

Short as he was, Serge nevertheless put an arm around Adam's shoulders and spoke to him rapidly in French. He needed to see Adam and Natalie together. He needed to see love. Was this understandable? He wanted everyone to go away for half an hour while he watched Adam and Natalie love each other in the sunshine next to the wall. He admitted to nerves. He could not remember what love looked like. Claude was a smarmy, proletarian, money-minded cretin – he wanted everything

266

finished yesterday. Natalie was a goddess, the discovery of a lifetime. He had never seen her so poised and ravishing, he said, in a way implying that Adam had a role in her transformation. He had the utmost respect for Adam as a man and as a potential business associate. For now, he needed him to embody love in the sunshine.

'Delighted,' said Adam.

Natalie skipped over in her bare feet and kissed Adam on the cheek. She was suitably deferential to Serge, but she could not conceal her pleasure in having done such a good morning's work.

'Come, over here,' said Serge. 'Everyone, be gone!'

His crew scattered. Claude glowered like Richelieu, then slunk away.

Adam and Natalie stood next to each other in front of the styrofoam wall. Serge paced back and forth without looking at him, rubbing his face with both hands. 'You may speak,' he said.

'I feel slightly self-conscious,' said Adam.

'I missed you,' said Natalie, her eyes huge.

'Did you? I mean, I missed you too.' Adam felt certain that Natalie was still acting, or half-acting. Whatever she was doing, it was for Serge's benefit rather than her own or Adam's.

'Oh, Adam. This short time we've had together, I . . .' Her bosom heaved, and she looked at her feet. 'I've never fallen in love so fast.'

Serge stopped pacing, stopped rubbing his face with his hands. He moved closer in a stooped, inquisitive posture. He extended his hands in a gesture of supplication. His eyebrows came together and his lips parted.

'Natalie, I'm . . . in agreement,' said Adam.

Natalie's eyes pleaded with him to play along with Serge's game; either that, or they expressed a sincere emotion of some other kind.

'Last night,' she said, smoothing her dress over her hips. 'Last night was something I'd only . . .'

Adam fell out of character and looked at Serge, who wore the expression of someone watching his house burn down.

'Natalie, not here.'

'I love you, Adam.'

'Well, of course. I love you, too,' said Adam, stiffly.

Serge appeared to like Adam's repressed delivery; perhaps his French lead actor's performance had been too superficial. The director clapped his hands and kissed Adam on the throat. Then he cursed, and punched a hole in the wall with his fist. He uttered the French word for 'whore' half a dozen times. He grasped Natalie's chin between his thumb and index finger and kissed her on the mouth.

Adam put his hands in his pockets and watched the director's emotions play themselves out, one by one. He glanced over at the thinning crowd of tourists behind the barrier, and shrugged his shoulders at them. He watched as Natalie soothed and manipulated her director back into near-rational thought. She touched his shoulder with her fingertips, and reeled him in until he sobbed into her bosom. Claude appeared from behind the wall, telephone tight to his ear, mouth spluttering dire tidings. He caught Adam's eye, and seemed to demand an explanation for Serge's tantrum. Adam shrugged again, and looked down at his feet.

After a minute or two Serge disengaged himself from Natalie's bosom and began to shout orders. He needed an hour alone. He needed a helicopter. He needed the Italian Coast Guard. He needed Claude to stop being such a coward. He needed a telephone. He needed a bottle of wine. He needed a piss.

Adam took one or two steps backwards, hands still in his pockets, and watched Serge blossom. The director had until today contained his frustrations so effectively that Adam had come to think of him as a gentle, sophisticated, philosophical craftsman.

Serge needed a woman. He needed his wife. He needed a particular kind of ham that even Italians could not provide. He needed a fast car. He needed Verdi.

Adam moved over next to Natalie and took her hand. 'Maybe we should get out of the way,' he said.

Natalie rolled her eyes. 'I hope he doesn't have a stroke.'

Serge wanted someone *trustworthy*. He wanted adequate support. He wanted a hell of a lot more money. He wanted to be in Los Angeles. He wanted to have worked in the Thirties. Whore, whore, whore.

Adam and Natalie backed away from the director. Claude mouthed his advice that they return to the hotel. To do so, they had to penetrate a crowd of rubber-neckers eight or ten deep. Natalie signed four autographs before they were through, with Adam pushing gently from behind and keeping an eye out for assassins.

'What do you think is bothering him?' Adam asked, as they walked quickly over open ground towards the hotel.

'You know him as well as I do,' said Natalie. 'He's upset about not being in love anymore.'

'I think it's you,' said Adam. 'He thinks he's in love with you. I thought he was going to lash out at me.'

'Now that would have been something.'

'Yes. I could have wrestled him to the ground and confirmed my reputation, prolonged my fame.'

'Someone showed me the cuttings, this morning,' said Natalie. 'Very classy, Adam.'

In the safety of the empty hotel, Adam and Natalie naturally repaired to the bar. She carefully unpinned the flowers from her hair and placed them on the

269

counter. When the waiter appeared, Natalie ordered a glass of water for herself and a glass of wine for Adam.

'I'm working, after all,' she explained.

'Let's hope so,' said Adam. 'I haven't seen your contract, but I wouldn't be surprised if in the event of the film's collapse, even though principal photography began yesterday—'

'Adam, please. Of course he'll make the stupid film. Why can't everyone relax? Anyway, I don't care if I'm paid or not. The experience is plenty.'

'As your lawyer, I have to advise you never to think that way.'

Their drinks arrived. Natalie was flushed with excitement and frustration. She changed her mind and asked the waiter for a bottle of champagne. In the interim, she shared Adam's glass of wine.

'What the hell,' she said.

The next few minutes caused Adam to lose most of his composure. The waiter brought Natalie a telephone, into which she spoke to Jane Wheeler in London. Claude blundered in to the bar, saw that Natalie was busy, then left again. Natalie finished speaking to Jane Wheeler, and rang her parents; a photographer; a friend in Barcelona; a British journalist she had stood up a week ago; Jane Wheeler again. Adam didn't know where to turn his thoughts, and wished he had a magazine to read. Claude returned and sat down next to him. When Natalie at last stopped talking on the telephone, Claude was ready with his instructions.

Serge had locked himself in his room, alone. Claude had been unable to find him a woman, even though he had offered quite a lot of money to a girl near the sea wall who sold freshly squeezed orange juice to tourists. Serge hadn't been kidding about the helicopter – at least Claude didn't think so.

Natalie crossed her legs and asked Claude for a

cigarette. Adam had not seen her smoke before. There was a certain imperious edge to her voice when she asked Claude what Serge could possibly want with a helicopter. Evidently it did not take long for actresses to take on board their vital importance in the world.

Claude said he had no idea about the reason for the helicopter, and added that in fact the helicopter had become *three* helicopters before Serge had finished with his demands. The helicopters were being arranged. There was an airfield just four miles north of town. Claude hadn't been told what kind of helicopters, so he had ordered the biggest ones that could be found on one hour's notice.

'I'm really in the way, aren't I, Claude,' said Adam, dejectedly. 'I ought to disappear.'

Claude looked appalled. 'My God, no,' he said. 'Serge is still firm that there will be a wedding. I just have a terrible feeling . . .'

'Go on, Claude,' said Adam. 'Tell us.'

'I have this feeling, you know, that the set has not met Serge's expectations. He said "plenty of fuel". I think he wants to go to Yugoslavia this afternoon. Anyway, he calls it Yugoslavia still. I have put the crew on alert,' Claude said, grandly. 'They have their passports.'

Natalie seemed to like this idea. Adam, on the other hand, had put Yugoslavia on the top of the list of the nearby countries he did not wish to visit. This was not cowardice on his part, but an easy moral choice. There was a density of hateful people over there, just across the water; if he could not separate the good from the evil, which even experts seemed patently incapable of doing, he wasn't going to take the chance of accidentally being pleasant to genocidal barbarians. There had been enough of that in his family.

Claude went away to continue trying to stem the tide

of chaos. Natalie stubbed out her cigarette and exhaled inexpertly into Adam's face.

'It's OK with you, isn't it?' she asked.

'It isn't as if I have a great deal of say. None of you have.'

'No, but that can be fun. Did you think we would come here?'

'No.'

'Did you think we would be getting married in Yugoslavia?'

'No.'

'Have you ever *been* to Yugoslavia?' she asked, as if visiting a foreign country might be on a plane with marriage, experiencewise.

'Actually, yes.'

'What is it like?'

'It's the same as anywhere else.'

'Oh, Adam. You're so jaded,' said Natalie, who was not badly travelled herself.

'What I meant was, it's like anywhere else in that ideally people eat chicken and swim in the sea and get tipsy and work hard most days and play board-games in the evening and gossip about their neighbours and sport and try to stop their children from doing dangerous things and die one after the other more or less according to a natural schedule. And like anywhere else, there are worse periods than others, when this sort of thing isn't possible, and when people like me have to sit around dinner tables talking about how ghastly it is.'

'Maybe we could do some good,' said Natalie.

Adam had long fantasized about holding forth in court when someone said something so fabulously naïve. He had deep resources of oratory, or so he had come to believe since his best man's speech. In this instance, he restrained himself.

'I rather doubt it,' he said.

'When this is over, we'll have good fun,' said Natalie, optimistically.

Adam thought of what excitement might be wrung from watching Natalie try to publicize *Te Deum*, and her unending protests that prolonged nudity and convincing, sweaty orgasms had been necessary to show her character's . . . *discomfiture* in the bloody maw of post-Holocaust Europe.

'We might,' said Adam.

'Cheer up, for heaven's sake. You could show some gratitude, you know.'

Adam raised a heavy eyebrow. Delicious ripostes welled behind his tongue. He thought of how often in his life he had swallowed his bile. He had invested good manners with such importance that people like Dick McDavis escaped with a deferential nod instead of grievous verbal harm. He had taken it on trust that politeness and reserve would out in the end; he had not been paying attention.

'I'm *awfully* grateful,' he said. His eyebrow remained contemptuously arched, like a sarcastic quotation mark.

Natalie gulped unattractively at her champagne. She said she wished Serge would decide what he wanted to do. The whole situation was wildly romantic, she said, but it would be a shame to lose the day's light. She still wore her acting make-up, which seemed to accentuate something hideous in her personality.

Adam was almost alarmed by the quick lucidity of his thoughts. He was a man of few talents, but he revelled in the consistently smooth and acute workings of his mind. He thought he might be a genius.

Natalie filled his glass, then her own. She uncrossed her legs, then recrossed them in the other direction. Here elegant posture was unaffected by increased fame. She had left her shoes back at the set.

273

'I think Bruno might have been the problem,' she said. 'Don't you agree? He seemed a little stiff. It's a leap for him, of course, not to have a gun in his hand.'

'I wasn't watching that closely.'

'And of course his voice will have to be dubbed over. He sounds like a surfer. I can't *imagine* why Serge cast him, unless it's for the publicity. It can't be worth the trouble. If Serge really knew what he was doing, he'd put *you* in the role.' Natalie had a thought. 'Maybe *that's* it. Do you think that's what he is going to do? He had you go through the motions. Oh, Adam, just imagine.'

'That isn't what Serge is thinking.'

'How do you know?'

'Because Serge is a professional. This isn't a game.' Adam felt wise.

'It seems like a game to me.'

If he had drunk one more glass of wine, Adam might have delivered a soliloquy in which he spelled out the reasons Natalie had been hired, in order of importance to the director's sexual and artistic needs. Natalie would have to find out for herself.

'Were you happy with your performance?' Adam asked.

'I enjoyed it a lot more than I thought I would. Acting,' said Natalie, who had acted for less than five minutes of printed film, 'is all about *chutzpah*.'

'Is it?'

Natalie replied by taking Adam on a syllable-by-syllable tour of the line she had spoken during the day's filming. She was particularly proud of the way she had stressed the interrogative '*Toujours?*', and the way in which a strand of hair had fallen from her coiffure into her eyes as she did so. She had blown the strand of hair away without losing her character – and the strand of hair had stuck to the tiny white flowers. It had been a precious moment, if Natalie was any judge. A lesser actress might have lost her concentration when the strand of hair fell into her face.

'And what did *you* do,' Natalie asked, 'to pass the time?'

Bruno came into the bar, a bodyguard on each flank. Still in ghost costume, he seemed to float along without moving his legs. He looked slightly dishevelled, as if his expedition through the adoring throng had caused him trouble. His bodyguards were not the hulking bouncers Adam might have expected, but dangerously lean and well-dressed black men with identical goatees and superior airs. They wore crisp white shirts and silk ties, and carried their jackets over their shoulders. They looked professional, alert, powerful, fast and utterly redundant in an empty hotel bar in the peaceful town of Sampara.

'Serge is ready to roll,' said Bruno, enthusiastically.

'What does that mean?' Adam asked. The bodyguards had not been introduced.

'He came back out to the square and told everyone to pack up and get ready to go.'

'The whole crew?' Natalie asked, waving flirtatiously at Bruno's men, who had staked out the entrance of the conservatory.

'I don't know. Definitely me, you, Adam.'

'I can't imagine I'm needed,' said Adam.

'Oh, sure,' said Bruno. 'He's really thrilled, you know, about your wedding. Congratulations, by the way.'

'Thanks,' said Adam and Natalie in unison, an octave apart.

'I had a word with Claude,' said Bruno, leaning on the bar. 'There are so many arrangements he has to make. Poor bastard, really. But he has to put up with it. Also the publicity will help. They can't have been making a lot of films in Yugoslavia, lately.'

Natalie reached over the bar and got Bruno a glass. She poured champagne for everyone, and proposed a toast: 'To Serge's whims.'

Adam didn't drink. He had never approved of frivolousness, and this was one aspect of his character that had gone unchanged during his trek into Europe. Only recently had he identified the paradox of his ambitions: he wanted things for himself that he disapproved of and despised in others. Subconscious motivations had propelled him along through life – he accepted that – and circumstances had dictated the majority of his practical decisions. To achieve Bruno's or Serge's or Claude's or Natalie's idea of success, one had to have a reckless personality and not a great deal to lose. This was missing in Adam; besides, he had always known his place.

Bruno drained his glass, snapped his fingers at his men, and went away to find out what was going on. He looked exhilarated, despite what Natalie had said about his performance. One of his bodyguards preceded him out of the room; the other walked backwards behind them, scowling.

Natalie rubbed Adam's shin with one of her bare feet. Adam was reminded of the black cat on the restaurant terrace.

'We'll, *I'm* excited,' she said. 'Don't look so glum.'

Adam smiled at her and stroked her knee with his non-drinking hand. He sometimes felt he could see people's future in their eyes, a product of his finely tuned, defensive powers of social observation.

'I won't be glum,' he said. 'I was just about to say that you have to be awfully careful.'

'Are you going to give me fatherly advice? I'm not *that* young, Adam.'

'I wouldn't dream of giving you advice.'

'Except to be careful.'

'Even that is probably counterproductive, in your line of work.'

Natalie looked serious. 'Do you think there is such a thing as being a natural actress?' she asked.

'Yes, I do.'

'I think that may be what I am.'

'I wouldn't be the least surprised.'

'There is a great deal of pressure on me,' she said. 'I'm just starting to feel it. I don't know what changes have been made in the script, but if Bruno's character has much more to do with things, I'm going to have to carry him.'

'You'll do fine, I'm sure.' Natalie's blossoming self-importance would have been even more offensive, had Adam not been exposed to the egotists who engendered it in her.

The production manager crashed into the bar, her clipboard and lorgnette in hand.

'Quickly,' she said, in French. 'To the airfield. We leave in half an hour for Dubrovnik.' She dashed away without making entirely certain they had understood.

'I can't *believe* it,' said Natalie. 'We're going to a war zone.'

'It isn't so bad, at the moment,' said Adam, who used to read newspapers.

'My parents are going to be amazed when they hear about this. We'll have a party with them, don't you think, in a couple of weeks? Whenever this is over. I'm sure your parents will understand. They're near by – we'll tell them to come to a nice party, just the families and a couple of friends. Didi will be back by then – she and Norman could come along, I suppose. That would be only right. My brothers really liked you, you know. I'm sure they did. My father did too, I could tell. Everyone will be happy, and we can go away somewhere and not be bothered by the telephone and the moving around and the whole . . . *business.*'

'Maybe we should go to the airfield. Do you know where it is?'

'That way,' said Natalie, pointing vaguely over her shoulder as she finished her champagne. 'Drink up, Adam. This is going to be great.' She kissed him moistly on the cheek, and hopped off her stool.

They went upstairs to collect what little baggage they had. Natalie emptied the contents of the drinks cabinet into a plastic bag. Adam said a silent goodbye to the suite, and closed the door.

Downstairs, in the hotel car park, a dozen or more members of the cast and crew milled about, awaiting instructions.

'At least we know *we're* going,' Natalie said, enjoying the way the men watched her walk past them.

Adam had not inspected his car in daylight, and had almost forgotten it had been damaged. It hurt him to see the shattered head lamp, and the buckled fender.

Behind the wheel, Adam put on his dark glasses. Natalie turned the rear-view mirror towards her, and adjusted her hair. Adam drove slowly out of the car park, and turned right towards the centre of town. The set had been opened up to traffic and tourists, and most of the equipment had been removed. There were at least three of Serge's people standing in the open square, speaking into mobile telephones. It was an atmosphere like that of a circus decampment. Too late, the crew had managed to get their fountain to spout a feeble jet of water into the air.

Adam and Natalie's moods were not in sync. She was happy to speculate optimistically about Serge's chances of success in Dubrovnik. Certainly, there would be fewer distractions from crowds of onlookers. There were likely to be plenty of journalists staying there, resting and recuperating, who might decide to write about a plucky troupe of European film-makers braving the war zone for the sake of authenticity. A celebrity wedding, mirroring the director's doomed marriage, was newsworthy in itself – never mind that Adam had stood up for his bride's honour against the world's most arrogant star. It had all fallen into place, according to Natalie.

Adam's palms sweated on the steering wheel. He felt important, shaping his own destiny for a change. He tried to imagine how he would explain his actions to the few people in the world who were truly interested in him. His newsagent, in particular, would be fascinated. Dick McDavis would savour every titbit Adam had to relate. Norman's reaction did not bear thinking about. Adam's little world would be shaken, briefly, which was more than he had achieved in the past.

The airfield was not far outside of Sampara, and Adam found it easily. It comprised nothing more than an office and a control tower beside a short, concrete runway. There were no more than five aeroplanes moored rather haphazardly on the grass, and the runway had been built so that planes took off straight over the first fairway of a flat, undistinguished golf course. Claude was already there, and rushed over to Adam's car to tell them the news.

The helicopters had not materialized, but Serge was content with three aeroplanes. Landing permission was the important thing, and this had proved quite easy to arrange. Not many people were flying into Croatia these days, it appeared. Serge had recovered his good spirits after a brief bout of tears. Claude had every confidence that filming would go ahead on schedule, and money might even be saved on cheap Dubrovnik hotels. Most of the crew would remain behind, building interiors in an old stone house inland from Sampara. Claude concluded his briefing by saying that a priest had been found, so Adam and Natalie could rest assured that their wedding would go ahead as they had planned. It was most romantic, Claude added, before moving away with a swish of his ponytail to perform more miracles with his telephone and cheque book.

A skeleton crew began to arrive in a variety of vehicles. They seemed to be in a playful mood, looking forward to their adventure in Yugoslavia. They began to load their equipment into two of the planes, the third apparently reserved for VIPs like Natalie, Serge and Adam. Natalie continued to look at herself in the mirror, as if she had seen something that worried her.

'You look fine,' Adam said. 'Don't worry.'

A slight breeze had begun to blow in off the Adriatic sea. Natalie still clutched the spray of white flowers in one hand.

'I don't see Make-up,' she said.

'Claude will have thought of everything.'

Bruno was driven up in an American station wagon – one bodyguard at the wheel, the other quick to jump out and scan the empty horizon for snipers. The French actor who played Natalie's mortal husband arrived on a motorcycle. Four extras, still in costume, drove up in a dirty white sedan. Serge bounced out of a white van and strode single-mindedly towards the largest plane.

'This is it,' said Natalie. 'Time to go.'

'I suppose so,' said Adam.

Natalie squinted at him, then had to smile despite herself.

'I still like you, Adam,' she said. 'Do you like me?'

'I like you fine,' Adam said, inarticulately.

Natalie seemed to think for a moment, which was not something she had done very often in Adam's company.

She shaded her eyes from the sun and looked at Adam with some severity. Decisions did not come easily to her.

'Well,' she said, '*I* would have gone through with it.'

'I don't doubt that.'

'You can't play around with a girl this way, you know.'

'I would hate it if you looked back on it that way. I'm sure you won't.'

'Now I think I'm going to cry,' she said, still smiling.

'No you aren't,' said Adam. 'Not unless Serge tells you to.'

'I don't get to London very often, you know.'

'And why would you? I know you're going to have a wonderful time.'

'I hope so.'

'And be kind to Bruno. He means well, and he's actually a good actor.'

'Do you think so?'

'In my humble, layman's opinion. Not so good as you, though. You've got Serge in quite a lather.'

'You think this whole thing is my fault? We're flying off to God knows where because of me?'

'Fault doesn't enter into it. Catalyst, more like. Serge is captivated. You have nothing to fear.'

'For now,' said Natalie.

With a practised gesture, she summoned a minion to carry her bags to the plane. When he had left, she kissed Adam abruptly and said she hoped her parents wouldn't be too disappointed. She got out of the car and walked, barefoot, to the aeroplane where Serge and Claude waited for her. Serge himself helped her aboard. They exchanged a few words. Serge looked back at Adam and waved, smiling rather too broadly for someone who had just heard supposedly shattering news. Natalie waved too, and disappeared. Serge's last step into the plane was jaunty and boyish.

The two planes full of crew and equipment taxied together to the runway. They took off one minute later. Natalie's plane waited beside the runway, vibrating with Serge's artistic indecision. Adam took the page of newspaper out of his jacket pocket, and put it face up on the passenger seat next to him. He looked into his own eyes and saw the gaze of a man who had already made up his mind.

Natalie's plane rolled towards one end of the narrow runway. Without pausing, it turned towards the sea and accelerated into the breeze. Its wheels left the ground, and almost immediately the craft banked to port. Adam did not wait for the plane to disappear over the horizon. Holding his breath, he turned the key in the ignition. The engine started instantly, as if eager to continue its journey. Adam shifted into reverse and turned his car around.

THE END

THE COVER ARTIST
Paul Micou

'OUTRAGEOUS FARCE IS TEMPERED BY A GENTLE WHIMSY AND THE CHARACTERIZATION AND PLOT CONSTANTLY SURPRISE AND DELIGHT'
Sunday Telegraph

'MICOU MANAGES TO HIT MANY TARGETS WITHOUT LOSING THE GENTLE FRESHNESS OF THE SATIRE'
Sunday Times

'MICOU'S GIFT IS FOR FUSING OUTRAGEOUS ELEMENTS INTO REFINED FARCE'
David Hughes, *Mail on Sunday*

Oscar Lemoine's artistic medium is the celebrity nude caricature; his ageing black labrador, Elizabeth, is a late-blooming exponent of Canine Expressionism. The minor notoriety of Oscar's covers for the New York based *Lowdown* magazine sends master and dog into exile in the South of France, where Oscar hopes to improve his primitive social skills – and to do what he can to develop Elizabeth's budding artistic talent. Oscar finds romance in Val d'Argent; Elizabeth paints a series of masterpieces.

Paul Micou's critically-acclaimed novel *The Music Programme* introduced an exciting new writer; *The Cover Artist*, the story of a man's social myopia and his dog's artistic triumph, emphatically confirms that remarkable début.

'IT'S QUICK, BRIGHT, CONSISTENT, AND PROBABLY HAS SOME SECRET INGREDIENT TO KEEP YOU COMING BACK FOR MORE'
Saul Frampton, *Time Out*

'*THE COVER ARTIST* IS AN EFFORTLESS READ, OF THE SORT THAT IS FAR FROM EASY TO WRITE'
David Honigmann, *Listener*

0 552 99408 1

BLACK SWAN

THE MUSIC PROGRAMME
Paul Micou

All is not well at the Timbali headquarters of the Music
Programme. The imminent arrival of US Congressional
envoy *Charles 'Crack' McCray* threatens the Programme's
funding. The panicking employees try to pull themselves
together to form a united and competent front:
Englishman *Dr Humphrey Lord*, Assistant to the Supreme
Director, Late Baroque, finds himself in the front line of
the Programme's defence. *Dan O'Connor*, putative
Irishman and prized speechwriter, hopes not to be too
distracted from his passionate pursuit of the French
Ambassador's teenage daughter. *Wendell 'Skip' Skinner*,
American jazz trombonist, nearly sinks the ship with a
characteristic drunken gaffe. *Ludvik Kastostis*, the
MAXIMALIST composer-in-residence, dashes recklessly
to the end of his latest, loudest work, *Flamedance of
Euphorion*, hoping to have something – anything – to
show for himself. And somewhere, above it all, looms
the mysterious, reclusive figure known only as the
'*Supreme Director*' . . .

0 552 99381 6

BLACK SWAN

THE DEATH OF DAVID DEBRIZZI
Paul Micou

'HUGELY ENTERTAINING. AN ODD, COMPELLING
BOOK WITH A SUPERB TWIST, AND ONE WHICH
SHOULD CLINCH MICOU'S REPUTATION AS A
WRITER TO BE RECKONED WITH'
Carla McKay, *Daily Mail*

Pierre Marie La Valoise is incensed. He has just read
with disbelief what he considers to be a criminally unfair
biography of David Debrizzi, the renowned French
concert pianist. He sees the book as yet another
self-serving attempt by its author, Sir Geoffrey Flynch, to
take credit for David Debrizzi's successes, and to glorify
himself by his association with his genius subject. Why
else, wonders La Valoise, would Sir Geoffrey's
recollections be so at variance with the facts?

Resting comfortably on the terrace of a Swiss sanatorium,
La Valoise takes pen in hand to rebut Sir Geoffrey's *Life*.
He weeds through its distortions and omissions, its
exaggerations and personal attacks, and supplies the
version of the truth that he had intended to incorporate
into his own biography, *The Death of David Debrizzi*.
'Never have I begrudged you your *Life*,' writes La
Valoise, 'any more than you would deny me my *Death* . . .
Given the state of my health, and the treachery of my
bastard of a British publisher – who loathes me merely
because I am French – I feel it is safe to say that your
Life will stand alone on the shelves for posterity, while
my *Death* will remain untold.'

With abundant wit and verve, Paul Micou's third novel
at last gives La Valoise his say.

'IT IS SO FULL OF MUSICAL FEELING THAT EVEN
THE TONE-DEAF WILL FEEL THRILLED . . . ABOVE
ALL, IT IS A GOOD STORY . . . I HAVE NOT ENJOYED
A BOOK SO MUCH FOR A LONG TIME'
Oxford Times

0 552 99461 8

BLACK SWAN

ROTTEN TIMES
Paul Micou

'*ROTTEN TIMES* IS AS LIGHT AND DRY AS GOOD
CHAMPAGNE'
Independent

Flying back to London from an Alpine holiday, Lloyd
James suffers an electric shock in the aeroplane lavatory.
He is stunned to find that his memory has opened up
for him like a vast filing cabinet: he has developed
Tourraine's Syndrome. Riffling contentedly through
knowledge he thought he had lost forever, he ponders
the social and financial potential of his newly
refurbished intellect. Warned of side effects, Lloyd is
nevertheless unprepared for the discovery that his new
condition has restored his emotional memory into the
bargain. He is overwhelmed to realize that he has been
in love for several years . . .

In *Rotten Times* one gloriously repressed Englishman is
forced to address and act upon his deepest emotions.
Paul Micou's magnificently entertaining novel gently
guides him to his fate.

'EXTREMELY FUNNY . . . MICOU'S FEVERISHLY
IMAGINATIVE DREAMS ARE SO EFFORTLESSLY
WITTY AND WELL-PACED THAT ONE IS EAGERLY
PROPELLED ONWARDS. A TALENTED OBSERVER,
MICOU IS ALSO HILARIOUS ON SEXUAL POLITICS.
SHARP AND SASSY, HE IS AN ENTERTAINER WHO
EXCELS IN A FAMOUSLY DIFFICULT GENRE'
Daily Mail

'*ROTTEN TIMES* IS WITTY, CHARMING, MAD – A
GRIPPING SEND-UP OF LOVE, SEX, SELF AND THE
INTELLECT'
Time Out

'GRACEFUL, SKILFUL, BRILLIANT . . . TO CALL
ROTTEN TIMES A SATIRE ON THE ANGLO-
AMERICAN SPECIAL RELATIONSHIP DOESN'T BEGIN
TO DO JUSTICE TO HIS GORGEOUS GRASP OF
CHARACTER AND THE CRISPNESS OF HIS WRITING'
Sunday Times

0 552 99501 0

BLACK SWAN

THE LAST WORD
Paul Micou

'*The Last Word* looks to me like about five novels.
Five sorts of novel. The home-coming one, and the
religious charlatan one, and the eccentric family one,
and the rich WASP small-town one, and the updated
Candide one, so that while you are reading and
relishing it, other voices keep breaking in on you –
Thornton Wilder, say, and Richard Condon and
Nathaniel West and J. D. Salinger and Sinclair Lewis
and Scott Fitzgerald and both Tom Wolfes and many
another very American novel besides . . . It is an
elegantly rollicking folderol, a fine daft fable, a great
American cartoon, and it has to be read for the sheer
knockout quality of the writing, the style, the wit, the
farce, the acuity, the brilliant mischievous social and
moral aperçus, all the clever, funny, tangential stuff
. . . Read it, in short, for Paul Micou; he is the only
thing that really matters, and he is, thank God,
everywhere, all over it, all of the time'
Alan Coren, *Spectator*

'PAUL MICOU CAN CHARACTERISE SO VIVIDLY,
AND WITH SUCH HUMOUR AND PANACHE,
THAT ONE IS SWEPT UP IN HIS FANTASY . . . HIS
CONTROL OVER HIS NARRATIVE IS TOTAL . . .
MICOU'S COMIC TALENTS, DESERVEDLY,
HAVE BEEN COMPARED TO THOSE OF EVELYN
WAUGH. HIS STYLE IS LANGUID, HIS TIMING
IMPECCABLE . . .'
Tim Willis, *Sunday Times*

'PAUL MICOU IS THE REAL THING: A SKILLED
PRACTITIONER, AND ASSURED STORYTELLER.
THE PAGES OF THIS NOVEL ALMOST TURN
THEMSELVES IT IS SO EFFORTLESS A READ'
James Friel, *Time Out*

0 552 99502 9

BLACK SWAN

A SELECTION OF FINE WRITING
AVAILABLE FROM BLACK SWAN

THE PRICES SHOWN BELOW WERE CORRECT AT THE TIME OF GOING TO PRESS.
HOWEVER TRANSWORLD PUBLISHERS RESERVE THE RIGHT TO SHOW NEW
RETAIL PRICES ON COVERS WHICH MAY DIFFER FROM THOSE PREVIOUSLY
ADVERTISED IN THE TEXT OR ELSEWHERE.